D0454141

ADMINISTRATION CAN BE

MURDER

Richard L. Baldwin

Buttonwood Press
Haslett, Michigan

Other Books by
Richard L. Baldwin

Fiction

A Lesson Plan for Murder (1998)
ISBN: 0-9660685-0-5
Buttonwood Press

The Principal Cause of Death (1999)
ISBN: 0-9660685-2-1
Buttonwood Press

Unity and the Children (2000)
ISBN: 0-9660685-3-X
Buttonwood Press

Non-Fiction

The Piano Recital (1999)
ISBN: 0-9660685-1-3
Buttonwood Press

A Story to Tell: Special Education in Michigan's Upper Peninsula 1902-1975 (1994)
ISBN: 932212-77-8
Lake Superior Press

Contribution Policy of Buttonwood Press

A portion of each book sold is contributed to three organizations serving people with a variety of needs. The three chosen for *Administration Can Be Murder* are: The Michigan Association of Administrators of Special Education (MAASE); Council Against Domestic Assault (CADA); and The Sparrow Adaptive Golf Clinic. One dollar from each book sold goes to a fund to be equally shared by these three organizations.

This book is dedicated to all special education administrators who maintain their primary focus on the needs of children and their families.

I also dedicate this book to Todd Blanchard, whose life was full of compassion for his students, MATEDC, and all who had the priviledge to know and work with him.

To Ed & Dorothy,
Please enjoy my story. When Hollywood calls - this is the movie. ☺

My best,
Rich

 Published by Buttonwood Press
PO Box 716
Haslett, Michigan 48840
www.buttonwoodpress.com

Publisher's Cataloging-in-Publication Data
Baldwin, Richard L.
        Administration can be murder / by Richard L. Baldwin. – 1st ed.
        p. cm – (Louis Searing and Margaret McMillan mystery; no. 3)
        ISBN: 0-9660685-4-8

        1.   School administrators–Michigan–Fiction.
        2.   Golf stories, American.
        3.   Detective and mystery stories, American. I. Title.

PS3552.A451525A46 2000   813'.54
                          QB199-1790

Printed in the United States of America

Acknowledgments

I wish to thank my wife, Patty Moylan Baldwin for her love, her support, and her behind-the-scenes efforts at Buttonwood Press.

Every writer is indebted to the many people who contribute some knowledge, information, skill, expertise toward the successful realization of a dream. This book could not have been written and produced without the support of the following. Thank you to:

Holly Sasso, *Editor*
Joyce Wagner, *Proofreader*
Marilyn "Sam" Nesbitt, *Cover and Book Preparation Services*
John Zink, *Exhibit Photography and Materials*
Scott Baldwin, *Buttonwood Press Webmaster*
Patty Baldwin, *Backcover Photo*

Several people answered a question, listened to or read selections in order to help me to be accurate. Thank you to:

Chuck Achterhoff
Jane Bickerstaff
Todd Blanchard
Gayle Brink
Robert Erickson
Gary Geisen
Joe Hoffmeister
Kerry Jones
Kathy and David Lengkeek
Jacqui Lowman

Jim McBride
Greg Morris
Dean Sienko
Elaine Stanfield
Kurt Theummel
Patrick Vaughan
Daniel Wilkins
Russel Wolfe
Paul Zimmer

ACKNOWLEDGMENTS

A few people read prepublication drafts and offered thoughts and advice. Thank you to Gloria Anderson, Patty Baldwin, Karen Blackman, Bert Donaldson, and Ben Hall.

In the 1990s I enjoyed a number of spring golf outings with Don Bollinger, Larry Campbell, Bert Donaldson, Regis Jacobs, Whitey Larson, Jim Palm, and Jerry Wright. These outings were full of laughter, great golf shots, and provided welcome breaks from my work. Thank you, men, for the memories of a lifetime.

I wish to express my sincere appreciation to Mr. Jack Bott, owner of the Marsh Ridge Golf Resort; Mr. Dick Weber, General Manager of Marsh Ridge; and Mr. Ron Grow, nationally known mystery script writer who conducts the world famous 'Mystery at the Marsh,' for their support and allowing me to use the Marsh Ridge Golf and Nordic Ski Resort as the setting for my story.

ADMINISTRATION CAN BE

MURDER

CHAPTER 1

Saturday, July 9
Marsh Ridge Resort, Gaylord, Michigan
The Day of the Murder

School administrators Bill Wallach, Reggie Macleod, and Dan Dillon, arrived at the 14th tee. It was a scorcher of a day. One golfer pulled ahead in his cart, took out his cell phone, and proceeded to call his answering machine for messages. Another went into the Port-a-John and the third was cleaning his golf ball at the ball washer. A golf cart suddenly and quietly approached the tee. The driver of the cart, dressed in grey knickers and white socks, wore a black bag with eyeholes to conceal identity.

The masked driver handed a note to the player at the ball washer. The note read, "Thanks for helping us with the murder mystery weekend. I'm the disguised murderer in the production. If anyone asks you if you saw me, simply say, 'The masked one stopped and gave me some lemonade to quench my thirst.' This is a clue in our weekend mystery. Please drink this cold and refreshing lemonade, fluid intake is critical in this heat. I offer it to you in good health and as a token of our appreciation for assisting us in fooling our guests." The driver poured the drink into a cup and handed it to the golfer.

As the masked driver pulled away, the golfer ceremoniously lifted the cup and drank the ice-cold, refreshing lemonade. Within seconds, he felt ill. Before he could cry for help, he fell forward like a heat-stricken Beefeater guarding the Tower of London. In a matter of seconds, the golfer was dead. It happened so quickly and quietly that the others didn't realize that their friend was down. When it became obvious that things were amiss, they thought that the golfer was playing a practical joke, or in a worse case scenario, had fainted.

ৎ৲

All golfers at the Marsh Ridge Golf Resort had been alerted to expect something different when they signed in at the pro shop. Each golfer was given a notice that prepared him to expect odd occurrences. It read:

> Attention Golfers
>
> *Marsh Ridge is entertaining 80 guests this weekend for one of four Murder Mystery Weekends. These very popular events are designed to provide an atmosphere of fun and suspense.*
>
> *There may be some interruptions in your game. We want to alert you to this possibility and to apologize for any disturbances. For example, you might see someone running across the fairway or you may hear sounds, including gunshots. Ambulance sirens may be a part of the production. You might see costumed characters or guests who approach you and ask a question or two. Please play along.*
>
> *If you are disturbed by this activity, we will give you a coupon for a free round of golf at a quieter time at Marsh Ridge. Please see our assistant pro, Wendy, if you think you deserve to be compensated.*
>
> *Thank you for understanding and again we apologize if any activity associated with our mystery weekend inconveniences you. Have a great round of golf at Marsh Ridge, the finest golf course in America."* The letter was signed by Bob Sanders, Head Golf Professional.

ADMINISTRATION CAN BE MURDER

꒚

As the golfer lay dead on the 14th tee of Gaylord's rustic Marsh Ridge Golf Resort, Lou and his crime-solving partner, Maggie McMillan, were signing copies of Lou's latest novel at McLean & Eakin Booksellers in Petoskey. Lou's wife Carol, recently retired from the public schools as a preprimary home teacher, was shopping and hoping to get a jump start on holiday gifts. For every dollar Lou earned with the sale of a book, Carol would turn it back to the citizens of Petoskey with a purchase here and there. Maggie's husband Tom, a retired, golf-crazed oral surgeon, had taken his chances to get on the Crooked Tree golf course. Successful in his efforts, he putted out for a birdie on the par 3, 15th hole.

Lou looked up to see a tall woman holding out his second mystery novel for a signature. "I'm a huge fan, Mr. Searing," she said. "I remembered when you were our State Director of Special Education. Are you enjoying retirement?"

"Yes, thank you. I'm busier than I was behind the desk. My writing has replaced the crisis, problem-solving, and bureaucratic side of education."

"You sure look relaxed and happy," she added.

"A smile comes a lot easier these days. To whom shall I autograph your book?"

"To me, I guess. My name's Alice."

"Are you a teacher, Alice?"

"Yes. I've been a teacher of children with hearing impairments for twenty-five years. I teach children here in Petoskey. I love it, it's the greatest job on earth."

"I'm sure your children are most fortunate to have you for their teacher," Lou said as he wrote: *Alice, thanks for all you do for children and their parents. I respect and admire your commitment to quality education. Please enjoy Lou and Maggie's second adventure.* He signed it *Lou* and dated it July 9, 2000.

Fans and curious bookstore customers spent most of their time talking to Maggie and asking her to sign their book too. Readers of the Searing and McMillan mysteries loved Maggie. She was attractive with a beautiful smile and always offered a nice word to everyone she met. Maggie was in her mid-forties and used a wheelchair. Her disability resulted from an attack by a disgruntled insurance claimant who went berserk when Maggie, a claims investigator at the time, shattered his alibi.

It wasn't that people didn't enjoy Lou, but Lou was Lou. He was pleasant, somewhat handsome for an older man, with a little hair on both sides of male-patterned baldness. He wore two hearing aids, and nervously flitted here and there. It was Maggie the people liked. In fact, when readers had a word or two with Lou, they would often remark that they enjoyed Maggie most in his stories. "Tell us more about Maggie!" critics and fans alike would comment.

It would have been easy for Lou to become jealous over the attention his readers gave to Maggie, but he could understand; she was interesting and fun to be around. Since he wasn't jealous, it left a little room for him to be envious. Not only did his good friend come up with the pattern to solve most of the mysteries, but she also won the hearts of his readers.

CHAPTER 2

Wednesday, July 6
The Natural Golf Course, Gaylord, Michigan
Three Days Before the Murder

The ball left the face of the seven iron with a destiny. It went high into the northern Michigan sky and made its way toward the green of the 156 yard par three eighth hole. It landed to the right of the flag, bounced and followed the curvature of the green until it fell into the cup.

"In the cup!" shouted Art Williams with more emotion than he had shown in all of his forty-nine earthly years. "It dropped, it dropped, it dropped! A hole in one, Billy!"

At the same time that Art was shouting words of surprise, the man who hit the lucky shot, Bill Wallach, was shouting for joy, arms raised to heaven as if thanking his maker, and smiling a smile that communicated pure joy. Bill's friends were going berserk with excitement. Bill ran toward the green to be sure that the ball actually had gone into the cup.

Matt Maloney was exploding with joy, "You got a hole in one!! You got an ace!" He joined Bill in jogging to the green.

The last member of the foursome, Walt Wilcox, stood in shock. "I can't believe it!! I've never seen a hole in one before!"

The other four in the outing were playing a hole behind and

heard the commotion. "Something's happened up there. One of them must've come close to getting a hole in one," Dan Dillon said to his cart mate, Reggie Macleod.

Walt jogged toward his friends, "Bill got a hole in one. Can you believe it? Knocked it right into the cup!"

"Incredible," said Reggie who passed on the word to the two men in the cart further back in the rough on the left side of the par 5, 7th hole. "Bill got an ace!"

"What happened?" Doc Lewis asked. Doc wore two hearing aids, but could rarely hear anything the first time it was said, and he never got it right on a golf course. Doc's partner was Jeff Gooch who interpreted Walt's joyful message, "Bill got a hole in one up there on eight!"

Jeff shouted back to Reggie, "Bet Bill's one thrilled guy!"

A less than excited Doc said, "I did that once. Big thrill. It really is, but watch his game go to pot. The adrenaline pours into the bloodstream and the timing and concentration get out of whack. I'm playing him dollar-dollar-dollar. He's got a great memory and I'll get three bucks. Guaranteed."

The game came to a halt as all four golf carts converged on the apron of the eighth green. Each of the seven showered Bill with joy and some jealousy. Bill promised a round of drinks at the 19th hole while he kissed the Titleist ball and put it into his bag for safekeeping and mounting. Bill planned to put the trophy in his office for friends and colleagues to admire for years to come.

☙

The eight golfers, six of whom were school administrators, were on their sixth annual spring golf outing. This year they returned to Gaylord which was becoming a golf mecca in the Midwest.

The small town of Gaylord, nestled near the top of Michigan's Lower Peninsula was booming with beautiful golf courses. Doc Lewis said that if he was privileged to get to heaven, he couldn't imagine it's being and more beautiful than the golf course located south and west of Gaylord, known as The Natural. Reggie retorted, "Only problem in heaven will be getting a tee time."

"Then it won't be heaven," Jeff replied. "In heaven there's a course for each person, and it'll look more beautiful than any in northern Michigan or even Augusta for that matter."

つ

After a few rounds at the bar, Bill picked up the tab. It was more than he wanted to pay, but he was celebrating a hole in one. He now had a story for life: memories of the experience with good friends on one of Michigan's most beautiful golf courses.

Bill Wallach was the superintendent of the Potawatomi Intermediate School District, located in a rural county in mid-Michigan. Bill came into educational administration via special education. He was a speech therapist in the 1960s. Back then, speech correctionists would see a ton of kids and be given credit for magically curing them of their misarticulations. In reality, if you just left the kids alone, they eventually pronounced every phoneme with ease. Most of them, anyway.

Bill was a large man. He was tall, good-looking, and muscular. He had played left tackle for Michigan State University in the '60s. As intimidating as Bill looked, he was a teddy bear at heart. He wouldn't intentionally harm a soul.

Art Williams was Bill's best friend. He was the undertaker in the town of Greenville, Michigan. He decided as a young man that his future should be a business that was guaranteed to be a sure thing. Art thought about becoming a barber. You could always count on hair growing, but small talk and working in human manes didn't appeal to him and neither did the Saturday workday. Saturday is a golf day and every golfer was meant to be on a course. Art believed this as strongly as Baptists believe that people should be in church on Sunday. Since he never heard of a human living forever, Art figured that undertaking would always attract customers. Funerals were held on Saturday, of course, but he'd learned to convince most families to conduct the service late in the afternoon. Art's staff handled visitations except for the town dignitaries, when he liked to be visible to handle the influential crowd himself.

Art was thrilled to be with Bill when he got his hole in one. The two had played in a golf league in Belding for almost 20 years. A hole in one was an experience to be shared with a good friend, and besides, Bill was the kind of guy who needed a credible witness. It wasn't that Bill couldn't be trusted, but he was known to participate in practical jokes and he often stretched a story a bit.

Dan Dillon was the scratch dresser among the eight players. He usually didn't shoot consecutive pars, but he looked good. Tall, handsome, and smooth, Dan was quietly stylish. He made a living as the superintendent of Twin Lakes Intermediate School District. Dan was popular, had a great sense of humor, and his good looks enhanced his reputation.

Doc Lewis, a dentist, was from Bay City, a fairly good-sized town at the base of the thumb of Michigan's mitten-shaped state. Doc's first name was Richard. His parents named him Richard so they could call him Dick, a name that Doc had never appreciated. He preferred the more dignified and formal Richard. When he went off to college, he switched to Richard or Rich and now only his elderly parents call him by the nickname.

Because of his hearing loss he wore two hearing aids. He often didn't wear his aids on the golf course, so he didn't understand much that was said. Doc believed the lack of mindless profanity and unnecessary chatter helped his concentration. The other guys couldn't see where a little sound hurt a good bogey golfer.

Walt requested the six to invite Doc to join the golf group when an opening came along three years ago. Walt and Doc were high school friends who had gone to Central Michigan University together.

Doc got his hole in one when he was in high school. He knocked it into the cup while playing in his first high school match as a sophomore in Bay City. Just like Bill, Doc got his ace on a par three using a seven iron. It was a match he'll never forget. The ace came on April 27, 1957. Doc's ace was on the second hole and as he predicted would happen to Bill, he came apart afterward. Doc's body kept on secreting adrenaline and for the rest of the round he didn't come down to earth.

CHAPTER 3

Thursday, July 7
Gaylord, Michigan
Two Days Before the Murder

On Thursday, the eight friends played the Rick Smith Signature course north and east of Gaylord. In the first group was Dan Dillon, Bill Wallach, Doc Lewis, and Art Williams. After playing the 12th hole, two players in the group in front of them confronted Doc and Dan, "You guys hit into us four times!" accused an elderly man who looked as if he had had major reconstructive surgery on his face. The man wore knickers and he looked quite fashionable. He was angry. "Don't let it happen again!" he scowled.

Doc, not clearly hearing his words or sensing his anger, thought that the old man was making small talk about the beauty of the day, so he nodded and smiled. The look on the old man's face and the intensity of his voice, lead Doc to realize that this wasn't normal small talk. In a second or two, Doc figured out what the man had said, and responded, "What are you talking about? We never hit into you guys."

"Four times. Don't let it happen again!" the man threatened. By this time Bill had come over and the old man's partner had joined them as well.

"What's wrong, Doc?" Bill asked.

"He said we've hit into them four times."

"You're nuts, and if I didn't have respect for my elders, I'd tell you what you can do with your two iron," Bill said, his anger welling up inside his huge frame.

"Four times you guys hit into us and I'm putting you on notice; don't let it happen again, and believe me, you don't want to force me to have to stand behind my word."

The man's partner seemed embarrassed about the confrontation and tried to get him to play on and forget it.

"You're crazy. You better keep an eye on us," Bill responded. "You've given me good reason to knock the ball where the sun don't shine. One more accusation and you don't want to force me to stand behind my word, either."

At this point, Dan Dillon tried to calm Bill down. Like hockey players coming over to keep a teammate from swinging at the opponent and getting a two minute penalty, Dan Dillon and Art Williams took Bill by the arms and pulled him aside. The old man and his partner walked over to their cart and drove off.

"What was that all about?" Doc asked.

"Beats me." Bill replied. "We never hit into them. I hate getting accused of something I didn't do."

Dan tried to calm his friend. "Settle down, Bill. People like that are crazy. There's no sense provoking them. He could carry out his threat. This is a crazy world, man. Even on this beautiful golf course."

Bill, Doc, Dan, and Art all thought of themselves as students of the game. They apologized if they ever hit into a group. The fact that they hadn't hit into the old man's group once, let alone four times, angered Bill enough to say some pretty strong words. You don't accuse Bill Wallach of doing something he didn't do, whether it is in his school district or on a golf course. Doc had the feeling that they hadn't seen the end of this unfortunate confrontation.

Dan was able to convince Bill and the others to stay clear of the foursome. They made sure that they didn't attempt any shot that might come close to the group ahead of them.

"Nobody wrongly accuses me without paying for the mistake," Bill said with authority.

"Doc's right, Bill, release it. They're nuts. We know we didn't do anything wrong. You're letting it control you." Art was feeling tense. He'd seen his best friend angry before. He knew it was all words and show, but he also knew that for his health, Bill needed to get over the confrontation.

Doc pulled Art aside. "When we finish, we gotta get Bill out of their way. We gotta get him into the car and outta here. I smell trouble. I might have to feign chest pains to get his attention off that man and onto me. The old man has made a threat and he could have a gun or something. The world's got a lot of nuts."

"You're right. We gotta do something."

When they got to the 18th tee, Bill said, "I'm hitting. Got some wind behind me. I'm goin' to challenge that guy. I'm gonna hit the cover off of this ball and we'll see what he'll do. Let's see if he's got the guts to take on Bill Wallach and his friends!"

"No, Bill! Don't upset them. We're goin' to finish and go back to the condo," Dan said, trying to convince Bill to use some common sense.

Bill teed up his Titleist and prepared to hit the ball into a couple of guys who were looking for a reason to carry out their promised threat.

"Listen to me," Doc said, offering one last plea. "Please don't hit that ball. I'm appealing to your sense of maturity here. Let it go. He's crazy. He's like a guy on the freeway who gets ticked when someone looks at him wrong. He just blows the guy's head off. Think of your family, it's not worth it."

Art looked on. His friend Bill was acting consistent with his personality. Art knew that it did no good to try to intervene where Bill was concerned. He understood Dan and Doc's trying to calm Bill, but it was for naught. Bill Wallach would have the last word, he always did. Whatever Art said would fall on deaf ears.

"Oh, they won't do anything. Threats are just that, threats. I'll hit into them, upset 'em a little," Bill said. "I'll teach 'em they can't unjustifiably accuse us. I'll have the last word."

The three probably could have grabbed his clubs and run away or tackled him and held him for a few minutes, but they didn't. Bill got up to the tee and knocked the ball up into the wind. Sure enough, it landed about twenty-five feet to the left of the twosome and rolled another fifteen yards. The old man looked at his partner and smiled. It was an eerie smile, a knowing smile. He glanced back to see Bill on the tee. The old man continued to play, but he thought, *that big guy, whoever he is, is definitely going to regret that decision. He's made a mistake, just like that surgeon who operated on my face in Miami.* People paid for mistakes against Dwight Austin.

"Take that, old man, and don't ever mess with me again!" shouted Bill, who now seemed to feel better for having what he thought would be the last word.

The round was finished. Dan and the others knew that alcohol and anger were a bad combination. They knew there could be no 19th hole for the group today. They decided to urge Bill back to the condo. There, they could drink all they wanted out of harm's way or at least out of the temptation to say and do something they would regret later.

⨌

Dwight Austin went to the pro shop after his two gin and tonics. "Larry, who were the guys behind us today?"

"Let me get the register out and look. Let's see. That was the Wallach party. Michaywé package people."

"Wallach? spelled W-A-L-L-A-C-K?"

"Close, Wallach, an 'h' instead of a 'k.'"

They're stayin' at Michaywé, you say?"

"Yeah, golf package. Eight of them under the name of Wallach."

"You know where they're staying?"

"Nope, Michaywé office calls up and requests a tee time for the leader of the group."

"Can I use your phone?"

"Sure, Dwight."

"What's the phone number for the Michaywé Rental Office?"

"Got it here. It's 555-4589."

The phone rang. "Michaywé Rentals, Beverly speaking. How may I help you?"

"Beverly, I'm trying to reach a friend of mine. I understand he's renting one of your places for a golf outing. Name's Wallach, spelled, W-A-L-L-A-C-H."

"Just a second." Fifteen seconds later he heard, "The Wallach party is staying at 100 Pebble Beach Way. The phone number is 555-9334."

"Thanks. Some of his friends are arranging a surprise reunion. It will be a visit Mr. Wallach won't soon forget."

"Glad to help," Beverly said, wondering if she should have given Mr. Wallach's address to a stranger. She knew that some people come up to northern Michigan wanting to escape from people and the stresses of life. Mr. Wallach might not be very happy about having his rental address released. Too late now, she realized. If Wallach complained, Beverly would apologize and indicate that she was just trying to be helpful.

⟐

When the golfers got back to their condo, they sat down with everything from a Diet Coke to straight bourbon and examined the score cards. It was their tradition to record the rounds, refigure handicaps, and pay bets before the next day's outing. Cards were being shuffled for some poker before dinner.

Mixed nuts, potato chips, and pretzels complemented the drinks. Walt Wilcox, munching on anything in reach, was the first to complain about his handicap. Walt was the special education director in the Tecumseh Intermediate School District in southeast Michigan. He had a goatee and a full head of white hair. Walt took pride in the fact that his waist size was still exactly what it was when he was a senior in high school, 36 inches.

"You're always complaining about your handicap, Walt," said Matt Maloney, the score coordinator for the group, often referred to as "the commissioner" or "the commish" for short.

"Only 'cause it's too low. I've not shot 76 in years. A four handicap is your way of taking my money."

"You seem to have forgotten last year's rounds of 75, 78, and

79. I suppose you think your 89 and 91 today would qualify for a couple of strokes up," Matt said with a smile.

"You betcha! Those out-of-sight scores were last year's. I was lucky. This is a new year and I'm back to bogey golf. My handicap ought to be up around 15."

Reggie Macleod had the opposite problem. He had a ten handicap but shot rounds of 78 and 77, which meant that he should have a 5 or 6 handicap. Art picked it up right away. "Looks like sandbaggin' Macleod needs an adjustment, too. He shoots a 77 and he's got a 10 handicap? Get real!"

"Hey guys, I get a lucky day and you get on my case," Reggie pleaded while indicating to Jeff that he wanted the pretzels passed.

"Lucky day? Give me a break! You been sandbaggin' up till now. You're a scratch golfer and you know it. Good thing we redo the handicaps otherwise you'd clean out our wallets. Get Macleod down where he belongs!" Doc bellowed.

Reggie knew that he had to get the discussion diverted before his handicap took a nose dive. Reggie, medium height, well-tanned, receding hairline and handsome, was the director of special education for the Sand Dunes Intermediate School District in the northwest part of Michigan's Lower Peninsula. Golf was a passion and Reggie was the consummate golf fan. He had every piece of equipment, and owned the latest in outfits and shoes. Not only did he have it all, he talked it all. If it weren't for a compassion for children, he'd have gone pro and lived his entire life around golf courses. Reggie looked at Jeff, "What'd you get today?"

"Eighty-six."

"Looks like Jeff is right on. His handicap is 14 and he hit it right on the nose."

Jeff Gooch, a tall, thin, and mustached man, lived in Allegan. He was retired after a long and distinguished career in special education. Jeff had done it all. He had been a teacher, a local director, an intermediate school district director, a state department employee, a university professor, and finally an executive director of the special education administrators' organization. He was highly respected.

Jeff turned to Bill, "What's on your mind? You look pretty low for a guy that got a hole in one yesterday."

"Can't shake the threats against us by that old guy."

"Stop it!" Doc interrupted with authority "It's over. You're letting it ruin our vacation."

"Nobody treats me and my friends that way."

"You got the last word, Bill. Bury it. Come on, shuffle and put your money on the table," Doc said, perturbed with Bill's incessant dwelling on the incident.

Just then the phone rang. Walt picked it up, "Hello."

"Mr. Wallach, please," said a man with a deep voice.

"Just a minute." he handed the receiver to Bill.

"It's for you. Some guy."

Bill listened, looked upset, gave short answers, and hung up.

"Who was it?" Doc asked.

"Guy from the pro shop at Marsh Ridge. They can't get us on The Loon on Saturday, so they switched us to eight-thirty at Marsh Ridge. He apologized saying a tour bus full of golf writers was in the area and management made the decision to bump several groups off the Loon and on to other courses. We're to play Marsh Ridge."

"A fantastic course, but we played Marsh Ridge last time we were here. We wanted different courses this year," Dan appealed.

"It's done. Like Doc told me, bury it. Out of our hands. Relax. We'll play it again. Ante and deal."

༄

A vote was taken and the majority wanted to eat dinner at the well-known Sugar Bowl Restaurant in downtown Gaylord. Doc didn't like to go on the dinner trips. He didn't like taking two hours to eat, and he had trouble hearing conversation in a noisy restaurant. He also didn't like the way some of the guys treated the waitresses. It was all harmless fun, but none the less, it bothered and embarrassed him to be in a group with a lot of loud talking. Doc usually went into town and got a baked potato and salad at Wendy's. Doc gave in this time, and he soon discovered that the group's meal at the Sugar Bowl didn't lack for excitement.

About halfway through the meal, Dan Dillon got up to go to the restroom. On the way, he was stopped by a couple with a young adult who was disabled. "Is that you, Dillon?"

"Well, what brings the Dailey family to Gaylord?"

"We live here now. Danelle is getting the program that you wouldn't provide. Won't ever forget you, Dillon. You guys set my daughter back several years."

"Don, don't make a scene here," Dorothy Dailey pleaded.

"Just wanted Dillon to know that he'll have to live with the decisions he made that ruined our daughter's life."

"Mr. Dailey, I'm sorry you feel that way, but -"

"Don't but me, Dillon. You and your administrative buddies knew you were screwing the Dailey family."

"Don, please calm down," Dorothy pleaded fearing a confrontation.

"Mr. Dailey, the process was followed -"

"No way, Dillon. My kid didn't get what she needed and you know it!" Don started to raise his voice.

"Don, stop it. People are looking at us." Dorothy grabbed his coiled fist.

"Dillon, I never got over your decision, and one day you'll pay big time. You do know that, don't you?"

"Hey, I'm sorry you have these feelings, but I followed the rules and our intermediate school district plan and what happened was the result of circumstances."

"Let's step outside, Dillon."

"Sorry. Not in my plans. Stoppin' in the restroom and finishing dinner with my friends."

"Don, one more statement and Danelle and I are leaving," Dorothy promised, realizing that things could get ugly.

"Looks like you're up here on a golf outing. Probably spending all of my tax money having fun. Dillon, it might be a good idea to look over your shoulder on that golf course. I'll even the score sooner or later. Bank on it."

People were beginning to stare. The waitresses could be seen talking to the manager. It was uncomfortable in the Sugar Bowl.

"Come on, Danelle, we've got to go." The two women walked out onto the sidewalk of Gaylord's Main Street and made their way to their old Ford Taurus. Dorothy had hoped that the beers Don had consumed before dinner would not lead to any confrontations. But the moon must have been full, because as fate would have it, Mr. Dillon's shadow crossed Don Dailey and that could only lead to a confrontation.

Dan walked into the restroom. When he came out, Don Dailey was being escorted out of the Sugar Bowl by the manager. Dan walked back to the table to join his golfing friends.

"Who was that, Dan?"

"That was the Dailey family. They used to live in my district. They were always arguing with the school, the guy especially. We just couldn't do anything right to serve their daughter. He often called to make threats and after awhile we just learned to accept that anger was a part of his personality. He never could accept that his daughter had a mental impairment and he was never pleased no matter what we provided."

"What kind of threats did he make?" Jeff asked.

"Oh, you know, verbal threats of bodily injury and damage to property."

"What'd ya do?" Matt asked.

"The first few times we called the police, but nothing ever happened. Cops said they'd gotten similar calls from his employer, neighbors, and others in his life. Tonight was more of the same. He's had too much to drink and seeing me brought back memories. He went into his 'woe is me personality.' I feel bad for his wife and daughter. He's gone. Back to normal."

჻

Don slammed the car door. "Dillon's goin' to get roughed up. If I'm goin' to do it, now's the time."

"Don't do anything stupid, Don. You hear me?"

"If I'm ever goin' to get revenge, this is the time. He's up here, and I can rough him up and people won't know."

"He's with a lot of friends. You're no good to me and Danelle in some jail, and we got no lawyer. Forget it, Don."

"Not goin' to forget it. We're sitting here till Dillon leaves; then we'll follow him to wherever he's staying and I'll just pay him back for messin' up Danelle's life."

"I don't know why I stay with you. You're nothin' but a pain in the butt, Don Dailey."

"You stay with me 'cause you know that my paycheck puts food in your mouth, and you got no place to live or money to spend if you do leave."

"Let's just go home and watch TV and put this behind us. Please."

"Sit tight. It's time to pay for Dillon's bad decisions." He reached under the car seat and took out a pint of scotch that was half-empty. He unscrewed the top and took a healthy swig followed by a smack of his lips. Danelle began to cry. Whenever she saw her daddy drink from a bottle like this, she knew she would get hurt.

"Shut up, Danelle! Daddy don't like you crying!"

The Daileys sat in the Taurus for about a half hour before the golfers came out of the Sugar Bowl. They got into two cars and headed south on I-75 to the 270 mile exit. The Daileys followed the cars toward Otsego State Park and the entrance to the Michaywé complex. The Taurus weaved a bit, but stayed in the lane. The two cars pulled up in front of 100 Pebble Beach Way. Don Dailey passed the condo. Now he knew where Dillon was staying. All he needed was some time and a plan – a plan to get even after four years of anger.

The golfers devoted the rest of the evening to poker with toothpicks equaling quarters. By the time the last hand had been dealt, Jeff and Art took in about twenty dollars. Dan, Doc, and Bill would have to wait until tomorrow night for the chance to win it back.

After dinner, Walt left for the casino in St. Ignace. The group didn't expect him to be back until three or four in the morning. Walt was into bigger stakes than toothpick quarters. He hoped to hit it big and pay for the entire outing in one evening.

CHAPTER 4

Friday, July 8
Gaylord, Michigan
One Day Before the Murder

Matt Maloney got the coffee going every morning. He was an early riser, always had been. All during his adult life he'd gotten up early, sometimes as early as 4:30, to read the morning paper, eat breakfast, and prepare for the day. Matt had worked as a supervisor of special education transportation for twenty years before being promoted to superintendent of the Porcupine Mountain Intermediate School District, located in the western portion of Michigan's Upper Peninsula. Matt loved the U.P. and the people he worked with, but he also had a cabin in southern Wisconsin. It added two months to his golf year.

The coffee was brewing as Matt tuned to the Weather Channel so he could alert the guys, as they awoke, to what the day held in store.

One by one the golfers got up and dragged themselves into the kitchen for donuts, bananas, coffee, and sweet rolls. Doc had to have his All- Bran, something about being regular. When Walt joined the group he said, "Never goin' to guess who I talked to last night?"

"Spare us playing 20 questions, who'd you see?" Jeff asked.

"Good lookin' chick who seemed to know me and asked if I was with my golfing buddies this week. Naturally I was surprised to have this stranger act like she knew me, but I answered truthfully. "I told her, 'yeah, as a matter of fact. I am.'"

"Who was she?" Jeff was curious.

"Didn't remember her name, but she said she knew you, Reggie."

"Didn't know Reggie was the ladies' type," Jeff joked.

Walt turned to Reggie as he continued, "She said she used to work in your district, but got a bad evaluation in her first year as a special education teacher. She wasn't asked back the next year. You probably know who I'm talking about now."

"Must have been Judy Austin," Reggie said. "That happened a year or so ago. She was upset, but she couldn't teach. She came unglued as I recall. She went on and on about it. Very angry lady! Worked her way through college and when she finally got a teaching certificate, I fired her. I can understand how she felt, but hey, she couldn't teach.

"I got the feeling she'd have spit in your face if you'd been with me, Reggie."

"Still mad, is she?"

"Hasn't gotten any work. She said you ruined her career and she won't forget what you did to her. What's more, her dad is even angrier than she is. She said that she did all she could to keep her father from putting a bullet in your head."

"Sounds like Bill and Reggie are a couple of adored guys. That old man yesterday and Judy's dad had better not team up. Worse yet, maybe they're the same guy. God help us if that's the case," Doc said.

"Anyway, how'd you do, Walt?" Jeff asked, wondering if the trip to the casino was successful.

"Took in about four hundred. Picked up my winnings and came back for a couple hours of sleep before going to the Lake course."

"Well, when we play Marsh Ridge tomorrow, you'll get to meet Judy Austin. She works there. She's the beverage girl and has other jobs at the course."

"Small world, huh, Reggie?" Dan said.

"I got nothing against Judy. I was just doing my job. She was a lousy teacher and the university people got no guts. They tell some students they can teach kids with disabilities when they can't. They figure if kids pay sky high tuition they have a right to pass courses and get through the program. If we want to hire 'em, that's up to us. I gambled on Judy Austin and she wasn't any good. I told her so and dropped her. Sometimes the truth hurts and part of life is realizing what you can do well and what you can't do well. For the sake of our kids with disabilities, I got her out of their classroom."

"Looking forward to seeing her tomorrow?" Dan asked in jest.

"I liked Judy. She just wasn't a teacher. I look forward to seeing her. I can't control her feelings much less her father's feelings about me."

"She said her father is playing more golf lately. He's taken a liking to Payne Stewart. He even wears knickers. She said he recently had cancer and that golf is good therapy after surgery," Walt said.

"What kind of surgery?" Bill asked, concerned.

"Didn't say. What difference does it make?"

"You just described the guy who confronted us yesterday – old man, knickers, cancer, playing golf. Getting a little too close for a coincidence."

"Not to worry. Lots of old men like to play golf in knickers." Walt began to realize that the two men were one and the same.

↭

The golfers enjoyed a delightful day on the links. Each man scored in a range to be expected for his handicap. The weather was perfect so the group played an additional eighteen holes. After showers and a cold drink or two, the eight decided on dinner at the Michaywé restaurant followed by some toothpick poker while watching the Tigers attempt to move a game up on the first place Yankees.

During the evening, Doc got a call from his answering service. A long time patient was involved in a car accident and Doc's advice was needed during emergency oral surgery. He packed up, wished his friends a fine round at Marsh Ridge and headed home thankful for at least a few days of golf with good friends.

The Weather Channel predicted another hot day on Saturday. The remaining group looked forward to the long, narrow fairways, and challenging greens; what every golfer had learned to expect at Marsh Ridge.

Meanwhile in Room 4 of a family-run, cheap motel on the outskirts of Gaylord, Dwight Austin was about to leave a woman in agony and pain, the victim of sexual violence. Forced to provide gratification or face public ridicule and humiliation, Stacy Hammonds took her turn at pleasing a controlling and powerful millionaire. She felt cheap and ugly, and she hurt, but she couldn't press charges and neither could the others. To do so would be worse than the agony she chose to endure during occasional encounters with a man who's deformed face and sick personality demanded her attention. She quietly left the motel, where a neon sign flashed "Vacancy" well into every night.

CHAPTER 5

Saturday, July 9
Gaylord, Michigan
The Murder at Marsh Ridge

The starter shouted, "Next up, Wallach party." Jeff Gooch walked right up, teed up, and with the confidence of a Masters Champion, knocked it right down the middle of the 420 yard par four first hole.

"Awesome, Gooch!" Bill remarked in admiration for Jeff's getting the round off in such magnificence.

"Did you see that, Art! Great shot, Jeff!" Matt stated with envy. Jeff responded nonchalantly but savored every word from his friends.

Art was next; his drive went far left into a grove of trees that seemed to swallow the ball like a rhino taking in a marshmallow. "I'll take my mulligan," Art grumbled. The accepted rule of the group was that a mulligan could be used on the first hole. Art didn't need the penalty of a lost ball to begin his day. His second shot wasn't pretty either, but it was playable. It landed left about 175 yards out. Walt connected and hit the ball straight as a die and long. He couldn't help think that this round was going to be one to remember. Matt put his ball in play to the right and out about 250 yards.

Walt and Art had a dollar-dollar-dollar bet which meant that the winner of each nine got a dollar and the man with the best total score got a dollar. Most of the guys kept small dollar bets on the side. It didn't break the wallet, and it was fun to have a little cash to look forward to at the end of a decent round.

The beauty of the area was incredible. Pines and birches lined the fairways. The blue sky reflected off the crystal clear ponds. The Marsh Ridge fairways were cut to perfection. Each green offered a unique picturesque setting surrounded by acres and acres of manicured fairways, undulating greens, and deep sand traps.

As if the plants, trees, and grass were not enough, plenty of wildlife accented the landscape. Deer peeked out of thick wooded areas, birds darted noisily overhead, and even a skunk made himself known. Fortunately, the skunk was playing a hole on the back nine. Fearing his scent, Walt said, "We may have to let him play through."

Jeff smiled, "When you got that odor in your bag, you play whenever and wherever you want. He'll get no challenge from me."

After the first group hit their second shots, Reggie led off with a towering home run ball that would be the envy of any golfer. Bill was next up and his swing left him feeling like an unhappy camper. He hit a sharp slice that found a pond thirsty for his Titleist. Like Art, Bill took a mulligan to erase the pain of a penalty on the first hole. Bill's second shot was like a pop-up to the shortstop, but at least it was in play.

Dan Dillon stepped up to the ball, concentrated, but seemed to almost miss it as it dribbled past the red tee markers. "Mulligan!" Dan declared, joining Matt and Bill in accepting the ego-soothing rule. Dan regrouped beautifully and hit a grand-slam homer right down the middle with a slight draw. It put him in perfect position for a shot to the green.

⟋꙳

Judy Austin arrived for work at about 9 a.m. She drove around to the back garage that was creatively hidden by a group of pine trees. Judy had applied for the job in early spring after seeing an ad in the *Gaylord Herald Times*. Some of the other employees thought Judy had gotten the job because of her influential father, but she had called the course on her own. She liked the outdoors and she had played golf on her high school team. She hoped the job would give her an opportunity to play some golf on a premier course.

Judy worked concessions. She liked that there was good variety to the job since she could work inside in the restaurant, or outside making hamburgers and hot dogs at corporate golf outings. Finally, she worked as a beverage girl, driving around the course in a club cart with soft drinks, beer, and candy for sale.

Judy knew the ins and outs of the golf course business, and that every penny counts. She learned that guys will more easily part with their money from an attractive young girl. The concessions manager could see Judy's success from the take at the end of the day. Judy sold three to four times more than the others in the concessions operation. It was no secret that she was attractive and could sell. Judy may have been a less than effective special education teacher, but she was great at selling herself and the beverages that she kept cool in her ice chest.

◈

Don Dailey pulled up to the maintenance garage of the Marsh Ridge Golf Resort at about nine fifteen. He expected to get chewed out for being late for work, but he knew he couldn't get fired. Don's hair was crying for a comb. His wrinkled T-shirt hung outside his dirty jeans. He could use a haircut and he hadn't shaved in a couple of days. In spite of his appearance and tardiness, Don was the best golf course groomsman in the region. Hook Avery, his supervisor, knew Don had had too much to drink the night before. It was always the reason Don was late. It did no good to discipline, threaten to fire him, or to get angry with him. So, Don's coming in late was to be expected. The result of Hook's leniency in allowing Don to come to work late was a beautifully manicured golf course.

"Late again, Don," Hook said. Hook wasn't Al's real name. When nine out of ten drives take a direct turn to the left, you automatically obtain a logical nickname. Such was the case with Al Avery.

"Yeah, had trouble getting up."

"We'll tolerate that around here 'cause we gotta have a good mechanic, but you're gonna have to change your ways."

"Hard to teach an old dog new tricks."

"Yeah, well maybe the old dog would learn a new trick if it didn't get fed for a few days."

"Don't hassle me, Avery. Be lucky I decided to get here. Until you find someone to do this job as good as me, then you'll take me on my terms."

Hook found it hard to take talk from a guy who had no respect for authority. But, Don had him over a barrel. With so many courses in the Gaylord area and with a shortage of experienced golf course workers, Hook let Don call the shots.

ᖇ

The seven golfers continued their rounds. Play was typical. Actually no one had played a hole in any way other than what was predictable for his game.

Bill, Reggie, and Dan realized that the old man from Thursday's confrontation was playing in the twosome behind them. And the old man knew that Bill Wallach was ahead of him. After two days to cool off and a constant distance between them, Bill felt he'd had the last word and there would be no further confrontation.

The day was getting quite hot. Judy Austin was selling at a record setting pace. Some guys were paying for ice in her cooler so they could feel the coolness on their foreheads with drips mingling with their sweat-filled golf shirts. Don Dailey suffered from the heat as he mowed the fairways, making sure the roughs were exactly two and one-quarter inches high, the height that seemed to effectively punish the golfer for straying from the fairway. Don avoided a higher cut that would incur the wrath of golfers.

At the end of nine holes it was time for a break. An early lunch was a soft drink to go with hot dogs and hamburgers. The starter was making sure that not too much time was taken before the players got going with their second nine. The score cards showed Jeff at 47; Art had a 46; Walt carded a 42, and Matt had a 44. In the second group, Reggie had a 39, Bill had a lucky 40, and Dan Dillon had a 49. The heat was overwhelming, but golf is a summer sport, serious players realize that a hot day goes with the territory.

Unbeknownst to the seven in front, Dwight's partner must have gone home at the turn. A man approached Dwight and asked if he could join him. There was no reason to deny the company. The two shook hands, shared first names and began to play the second nine.

❧

There was drama on the 12th hole. Reggie and Bill shared a cart while Dan had one all to himself. When the players arrived at their tee shots, Bill went into the woods to find his ball. Soon thereafter, a ball landed about ten yards to Reggie's left. No one shouted "fore." The ball rolled forward about ten yards. Reggie wheeled around to see the old man on the tee. There was no wave, no shout of apology. Dwight walked over to his cart and put his club in the bag.

Reggie made a quick decision to keep this to himself. Sharing it with Bill would incite a riot and this wasn't what anyone needed. Dan didn't notice the long ball either, he was looking at players on another hole. Reggie decided that some revenge was needed. When Bill got back in the cart, Reggie drove over to Dwight's ball, got out of his cart and stomped the ball into the spongy turf. "What was that about?" Bill asked.

"Just needed to get somethin' off my chest."

"Did the old man hit into us?" Bill asked.

"Naw, the ball came from the other fairway, but you would think the guy would have at least shouted 'fore.'" The two took long drinks from their water bottles and moved on to the next shot.

The 13th hole was uneventful, but it was getting so hot that playing golf was uncomfortable. In order to get to the tee for the 14th hole, the players took a long cart ride through a beautiful grove of trees. A doe with her fawn peered out from a clump of poplars but quickly scooted away at the sound of the golf carts and men's voices. The tee for the 14th hole was elevated and the players looked out onto a carpeted fairway that took a sharp dogleg to the right. When Reggie, Bill, and Dan got to the tee, they could no longer see the first group of friends ahead of them. The first group was picking up the pace and was about a hole ahead. The twosome playing behind them was about a hole back. The guy playing with Dwight got himself into a lot of trouble. He was often taking his full five minutes looking for a lost ball.

The three arrived at the beautiful 14th tee. Flowers were planted in decorative pots. The sign was full of information. The 14th was a short par 5 dogleg to the right, 460 yards, traps on both sides of the fairway about 200 yards from the tee. The distance from the blue tee was 480, 460 from the white, 440 from the black tee and 400 from the red tee. The ball washer stood available with a damp towel hanging down from its hook. On the bench, close to the tee, was a container of styrofoam cups and an orange cooler with a sign that read, "Free Lemonade! Thanks for being at Marsh Ridge."

"That's a nice gesture," Reggie said, pouring himself a cup of lemonade. It was not very cold, but it was wet and refreshing.

"Better get something for free. We pay a lot of bucks to play these courses," Bill remarked, as he headed for the Port-a-John. The drinks to keep him from becoming hydrated caused him to use the facilities often. Dan moved his cart ahead and into the shade of a large maple. He took out his cell phone and proceeded to make a call.

Just as Reggie Macleod was beginning to wash his ball, a golf cart pulled up with a masked driver. A note was handed to Reggie. He read it, smiled, and said, "Hey, I get a part to play in this crazy murder mystery? An actor at last, this will probably be my fifteen minutes of fame."

Reggie accepted the cup and drank the cold lemonade as asked to do by the masked driver. As soon as the drink was served, the driver turned to head back toward the 13th hole. Reggie put the cup down and moved toward the tee. He collapsed. Dan was still on the phone and didn't notice anything. When Bill came out of the Port-a-John, Reggie was down. Bill caught a glimpse of a cart leaving the bench with the cups and cooler. He saw one person in a golf cart, a black bag was over the person's head and he thought the driver was wearing grey knickers and white socks. Bill called to Dan, "Either Reggie is playing a practical joke on us or he's fainted."

Dan had been a paramedic when he was in college. He immediately went to Reggie and checked for vital signs. There was no pulse, no breath. "I think he's dead, Bill, must've had a heart attack."

"Call 911 on your phone, Dan. I'll take a cart to the pro shop and tell them what's happened," Bill said. "You stay with Reggie. I'll be back with help."

کئ

Wendy, the assistant pro, stayed at the pro shop to direct the ambulance to the 14th tee. The golf pro, Bob Sanders, took a cart and drove out to the tee after calling 911 and asking for immediate assistance. The initial report from Bill was that the golfer was probably dead.

Bob Sanders was a handsome, light-complected African American who was enjoying his first experience as head professional at a major resort. He had worked his way up to this opportunity by graduating in the top five of his class at the Golf Management Program at North Carolina State where he was the best golfer on the team. He tried the Nike tour and came close to earning his card which would have allowed him to play on the PGA tour. He was an assistant pro for a few years in the Lansing, Michigan, area and then was the successful applicant for the job at Marsh Ridge two years ago. Bob was tall, thin, a stylish dresser and a fine teacher.

A crisis on a golf course was not unique. He had experience with heart attacks, fainting, and people getting hit with errant golf balls. Dealing with this problem on the 14th tee was simply one more activity on a very hot and busy day.

Sirens could be heard in the distance, and the sound got louder as the vehicles got closer and closer. With lights flashing and sirens blaring, the ambulance followed a deputy sheriff who pulled into the pro shop area. Wendy got into the ambulance and directed the deputy and paramedics along cart paths to the 14th tee.

When they arrived, Reggie was motionless in the hot sun. A few golfers and golf course staff stood around. Art, Walt, Matt, and Jeff hadn't gotten the word. They heard the ambulance sirens, but didn't pay any attention. They remembered the note telling them to disregard disturbances related to the mystery weekend.

They did notice that their friends were not behind them, but they figured that a couple of lost balls in the woods would be enough to stall the group and put them a hole or two back.

The paramedics were in touch with their dispatcher who passed along information that was known about the victim, "Middle-aged male, no pulse, no respiration, body was discovered about five minutes ago."

"Any evidence of wounds?"

"Negative."

The paramedics figured it was a heart attack. No wounds, hot day, quick death. They would, upon arrival, do their own check for vital signs and if the doctor at the hospital directed, they'd take whatever action was necessary to try to revive the man's heart.

The paramedics sprang into action and quickly determined Reggie to be dead and beyond the point where any action on their part would revive him. They forwarded their information to the doctor at the hospital who agreed with their assessment and directed that no action be taken. The doctor released jurisdiction of the body to the police and the medical examiner.

The deputy called Detective Sergeant Harrison Kennedy. "I suggest you get out here, Detective. Got a middle-aged man dead on the 14th tee of Marsh Ridge. No obvious body wounds, no witnesses to the death that we've been able to determine. He's probably had a heart attack, but there could be foul play. A golfer at the scene claims an old man in knickers killed the guy."

"Be right there. Fourteenth tee of Marsh Ridge?"

"That's right. I'll call for a backup. We're goin' to be here for awhile," the deputy remarked.

Harrison called the medical examiner. He'd need the death

certified and an autopsy ordered. He also called the prosecutor's office. Warrants may be needed and besides, if everyone was represented at the crime scene, he'd have all the bases covered. His final call was to the State Police Forensic Lab in Grayling. If this wasn't a coronary, and murder was possible, he'd need support from the lab.

While Harrison was en route, the deputy went to work processing the crime scene. He set up a 500-foot radius from the dead golfer with yellow "POLICE LINE DO NOT CROSS" tape. This would keep the curious away. Out of respect for the dead man, the deputy strategically placed a few golf carts so that the bystanders could not easily see the body. He then talked with Bill and Dan to hear what information they may have as they were the first to find Reggie down.

"I told you, the killer is the driver in knickers," Bill said, getting angry again.

"What driver in knickers?"

"There was an old man wearing knickers behind us. The guy's nuts. He's getting revenge for an incident a couple of days ago. He did this to my friend. You won't have much investigating to do."

"Is this guy here?" the officer asked looking left and right at the gawkers.

"Are you kidding? Do killers usually stand around and watch you guys do your work?"

"It's been known to happen."

"No, I don't see him. Don't know his name, but he did it!"

The deputy noted his observation and assured Bill that he would give it attention. Reggie's wallet was removed so the officer could find identifying information about who to locate in an emergency. The deputy shared this with Detective Harrison who had jurisdiction of the crime scene.

When he arrived, Harrison immediately took charge. The paramedics briefed Harrison as he closely examined the dead man. Once assured that sufficient photographs of the crime scene had been taken, Harrison picked up the Dixie cup, noticed some fluid and kept it as evidence. He smelled the contents and got a whiff of an almond scent. Cyanide was his quick assessment of the cause of death, but of course, an autopsy would need to validate his hunch. His next thought was, *if this guy was poisoned, how was he poisoned, and by whom, or was it suicide?*

The 14th tee was busy with sheriff's department personnel, state police forensic lab technicians, curious golfers and even the murder mystery weekend guests milling about ironically finding all of this rather comical. After all, the production company used for the mystery weekend was reputed to go to great lengths to put on a realistic performance. Most weekend guests thought that the company was certainly pulling all the plugs this time. What they were seeing was more real than an episode of COPS on television. Most would never be convinced that a man was really dead on the 14th tee.

⇒

Matt, Jeff, Walt, and Art were about to play the 18th hole when Dan approached. He called them together. "Need you guys over here for a few minutes."

The foursome joined Dan who by this time looked emotionally drained as all that had happened set in. "Got some bad news. Reggie's dead." Dan sounded to the point and factual, but he had no experience in telling friends about a death. He just blurted it out.

Dead? The reaction was mixed. They half thought this was one of Bill's practical jokes and half thought, because of Dan's credibility and serious tone, that the shocking news was true.

"We read the letter, the sirens and stuff are phony. You're going along with the weekend play, aren't you, Dan?" Jeff asked.

"Afraid not. He's dead. We think he was poisoned with lemonade back on the 14th tee."

Again, a mixed reaction. "Poisoned? By that lemonade? We all drank it and we're fine," Walt said, in an obvious state of denial.

"That old man in knickers got his revenge, didn't he?" Art asked, shaking his head.

The five were dazed, shocked, and unable to accept that their friend, so full of life only minutes ago, was dead. A few seconds later, Matt suggested they go to the 14th tee to join Bill in grief. They realized there was nothing they could do, but for some reason, being together was important.

The medical examiner arrived, certified death, and ordered an autopsy. Normally, a death scene where murder or suicide is suspected can be active for hours with the body remaining exactly where it was found. After he was certain that the evidence was catalogued, Harrison directed that Reggie's body be taken to the Otsego County Memorial Hospital where DOA procedures could be followed.

The paramedics placed Reggie in the ambulance and quietly left the area. Detective Kennedy ordered an analysis of the contents of the lemonade cooler. He also ordered a full inspection of Reggie's golf cart and golf bag. He wanted all medications, candy, the contents of any beverage can or any substance found to be recorded and prepared for analysis. He took thorough notes on the conditions at the scene; the weather, the temperature, the wind direction, and a description of the surrounding area. He also talked with Bill and Dan and anyone else who had a theory about Reggie's death.

Detective Kennedy was a bit surprised when an onlooker told him, "You're doing a good job making all of this look real." The onlooker had been to many of the 'Mystery at the Marsh' weekends and this production he rated tops. He said, "I think the lifeguard was killed by a jealous sunbather, but this phony death on the 14th tee threw me for a loop and certainly caused me to reconsider my theory." He thanked Harrison for a good show, "Very real, Officer, very real, good job!"

↫

Investigating a murder was uncommon in Gaylord. Murder wasn't rare in Detroit, however, where Harrison had lived and worked for twenty-five years prior to relocating in the north. Harrison and his wife decided it was time to get to a lower stress climate of Michigan so they had moved to Gaylord two years ago. Harrison applied for a position at the Otsego County Sheriff's Department and was hired on the spot when the sheriff learned of his extensive law enforcement experience in Detroit.

Harrison knew that there was a good chance that the death was not the result of murder. It was possible that Reggie had had a heart attack, middle-aged men die everyday from arteries packed with cholesterol. He also suspected suicide. But, Bill was convinced that an old man in knickers was the murderer. Harrison also considered the possibility that Bill might have killed Reggie and immediately put the blame on a guy behind them. Stranger things had happened, he knew that it was textbook to look at a variety of angles in an investigation. He was challenged.

Jeff Gooch left the scene, took a cart to the pro shop and called his wife Norma. After telling her about the tragedy at Marsh Ridge, he asked her to call Lou Searing and ask him to call the Marsh Ridge Pro Shop, area code (517) 555-2341.

In a matter of minutes Jeff was paged. Norma was on the line. "I called Lou. He wasn't home. All I got was a voice message. He may be connected to a pager so I asked him to call you at the number you gave me."

"Thanks. Please try every hour or so. I need to talk to him."

"I will. Are you okay, Jeff?"

"I'll be all right. It really hasn't hit me yet. I keep telling myself that this can't be happening."

"Do you want me to come up?"

"No, I'll be coming home late tonight."

"Okay, very sorry, Jeff. Tell everyone my thoughts and prayers are with them."

"Will do."

Chapter 6

Saturday, July 9
Petoskey and Gaylord, Michigan

Lou finished signing a book and asked the next
person in line to please wait. He noticed a message on his pager. Lou
dialed the number and heard that Norma was trying to reach him.
As soon as he heard the word, 'emergency,' he wrote down Jeff's
number and dialed. Lou contacted the bookstore manager, Julie
Northoek, to explain that he had to deal with an emergency. He asked
her to inform the folks waiting in line that he had to take an important
call.

"Jeff? This is Lou Searing. Norma left me a message on my phone.
What's the problem?"

"Well, there's been a tragedy here in Gaylord, Lou. One of your
friends may have been murdered."

"Oh, no!" Lou gasped. "Who?"

"Reggie Macleod."

"Oh, my God. This is terrible! What happened?" Lou asked, as
he pulled a chair over to sit down. Maggie glanced over at Lou and
could tell that he was receiving some distressful information.

"I guess he was poisoned at the 14th tee of the Marsh Ridge
Resort. A detective from the sheriff's department is on the case."

"Maggie and I will be right over. We're in Petoskey, having a book signing. We have to locate Carol and Tom first."

"I'd sure appreciate it, Lou. I knew you would want to know. I also thought you might want to help the police."

"I'm glad you called. Where are you now?"

"I'm at Marsh Ridge Resort in Gaylord. I'm with the rest of our group."

"Please tell the detective we're on our way. We have to finish this book signing and then we'll come right over. Maggie and I'll be there in an hour. Carol and Tom will probably follow."

Lou hung up, took a few seconds to pray for his friend and his family. He then asked the manager for a few seconds alone with her and Maggie. He briefed them on the situation. It was agreed that he would sign books for the people in the store at the time. In addition, the owner would promise folks who came later that an autographed book would be provided to them, but the detectives had to attend to an emergency. Carol, by chance, had stopped in the bookstore to see how the signing was going. Lou briefed her. She agreed to find Tom, check out of their hotel, and follow Lou and Maggie to Gaylord.

⌁

Jeff returned to the others." I just talked to Lou Searing. He and Maggie are in Petoskey. They'll be over in about an hour."

"Who's Maggie and who's Lou?" Art asked.

"You probably haven't heard of Lou, but most of us know of him because he has been solving some murders involving special education. He's a retired State Director of Special Education. He and a good friend went on a motorcycle trip a few years ago. They were attacked by some thugs. The knife couldn't get through Lou's leather jacket so he wasn't killed. His friend was not so lucky. Lou and Maggie McMillan, a former insurance claims investigator, went to Kentucky and solved the murder of Lou's friend. Since then, they have been involved in a few cases. They're good. Since Reggie is an education administrator, I was thinking that perhaps the murderer, if there was a murder, might be wanting him killed because of something in education. So, I got ahold of Lou."

"Fine with me, but the killer is that old man with the deformed face and knickers," Art said. "He was closest to him and the old man is getting revenge for Bill's hitting into him a couple of days ago. You'll never convince me otherwise. Bill and Dan would be dead now, too, if they'd have been near Reggie when the poison was given to him."

༄

Lou and Maggie arrived at the pro shop just short of an hour from when Lou talked to Jeff. Maggie parked her van in a space for persons with disabilities. She activated her automatic lift and the side of her van slid back allowing the lift to position itself to take Maggie to the pavement. Once on the pavement, she activated her device that allowed the lift to be swallowed up into the van again. She drove her wheelchair to the pro shop. Lou introduced Maggie to the men present. All shook hands and shared words of sympathy.

"Have you met with the detective yet?" Lou asked.

"Yes. His name is Harrison Kennedy. He's with the sheriff's office. He briefly talked to us and left to make some phone calls. He said he'd be back to talk with us later," Art explained.

"I told Mr. Kennedy that you would be coming up. He asked that you find him and introduce yourself," Jeff added.

"Okay, I'll find him. Thanks," Lou responded.

༄

The death of Reggie on the 14th tee created quite a bit of conversation. The staff of Marsh Ridge did not lack for something to talk about. Most thought the commotion was related to the resort's murder mystery weekend. Bob told the staff that Detective Kennedy wanted to talk with them.

Judy Austin told her boss that she wasn't feeling well. It was probably a combination of the heat, the death, and getting little sleep the past few nights. Her supervisor Betty Battles told her she could go home. Before leaving, Betty said, "The detective will want to know how to reach you."

"You've got my phone number, and I'll be back tomorrow morning."

"What do you think happened, Judy?"

"I think somebody wanted the guy dead. I knew him. His name was Reggie Macleod. He was a special education administrator and I was a teacher in his program. He fired me. I won't ever forget it. He ruined my career."

"I didn't know you were a teacher."

"I'd still be teaching if the dead guy on number 14 hadn't been mistaken about my ability. Gotta go."

Judy got into her 1990 Plymouth and sped away to find some rest and a break from the ugly scene. As she took off down the road, Don Dailey was finishing his mowing. He put the tractor into the maintenance garage. "Kind of a different day, Don," said Phil Riggins, the superintendent of the course.

"Yeah, you don't see a guy keel over on a tee everyday."

"What do you think happened?"

"Oh, it could've been lots of things."

"Like what?"

"That lemonade could have been spiked like the cop said. It could've been a suicide. Someone in the group behind his could've had a part to play in it. Someone could have come onto the course and hid in that area till his group came up and then killed the guy."

"Why?"

"How should I know? Lots of people hate people."

"Where were you when it happened?"

"I heard the sirens when I was mowing number 3 rough. I figured they were going on by the course, but then I saw them come in and then I seen them going out toward the back 9 following the cart paths."

"Where were you before you heard the sirens?"

"What's going on? You playing detective or somethin'?"

"Just needing to account for my staff is all. I know the cop will want to know where everyone was. I'm talking to the other guys as well."

"Before I heard the sirens I was having a smoke over by number 4 in the shade."

"Gus said he saw you driving a cart away from the 13th green before he heard sirens."

"Well, old Gus got his memory off a bit. I'll have to have a talk with him. Now that you mention it, I think I saw Gus buzzing around number 13 or 14. I can play that 'put some guy at the scene to cover your butt' game, too!"

࿐

"Excuse me," Lou said. "Are you Harrison Kennedy?"

Harrison looked around. "Yes, and you must be Mr. Searing?"

"Yes, call me Lou. Pleased to meet you, Detective."

"Thank you."

"The guy who was murdered was a friend of mine. Maggie and I want to be available to help you if we can."

"I appreciate it. I've got a real mess on my hands."

"You'll solve it, of that I'm certain."

"Maggie. You said Maggie, right?"

"That's correct."

"Didn't you and Maggie solve the murder of a school principal down in Shoreline nine or ten months ago?"

"We did."

"Just last week I was talking with a friend who told me about the two of you and how you skillfully figured it all out. That was quite a feather in your cap."

"Thanks. We put a lot of information together and we got lucky."

"Listen, I could use your help. I'll brief you and if you and Maggie can help, fine. I've never been one to turn down help, especially from the two of you who have such a good reputation."

"Thanks, Detective Kennedy. Maggie's up at the pro shop. We're ready to go."

"Thanks, Lou. Oh, call me Harry, short for Harrison."

༄

The 19th hole for the golfers at Marsh Ridge was Jac's Place. The only topic of conversation was the death of a guy down on number 14. Murmured questions moved around the room, was it murder, suicide, a heart attack, a guy dying of heat stroke? Bob came into the restaurant. He looked around and came over to the table where an old man with knickers and a deformed face sat with his friend Billy. Billy didn't go home after the first nine holes. Instead he drank and played cards in the bar area. "Dwight, the cops are goin' to want to talk to you."

"Why me?"

"You were playin' behind the guy who died."

"For cryin' out loud. Why talk to me? I know nothing about a guy dying."

"Just routine. You might have heard or seen something. You were closest to the scene, Dwight. Cops gotta look into this and talk to anyone who even remotely might have some information."

"Got nothin' for 'em. By the time me and the guy who joined me at ten got to the 13th green, the ambulance was arriving at the 14th tee so we didn't even go to there. It was so hot, we just took our carts back here. That's all I know, Bobby."

Dwight Austin was not happy to be told to stay around. He was used to coming and going as he pleased. He motioned for the waitress to come over. "Bring me another martini, drier than the last one."

"Dwight, be careful. You need a clear head when you talk to the detective. He'll probably be out here soon," Billy said, afraid of what more alcohol could do to Dwight's personality.

"They can't keep me here. I got golf to play. Haven't we got a four o'clock tee time at Black Forest, Billy?"

"Yeah, but the police want to talk to you about that guy dying."

"Not if it interferes with my afternoon tee time. If he wants to talk to me, it will be on my time," Dwight said with an air of defiance.

༄

The six golfers realized that there was nothing more they could do at Marsh Ridge. They wanted to go to the condo, gather up their things, return to their families, and be in the comfort and security of their homes.

Harrison brought the group together before they left. "Thanks for being patient, men. I need to talk with you while we're all still here so I can get your thoughts about motives. I know you want to get on home to families and friends and I'll get you outta here as soon as possible. Maggie and Lou will listen in and participate, if you don't mind."

"We're glad they're here," Matt said.

"Assuming Reggie was murdered, we won't know till the autopsy is complete. Do any of you have any idea who would do this?"

"He was well-liked, but something happened two days ago that you both should know about," Jeff said, anxious to support what Bill had already told them.

"What was that?" Harrison asked.

"Bill got very upset with an older man with a deformed face who was wearing knickers. The old guy said Bill and others in his foursome had hit into them four times. Bill said they never hit into the old guy and then he said some pretty heavy stuff. The two got into an argument. Bill just couldn't put it aside. Then he hit into them on purpose. The old guy didn't do anything, but I had a feeling that trouble would be coming."

"What was the old guy's name?"

"Don't know. He was playing in front of Bill and the others Thursday at The Natural. In fact, he was playing in the group behind Bill today. The club pro should have his name. You can't miss him. He has a deformed face, like he had cancer surgery. He wore knickers like Payne Stewart. He was quite fashionably dressed. Any of us could pick him out in a crowd." Harrison and Lou were taking notes.

"Then, Thursday night, we were eating at the Sugar Bowl in Gaylord and Dan Dillon got into a verbal altercation with some guy," Walt offered.

"Tell us about it."

"Dan got up to go to the restroom. He passed a table where a couple and their daughter were having dinner. The man recognized him and started confronting him about some problem back where Dan is the superintendent."

"Who was he?"

"Have no idea. The mother and daughter got up and left. The manager of the place showed the guy to the door. We didn't see him after that. Dan was a little upset by it, but he told us that this kind of confrontation had occurred several times when this family lived in his school district."

Harrison made a note to see the manager of the Sugar Bowl to see if they knew who the guy was. "Anything else, men?"

"Don't think so. Reggie may have somebody in his personal life who has it in for him, but we wouldn't know about that," Matt said.

"Listen, guys. Here's my card. If you remember anything else you think I should know, give me a call. I've got an officer going through Reggie's golf bag looking for medication, food, or anything else that might give us a clue as to what happened. I've also obtained a search warrant for your condo. When you arrive, an officer will be looking at Mr. Macleod's belongings; you know, notes, phone numbers, or anything else that might give us a clue to this tragedy. You're free to go. Please cooperate with the officer at your condo. Sorry, guys. Thanks for helping me."

"I know you're upset and still in shock about this tragedy," Lou said sympathetically. "Maggie and I are going to get involved. Mr. Kennedy has made us feel welcome. If any of you have any need to talk with Maggie or me concerning any thoughts you have, anything you heard, even an intuitive thought, give either of us a call. And the reverse is also true. You can expect a call from us if we think you can help. We may want to run clues and hunches past you. I know you'll help in any way possible."

"We sure will, Lou," Art replied. "You're the detective, but I'll tell you this, like we've told you before, that old man in knickers killed our friend. You can come up with all the theories in the world, but that old man killed Reggie. And I'll tell you this, friends watch out for friends. That old man won't be playing much more golf, we're going to see to that. All of us go way back."

"I know you guys are upset, but justice will prevail. Art, I know your grief, I had to deal with the loss of a good friend in Kentucky a while back, grief and loss are right up my alley. Take care of yourself and leave solving this thing to the sheriff. Understand?" Art nodded, but inside he felt differently. A long-term friendship was a strong bond. The men knew deep in their souls that the old man in knickers had taken their best friend.

"You guys probably want to pack up and get on home," Lou said.

ॐ

Once Lou, Maggie, and Harrison were alone, Harry began, "I think we've got a murder on our hands."

"Heat stroke or a coronary seems a bit remote," Maggie said a bit sarcastically.

"I'm fairly certain that the autopsy will show poisoning as the cause of death, and then all we'll have to do is figure out who did it."

"Any witnesses?" Maggie asked.

"Not that I know of. Bill Wallach said he saw somebody pull away from the bench area. The driver had a black bag over his head and he thinks he saw grey knickers and white socks on him."

"Do you trust the pro at Marsh Ridge?" Maggie asked.

"Have no reason not to. Why do you ask?"

"No particular reason. He's the captain of the ship so to speak. He's responsible for all employees at the golf course, he knows who's on the course by tee times, he knows the access points. I imagine we'd want to rule him out as a bit or a major player in the case."

"I see what you mean. My guess is that he's an innocent bystander, but we'll interview him and see if my hunch is right."

"One thing's for sure," Lou said. "I'm looking forward to talking to the old man in knickers. He seems to be our best lead."

"By the way, Mrs. Macleod has been told of her husband's death. She took it hard, as you can imagine. He's got three kids and some grandkids."

"Yes, I know the family," Lou said respectfully and with head bowed. "They'll be devastated. Who's coming over?"

"His oldest son, Jerry. Reggie's body will be released to the family following the autopsy, probably early on Monday. The other kids will stay with their mother and try to provide some comfort."

❧

Don Dailey called home during his break. "Hello," Dorothy answered.

"A golfer died out here this morning."

"What happened?" Dorothy asked, the anatomical juices associated with panic and fear flowing through her body.

"Dead on the 14th tee."

"Did you do it, Don?" she asked quietly.

There was a telling pause before Don spoke, "Let's just say that one of the golfers we followed from the Sugar Bowl is dead, okay?"

"You said you were going to get him. That's what you said Thursday night."

"Gotta get back to work."

"Are you coming home after work?"

"Goin' to the Yellowjacket first."

"Why don't you just come home for once, Donny."

"A workin' man deserves a few cold beers and some time with friends at the end of a work day."

Dorothy Dailey knew her husband had violent tendencies, but she never thought he'd actually murder anyone. She momentarily thought of the pain in the lives of the victim's family. She prayed with all of her heart that her husband had had enough sense to keep his emotions to himself.

❧

"I think we shoulda waited for the cop back at Marsh Ridge," Billy said.

"Haven't got time to stand around and wait for some cop," Dwight replied. "I got golf to play. Let's see, who's up? If you didn't get a par, I'm up."

"Still think we made a mistake in leaving."

"Get your mind on the game, Billy."

"A guy died back there. You were right behind him. You should have waited for the cops and explained what you saw. This is like leaving the scene of an accident."

"Billy, quit your stammering. I'll talk to the cop. I'll do it on my time. I got a tee time and I'm sticking to it. People die all the time. I came close with my cancer. I've got a new perspective on life. The cop has got all the time in the world to ask questions and figure out the murderer, if there was a murder. I'm thankful for every day I got; and this afternoon I got you for a friend, blue sky, and a tee time. I'm playin' golf and talkin' later."

"Looks like we're running from the cops."

"We ain't running from nobody. We're in the Gaylord area. Sanders knows me. I'm talking to the cops. Now, get up there and hit it down the middle, Billy. You're a worry wart." Billy shook his head and drove two hundred and fifty yards straight down the middle.

❧

Detective Harrison, Maggie, and Lou turned their attention to interviewing the staff at Marsh Ridge. Harry told Bob Sanders, "I need to talk to you, your assistant pro, your maintenance supervisor or grounds superintendent, and your supervisor of food. We'll want to talk to 'em, one at a time. We also want to talk to an old man, a golfer who wears knickers, and has a deformed face. Apparently he was playing behind the dead golfer."

"That's Dwight Austin. I think he left already."

"What do you mean he left already? I thought I made it clear that I wanted to talk to people."

"Well, Detective, you're going to learn that Mr. Austin does things on his own terms. He won't run from you, but he'll decide when he talks. That's Dwight."

"Local guy?"

"Yeah, plays out here all the time. He's easy enough to locate."

"We'll need to talk to him. For now, let's talk to your staff."

"Sure. Any particular order?"

"No, you bring 'em in and we'll take it from there."

"Okay. If you want any soft drinks, help yourself. I'll call Hook Avery. He's the course supervisor." He picked up the phone and told Hook he was wanted in the pro shop.

Bob arranged for the men to talk in his office. Al arrived and was introduced. "Al, this is Detective Kennedy," Bob said.

"Hello, how can I help you?"

"Just have a few questions for you, Mr. Avery. By the way, this is Lou and Maggie. They're working with me on this case."

"Nice to meet you folks. I'll do my best to answer any questions you've got."

"When did you first hear about the deaths?" Harry asked, leading the questioning.

"I got a call from Bob. I heard the sirens in the distance and figured they'd be coming here."

"What did Bob say?"

"He said something like, 'Hook? Got a guy down on 14. I think he's dead. I've called 911. Just wanted you to know.'"

"What did you say?"

"I said something like, 'Oh no, not again. What do you want me to do?' He said, 'Nothing at this time. Try to know the whereabouts of your staff.'"

"Why did you say, 'Not again?'"

"Because about a year ago a guy had a heart attack on number five. The same emergency procedures were followed then."

"Which were?"

"911 gets called. The ambulance comes to the pro shop area and follows the most direct cart path to the scene."

"Which of your staff would be in the area of the 14th tee?"

"That'd be, let's see, this is Saturday. That would be Gus's crew."

"What makes up a crew?"

"The head man, in this case, Gus, and five guys. The work is divided between the five at Gus's discretion."

"Mowing, raking bunkers, changing cups and stuff like that?" Harrison asked.

"Yeah, except this is Saturday and we get off the course after the greens get mowed, cups get set, bunkers raked. The men will be off the course by nine in the morning. We don't mow on the weekends. Dailey might do some mowing if it's needed, and then he'll switch to mechanic and work on the mowers and tractors most of the day."

"I'll need to talk to Gus."

"He's not here. He had a dental appointment. I let him go. He's a real cooperative guy. You'll find him very helpful."

"Who heads up the other crew? I assume they work the front nine?"

"Yeah. That crew chief is Hack Babcock. He also has five guys working with him. He'd only have a couple today, being it's Saturday. They hand water around the greens. We try to stay out of the way of the weekend golfers."

"We'll want to talk with Hack as well."

"No problem. Hack is down in the maintenance garage. Want me to send him up?"

"Not yet. Just tell him that we'll want to talk with him."

"Got any idea who did this, Mr. Avery?"

"No, sir. If it was done by an employee of Marsh Ridge, I sure hope it wasn't one of my men."

"Could it have been one of your men?"

"Well, I suppose it could be anybody. I don't think any of my staff would do anything like this. Don Dailey comes off as a pretty angry guy at times. He drinks too much and shoots off his mouth a lot. He's usually upset with some person in authority. Mind you, I'm not saying he did it, I'm just saying that of all my guys, he's the only one who seems angry a lot and who may have a tendency to lose control. Know what I mean?"

"Is this Dailey here now?"

"No, he's kinda his own guy, too. He comes and goes when he feels like it. Anybody else would fire the guy within three days of work, but Don is the finest course maintenance worker in the midwest. He's also a mechanic. In this day and age, you fire a guy with a drinking problem who shows up late for work in a minute, but Don knows mowing machines and he's a top-notch mechanic. Plus he knows how to keep a golf course groomed. Sounds strange, you'd think grass cutting and green trimming is fairly routine and a job for high school kids in the summer, but it's Don's work that makes Marsh Ridge one of the premier golf courses in the country. With his talents, he's earned the right to stay pretty much on his own. My guess is that about now, he's on his fourth or fifth beer at the Yellowjacket, a bar between the course and his home."

The next person to be interviewed was Betty Battles, the foods supervisor for the restaurant and the on-course beverages. Betty was a large woman, pear-shaped with a lot of weight from her waist to her knees. Betty, her hair bunched up under a net, was very nervous and upset. Rumor had gotten around that the golfer had been poisoned and that the poison was in the lemonade. Whether this was true or not, it was the opinion of the moment. This meant that the cause of death was in the lemonade cooler, and the lemonade cooler was the responsibility of Betty Battles.

"Try to relax, Miss Battles. We have a few questions for you," Harry began.

"I didn't do anything."

"I'm sure you didn't. But, we need to ask you some questions."

"How did the poison get in the cooler?" Betty asked frantically.

"Well, first of all, we don't know if the lemonade in the cooler was poisoned. There are several possible causes for the death. One possibility is that the man consumed some poisonous food or drink on the course. He could've brought the food or drink with him or he may have purchased it on the course. I'm not accusing you, I just need you to answer a few questions."

"Okay." Betty seemed to calm down a bit.

"How did the lemonade cooler come to be at the 14th tee?"

"We knew it would be a very hot day. I suggested to Bob a few weeks ago that on weekends we do some public relations by giving free lemonade to the golfers. We decided to put the coolers and some styrofoam cups at numbers 7 and 14. We hung a sign that said free lemonade with our appreciation for playing golf at Marsh Ridge."

"Where's the lemonade made?"

"In the kitchen."

"Who made it this morning?"

"Judy Austin."

"Who's she?"

"She works a variety of jobs. She's my best beverage girl on the course. She also works the restaurant once in awhile. So, she does food preparation, cart selling, and waitressing. All my girls do a variety of jobs."

"We'll want to talk with her. Is she here?"

"No, I let her go. She said she didn't feel well."

"How does the distribution work?"

"Judy made the lemonade around ten this morning. She made four coolers full. She took one cooler to 14 and the other cooler to 7. After a couple of hours she took the fresh coolers and replaced the used ones. She also adds new cups, if the supply is low. She made more lemonade and kept up the cycle for the rest of her shift."

"So, at about two o'clock she changed the coolers at 14?"

"Well, not on the exact hour, but in that area. Sometimes we get a call that a cooler is empty and then we'll take a fresh batch right out. I don't think that happened today."

Harry asked, "Do you know if she brought the unused lemonade back to the kitchen, or do you think she tossed it out at the 7th and 14th tees?"

Betty replied, "You'll have to ask her, but my guess is that she tosses it out there. The coolers would be lighter and she'd have to throw out the unused drink when she got back to the kitchen anyway."

"Before refilling, are the coolers washed?"

"You bet. Public Health Code requires it. There are so many regulations in the kitchen that it's a wonder that bacteria still make the kitchen their home."

"That's all, Betty. Thank you."

"Now what happens?"

"What do you mean?"

"Are you going to shut down my operation?" Betty asked nervously.

"No, why would you ask that?"

"I expect the Public Health Department to come here and go over the place with a fine-tooth comb. People won't eat here for months. I might as well resign and get another job."

"I don't know about that. I'm only interested in finding out who did this, and if the lemonade was, in fact, poisoned. I still don't have autopsy reports, you know."

Harry turned to Lou and Maggie, "We need to find out where the unused lemonade was poured onto the ground. We may need a soil analysis conducted. If an analysis of the cooler, present at the scene, shows no tainted drink, and the soil sample shows evidence of the poison, then someone changed the coolers between the time the victim went down and I got here to investigate. If the soil sample is free of poison, then it's probable that the lemonade in the container was not poisoned, and the individual cup was somehow tampered with."

Harry swung back to Bob and asked him to give him Judy's phone number. "We'll need the crime lab techs to help with this. We'll need a good soil sample taken as well, assuming I can trust Judy's memory and honesty." Harrison picked up his two-way radio and directed a deputy to ask the lab technicians to stay awhile longer.

え

The three investigators interviewed Bob and Wendy. Harry began, "Not a good time for you both. You'll get many questions from the media and many more from us, I'm sure. I appreciate your cooperation."

"How can we help?" Bob asked.

"First of all, we need to know about the pairings for the golfers this morning."

"Sure. Got a call from the pro at The Loon late Thursday afternoon. He said that they were having a bus load of golf writers on a tour and he asked if we could take several groups who were scheduled to go on The Loon. We were having a light turnout for a Saturday so I said I could accommodate some of his people."

"Is this common?"

"I wouldn't say it's common, but it's happened before."

"So someone contacted the groups, including the one we're talking about?"

"Yes. I did. I said they would be teeing off at eight-thirty at our course."

"Anything to add?"

Wendy spoke up. Wendy, the assistant pro at Marsh Ridge, was stunning, blonde, and well-tanned. She was among the 30 or so women hired as an assistant pro for the 800 plus golf courses in Michigan. Wendy earned her position with excellent steady golf on the women's tour for two years and straight A's at the University of Missouri's Professional Golf School. "I got a call from Dwight Austin who wanted to tee off following the Wallach party."

"What was his name again?" Lou asked.

Wendy continued, "Dwight Austin. Dwight's a steady player up here in Gaylord. He's out on a course in the Gaylord area every playable day. He's a multimillionaire. Word has it that he sued a major hospital in Miami for malpractice following some facial surgery related to cancer. The guy is worth millions, but, if you'll pardon the expression, he's a pain in the butt. Anyway, he wanted in around 8:37, so I put him in right after the Wallach party."

"This is the old guy in knickers?" Maggie asked.

"That's him. Says he and Payne Stewart's father were good friends in their youth. He apparently told Payne at a tournament a few years ago that he would wear knickers for the rest of his playing days as a tribute to his father's friendship."

"You said he left the course, right?" Lou asked.

"Yeah, he and his good friend, Billy, had a tee time at the Black Forest course so they left."

"That was the group that found the body?" Maggie asked.

"No, Reggie's playing partners, Bill Wallach and Dan Dillon saw him down," Bob added.

"I'm sure we'll have many more questions and we'll be seeking your help in the future," Harry said. "You can be proud of the way your staff responded to the emergency today, Bob."

"Thanks. We have periodic drills to cover heart attacks and possible accidents like getting hit with a club or a ball, but murder isn't something we anticipate. The staff is a good group of professionals."

"We're going to need to talk to Judy and then to take a soil sample for analysis yet today," Harry said to Bob.

"No problem. I'll get you Judy's phone number and just have whoever is going to do the soil sample see me and we'll cooperate in every way."

Bob had reporters calling from *USA Today, The Chicago Tribune, The Detroit Free Press,* and he'd just gotten a notice that a film crew from Channel 12 in Traverse City would be arriving soon for a broadcast to its NBC affiliates. Not exactly the kind of publicity Marsh Ridge strives for, but it was the card that got played today.

⌇

"This is Harrison Kennedy of the Otsego Sheriff's Department. Am I speaking with Judy Austin?"

"You're probably calling about the guy who died on the golf course."

"Yes."

"I didn't do it, if that's what you're wondering."

"Actually, I just want to ask a few questions about the lemonade."

"What do you want to know?"

"I'd like you to come over to Marsh Ridge so we can talk."

"I'll be there as soon as I call my lawyer." Judy didn't have a lawyer and couldn't afford one. She thought telling Harrison that she needed to call her lawyer would explain any delay in getting to Marsh Ridge.

Judy Austin was short, thin, shapely, and beautiful. She arrived about thirty minutes after Harry called, and was invited into Bob Sanders' office. "Thank you for coming out here," Harry began. He introduced Judy to Lou and Maggie and continued, "I have some questions and then we'll want you to go with us to the 14th tee."

"What do you want to know?"

"Please describe your lemonade-making and distribution."

"I got to work around nine o'clock. Betty told me that she and Bob decided to put out free lemonade for the golfers since it was supposed to be very hot today. She asked me to do what I do every weekend, make up a big batch of lemonade and prepare two big coolers. I put one cooler on the 7th tee and the other at the 14th tee. She told me to replace the cups and lemonade every couple of hours."

"And, you did this?"

"Yes. I got several packages of lemonade from the storeroom. The powder comes in big packages. You just add water, ice, and stir. Nothing to it. I took one cooler to number 7 and the other to number 14. I took the first coolers out at about ten this morning."

"I have a cooler here. Is this one of the coolers you used?"

"Yeah. They're all the same. We have about a dozen of them for various events at the course. They hold five gallons and the spigots are very good. Very little drippage."

"When you changed them, did you throw out the extra before putting the fresh one on the bench, or did you take the cooler back to the kitchen to empty?"

"I threw it out."

"Because?"

"Because it's lighter to carry, and I have to throw out the extra when I get to the kitchen anyway."

"Would it be possible for someone to poison this batch of lemonade on the 14th tee?"

"Oh, sure; you just snap up these two hooks and it opens at the top. Here, I'll show you." Judy demonstrated and waited for the next question.

"Please describe what you did the last time you changed the lemonade on the 14th tee."

"When I pulled up to the 14th tee with a fresh supply of lemonade in a new cooler, the sound of the ambulance was getting closer to the golf course. I got a glimpse of the guy down on the ground. There was a man sitting at the tee in a golf cart. He said that his partner had gone to the clubhouse to get help.

"I did what I came to do. I took the top off of the cooler by unhooking it. I tossed out the unused lemonade. I put the top back on and placed the cooler in my cart. I put the full cooler on the bench and then left to return to the kitchen."

"You didn't stay to watch the drama unfold?"

"I don't like these things. I get to feeling nauseous around accidents. So, having done what I came to do, I left."

"Okay. Now we'd like you to go with us to the 14th tee to reconstruct how you changed the coolers early this afternoon."

"I don't understand; why is this necessary?" Judy asked.

"Because if the soil where you say you threw out the unused lemonade contains the poison, we know that the batch was poisoned between the time the foursome in front of these guys drank it and Reggie died.

"If that isn't the case?"

"If that isn't the case, then it seems to me that the lemonade in the cooler was not poisoned when Reggie and his group arrived at the 14th tee. So, let's go get a sample of the earth where you threw out the unused lemonade."

They arrived at the 14th tee in three golf carts. The State Police Forensic Technician was prepared to videotape Judy's demonstration and then to lift a section of the soil where the lemonade had been poured. Harry said, "What we want you to do now is recreate, to the best of your knowledge, your actions when you came up to this tee to replace the lemonade cooler this afternoon."

Judy began, "I pulled up. The dead guy was over there on the tee. A man was in a cart waiting for the police and an ambulance. I drove up to about here. I opened the cooler, took it like this and then tossed out the remaining lemonade over here." Judy demonstrated how she actually moved.

"So, the leftover lemonade was thrown about here, ten to twenty feet away from the tee and across from the cart path?" Harrison summarized. "Two feet farther than the ball washer."

"Yes. I threw it right in that area," Judy said pointing to where Harrison was standing.

The forensic technician videotaped the demonstration and then took a soil sample in a variety of areas near and exactly where Judy said she threw the lemonade.

"Then what happened?."

"I put the fresh cooler full of lemonade onto the bench where the emptied one was."

"And then...."

"Then I saw the ambulance and golf carts coming toward the 14th tee and I left the area to go back to the kitchen."

"You weren't curious? All of this excitement and drama and you just drove away?"

"As I said, I don't have a good stomach for being around accidents and stuff like that. I didn't want to be here. It bothered me seeing the guy. I'm surprised I even switched coolers once I knew there was trouble there. Very unlike me."

"Did you know who died?"

"No. Still don't. Hundreds of guys come through here everyday."

"Does the name Reggie Macleod mean anything to you?"

"Yeah. I taught in his district when I was a special education teacher. Is he the dead golfer?"

"Afraid so."

"I'm sorry the guy died, but if you're looking for a lot of sympathy, you won't get it from me. The guy ruined my career."

"Tell me, in detail, what you were doing ten minutes before you came to this tee," Harry continued his questioning.

"I was working the front nine. I made a beverage round. I started at number 1 and drive the cart paths around the first nine holes. After I did that, I went to the kitchen to make up a new cooler of lemonade. I drove it to number 7 and switched coolers, just like I described to you here. I went back to the kitchen to wash out the cooler and to make up a new batch of lemonade. While there, I heard some sirens in the distance and one of the girls said she heard that there was a problem on the course. I put the new cooler on my cart and headed out to the 14th tee."

"So, for the ten minutes prior to being here, you were either on the front nine or in the kitchen."

"Yes, but it was more like forty-five minutes to an hour."

"What did you do after you left here?"

"I went back to the kitchen, washed out the cooler and then I took the beverage cart out for more sales. I finished my work and went home."

"Thank you, Judy, we appreciate your cooperation."

Lou and Maggie were sponges during the interview. They didn't want to intervene in Harry's questioning. They were grateful to be asked to watch Harrison work. It was a treat. Harrison was a pro, there was no question about it.

"I think that's all for today. Let's see, you folks got a place to stay?" Harrison asked.

"We'll find something. We'll hope for a motel that has a room that is accessible for Maggie and Tom. Carol and I can go anywhere."

While Lou and Maggie were with Harrison, Carol and Tom were already looking for a motel with a vacancy and an accessible room. As luck would have it, they got adjoining rooms at the brand new Hampton Inn. Carol paged Lou to let him know that she and Tom were window-shopping in downtown Gaylord. They planned to be back at the motel around six-thirty.

Carol made it a point to stop in and see Jackie and Jill at the Saturn Bestsellers Bookstore. She told them that Lou and Maggie were in town and would hope to visit in a day or two. She knew that Lou loved bookstores and the people who supported him in selling his mysteries.

Before parting for the evening, Harrison identified the people he wanted to talk to. First, he wanted to talk with Dwight Austin. He wanted to talk with the kitchen help to see if they would vouch for Judy being in the kitchen when she said she was. He also wanted to talk to Gus and his men, to Hack Babcock and his men, and especially with Don Dailey, the guy who he had discovered had had the confrontation with Dan Dillon in the Sugar Bowl. Harrison asked Bob for all names and phone numbers.

Bob and Wendy had no trouble finding the numbers of the people on their food and maintenance staff. They suggested that Dwight Austin's number might be in the Gaylord phone directory.

"Dwight and Billy often play together," Wendy offered. "Billy is Billy Wingate. He lives in Gaylord, too. His name should also be in the phone book."

Once Carol had reached Lou to explain their motel arrangement, Lou let Harrison know that they would be staying at the Hampton Inn and to be sure and call if they could be of any assistance.

"Think this will do it for today," Harrison said, taking a deep breath. "All the evidence has been catalogued, photos taken, possible suspects identified, death certified, autopsy ordered, family notified, search warrant secured, and the Michaywé condo searched for clues. Now we have paperwork and the job of tying a lot of loose ends together. We'll get a fresh start tomorrow. Enjoy your evening in Gaylord."

Before they left Marsh Ridge, Lou told Maggie that if she didn't mind waiting a few minutes, he'd like to go to the 14th tee. He'd take a golf cart and be back soon. Maggie understood and said, "You take whatever time you need, my friend."

Lou drove to the 14th tee. He stood where only a few hours ago, his friend Reggie Macleod had died. With beauty all around him, Lou remembered many joyful rounds of golf with Reggie. The two had shared excellent shots, a few missed putts, and some good soul searching conversations between shots or waiting for golfers to move ahead. They also shared a profession of helping children with disabilities, their families and teachers. They did the best they could given a host of barriers, emotions, and conflicts.

Lou knew that if Reggie had to die, there was no better place to do so than on a golf course. The game, friends, and the beauty of the courses were in his soul. There simply was no other place Reggie would rather be than on a golf course trying out a new ball, a new iron, the latest driver guaranteed to give him a few more yards, as if he really needed to be any closer to the flag than he usually was.

With his head lowered and his eyes closed, Lou paid his respects to his friend in a very private and solemn way. He said his farewell knowing how delicate this thing called life, so often taken for granted, really is. Reggie was a good man who had dedicated his career to helping others, but he also knew how to have a good time. May he have his own course in the afterlife where birdies and eagles come at will. Such would be Lou's wish for his friend. He lifted his head to see the western sky aglow with bright oranges and yellows. Streaks of sunlight forced their way through scattered clouds bringing a host of beautiful lights and colors to all privileged to see it. It was as if Reggie and Lou's father were telling Lou that all was well.

Lou took a deep breath, turned toward his cart, got in and returned to the clubhouse. He walked over to Maggie's van, got in, and said, "Thanks, Maggie. I simply needed a little time alone with Reggie."

"I understand, Lou."

As Maggie pulled out of the parking lot, Lou's thoughts turned to the joy he had personally received on a golf course; his high school and college competitive golf, playing with friends over the years, and more recently playing with his son Scott, watching him develop into a good golfer with potential yet untapped. Lou recalled the many times he had played the game with his father. Lou and his dad didn't hunt or fish. Their shared activity was golf, and it was through many holes of golf that the bond between father and son took hold.

"Let's go find Carol and Tom. They've been patient souls today. We need to give them a little attention," Lou said as they headed north into Gaylord.

"We'll solve this, Lou. It's tough to lose a friend and my gift to you will be to do whatever I can to see that justice is brought to this tragedy."

"Thanks. I know we'll solve it, or I should probably say, you'll solve it, you usually do. Let's go home, wherever home is tonight."

CHAPTER 7

Sunday, July 10
Gaylord, Michigan
The Day After the Murder

Early the next morning, unbeknownst to one another, both Lou and Harrison were out jogging before six o'clock. Lou was in downtown Gaylord, and Harrison was in his neighborhood on the outskirts of the city. Lou rarely missed his morning run along the shore of Lake Michigan, in all kinds of weather. The result was a fit 175 pounds on a six-foot frame. Lou took a great deal of pride in having his doctor tell him that he was a model patient. Lou chose not to smoke, drink, or eat a lot of fat foods. He tried to eat more than the average man's intake of fruits and vegetables. In spite of his addiction to chocolate and an active sweet tooth, Lou Searing was physically fit and in pretty good health for a young 58.

Harrison didn't run as regularly as Lou, but he put in many more miles. He was an ultramarathoner – he raced in events that took participants beyond the marathon distance of 26.2 miles. Harrison often traveled to Wisconsin or Ohio, or even into Iowa to compete in ultramarathons. He didn't carry much body fat either. Harrison's five foot seven inch frame wouldn't put him on a high school basketball team in this day and age, but if the coach wanted a scrappy guy with a lot of hustle, Harrison was the man.

Harrison also trained for triathalons. He wasn't a fast swimmer, but he plied through the water fast enough to give him a good start in a swim, bike, and run event. Never one to win a trophy, Harrison was a strong finisher and proud of his ability to compete in three sports and feel good at the end. Harrison offered a stark contrast to Lou. He was short with a full head of hair, normal hearing and the ability to walk by an M&M and leave it alone.

Lou and Carol went to the eight o'clock Mass at St. Mary's in Gaylord. Sharing Mass had been important to Lou and Carol over the past twenty-six years, Sunday after Sunday, in Kansas, Ohio, Texas, and now Michigan. Lou felt blessed to share his life with Carol. If angels spent time disguised as humans, Lou knew that Carol was an angel. She brought him much joy and happiness.

Most of Lou's thoughts were of Reggie and his friends. It was difficult to pay attention to the scripture readings and the homily. While thinking of Reggie, Lou realized that everyone else in church also had some burden to bear. When the congregation turned to another following the Lord's Prayer and said, "Peace be with you," it wasn't to be a rote phrase said as part of a ceremony, it was a sincere blessing meant to bring hope, compassion, and peace of mind to whatever was troubling the next person. On this holy morning, the death of a friend was very troubling to Lou Searing.

After church, Lou and Carol agreed to meet Maggie and Tom for breakfast at Diana's Delights. The four chose the buffet and shared various sections of the *Detroit Free Press* while consuming coffee, pancakes and orange juice.

Lou and Maggie planned to spend the day with Detective Kennedy. Tom said he was going to try to play 18 or maybe 27 holes of golf at the Gaylord Country Club, if he could get on. A cold front came through Gaylord overnight bringing rain and a relief from the very hot temperatures. Carol planned to visit a teaching colleague and perhaps do some shopping. In fact, she told Lou she'd page him if she decided to spend the day and evening on Mackinac Island. She knew she would have the time with Lou and Maggie working well into the evening on the case. Carol was used to the long hours that private investigators put in.

๛

Lou's cell phone rang after he paid his breakfast bill. "Hello."

"Lou?"

"Yeah."

"Harry Kennedy here. How're you today?"

"Good, Harry. The four of us just finished breakfast and were wondering when we could get together to continue our work."

"When we meet I'll tell you what I learned after you two left, but I wanted to call because I said I would, and to let you know that we'll be talking to Dwight Austin and Don Dailey at about one o'clock today. They're to meet us at the sheriff's department in downtown Gaylord."

"Okay, we'll be there."

"See you in a couple of hours."

Lou and Maggie were inside the sheriff's office at twelve forty-five. Harrison was on the phone when they arrived. A few minutes later he emerged. "Hello again. Want some coffee?"

"Sure."

"Let's go back to our meeting room. Neither Dwight nor Don is here yet. I want to brief you." The four entered a bland room containing a table and six chairs. The walls were bare except for a clock. There was a two-way mirror and a camera mounted on one of the walls for videotaping interviews.

"After you two left late yesterday afternoon, I received a call from Walt Wilcox who wanted me to know that Judy Austin talked with him at the casino a couple of evenings before the murder. I guess he felt that we should know that she knew the golfers were in the Gaylord area and she would have some time to plan a murder. I thanked him for the information and told me I would share it with the two of you.

"What we're seeing is an angry and bitter young woman. She knew that the man who ruined her career was in town for golf, playing the course where she worked," Maggie replied. "Judy may have seen a good chance to get revenge on her own turf, so to speak. Using good timing, she may have mixed poison in the batch of lemonade just as Reggie's group approached. He drank the poisoned drink and died. Judy takes away the tainted batch, plays innocent, and lives happily ever after."

"That does make sense," Lou offered, always proud of Maggie's reasoning.

"Yeah. The imagination is a wonderful tool in any investigation. The prosecutor's gotta have more than theory, you know," Harrison remarked.

A deputy interrupted, "Mr. Austin is here."

"Bring him back."

Dwight Austin came into the room with the same chip on his shoulder that he had carried with him on the golf course. "Gotta be outta here in fifteen minutes."

"You'll get outta here when we're finished, Mr. Austin." Not exactly a pleasant way to open the dialogue, but Harrison needed to establish his dominance right away. "This is Mr. Searing and Mrs. McMillan." Dwight looked at Lou and Maggie and nodded.

"We do thank you for coming in and we know you'd rather be doing other things, but a guy died yesterday, as you know. You were playing right behind him, at least that's what we've been led to believe. So, in doing our investigation, we need to talk with you to learn what you saw and did that day, in detail."

"Go ahead and ask your questions."

"For our records, your name is Mr. Dwight Austin. You live at 2263 Lake Otsego Drive. Correct?"

"That's right."

"Okay. We'd like you to recreate your activities that day, beginning when you called for your tee time."

"Billy and me, we..."

"Who is Billy?" Harrison asked.

"Billy's my friend and my golf partner. His name is Billy Wingate. He lives in town here."

"We'll want to talk with him, too. Got an address?"

"I don't know the number. He lives on Elm Street, a couple of blocks north of Main Street."

"We can locate him. Go ahead."

"Well, I called Wendy to get a tee time on Saturday. She said that she could fit me in at eight thirty-seven."

"You didn't make any special requests? You just asked for an open time and she said eight thirty-seven?" Harrison quizzed.

"That's right."

"Okay, then what?"

"We got to the course at about eight-fifteen. We got our clubs out of the car and put on our golf shoes. You know, doing what you do before a game."

"Okay, go ahead. Then what happened?"

"Nothin' much else to tell. We played all morning, took a break at the turn and then played up to 14. Billy said it was too hot for him. He quit after nine holes and said he was going to Jac's to play cards and have a couple of drinks. Some guy came up to me and asked if he could play along. I said it was okay with me."

"What was his name?"

"Haven't a clue. He introduced himself and we shook hands, but I didn't catch the name and I never saw him before."

"Did he say where he lived?"

"We didn't talk much. I was alone on the 10th tee and he saw a way to get in the flow of the people playing, that's all."

"Did you drive to the 14th tee?"

"No. While we were playing 13, the ambulance and sheriff's car came toward 14 and we could tell that we'd be going into a mess. We agreed to call it an afternoon and went our separate ways. I drove back to the cart barn and joined Billy in Jac's."

"Did you know the guy who died?"

"Never saw him."

"Are you related to Judy Austin who works as the beverage cart woman at Marsh Ridge?"

"I'm not her father, if that's what you mean."

"Any questions, Lou or Maggie?" Harrison asked, as he wrote Dwight's responses on his notepad.

"One more question please, Mr. Kennedy," Lou said, as he looked Dwight in the eye. "While playing the back nine, did you ever go toward the 14th tee?"

"What do you mean?"

"I mean, did you take your cart and drive up to the 13th green or the 14th tee? Or said another way, did you just play shot to shot, tee to green on number 13 till you finished the hole?"

"The latter."

"That's all, Mr. Kennedy," Lou said.

"Maggie, anything to ask?"

"Nothing at this time, thank you."

"We appreciate your cooperation, Mr. Austin. You may go," Harrison said, not happy with the information he had heard.

Harrison, Lou, and Maggie took a few minutes to check perceptions before bringing Don Dailey in for questioning. "Well, what do you think?" Harry began.

"I kept score. He lied two times for sure," Lou offered.

"Wrong," Harry quickly responded. "He lied three times and probably more. It was pretty obvious, assuming that Wendy and Bob were telling the truth."

"First of all, they told us he specifically asked to follow the Michaywé group. Secondly, he said he never saw Reggie yet he purposefully placed himself behind these guys. Which one did I miss?" Lou asked.

"You didn't hear it. I asked the question of Bob Sanders late yesterday afternoon, and he said that Judy Austin was his daughter. He said that Dwight thanked him personally for giving his daughter a job when she needed some work. So, if we can trust Bob, this Austin character is hiding stuff from us, is a pathological liar, or he's well on his way to classic Alzheimer's."

"I told him he might want to bring a lawyer because the things he said would be recorded and could be used against him in a trial. He said that was ridiculous. Then he said, 'I won't see the inside of a courtroom, and I'm not paying a lawyer to sit with me while I answer questions.'"

Harrison said, "Well, let's see what we get from Mr. Dailey." A deputy announced Mr. Dailey's arrival and was told to bring him to the conference room.

Harrison greeted Don Dailey, "Good afternoon. This is Mr. Searing and Mrs. McMillan who are assisting me." All shook hands and sat down.

"Thank you for coming in. We have some questions for you, Mr. Dailey. Shouldn't take too long," Harrison said.

"Mr. Dailey, for the record, state your name and address."

"My name is Donald Dailey. I live in a trailer park south of town here. My address is 60987 Country Lane."

"What's your job at Marsh Ridge?"

"I'm a mechanic and a member of the grounds crew."

"Specifically, you do what?"

"I maintain, repair, and keep the mowers and tractors in working condition. I mow the fairways and roughs. I mow the greens. In the fall there's tree trimming, raking, drainage work, tree planting. We also flush out and clean the underground watering system. In the spring there are flowers to plant and some landscaping."

"Did you know the victim?"

"No."

"Did you see the victim before he was found dead yesterday afternoon?"

"Yeah. I seen him in the Sugar Bowl. Me and the family was having dinner there and he was with his golfing buddies. He was with Dan Dillon. Me and Mr. Dillon had a run-in because he didn't help my daughter. I got kind of loud. I upset the Mrs. 'cause I was making a scene. She and the daughter left and the manager had to tell me to pay my bill and leave."

"What did you do after you left the Sugar Bowl?"

"We waited in my pickup till Dillon and his friends came out. We followed them to their rented home in Michaywé."

"Why did you follow them?"

"Wanted to know where they was staying."

"Why did you want to know where they were staying?"

"I was going to rough up Dan Dillon. Just needed to get the anger out. He messed up Danelle's life and he needed to get messed up. I wanted to know where he was staying so I could sort of get revenge."

"You realize this doesn't look too good for you, don't you? You have an altercation with a guy and within two days a good friend of his dies on the course where you work."

"I know that. I'm clean and I'm telling you the truth. I had nothing to do with it."

"The victim died around 1:30 or 1:45 p.m. Where were you at that time?"

"On Saturday, I usually work on the mowers and tractors in the garage. If my supervisor wants some selected mowing done, I do that."

"Were you doing any work on the course when the guy died?"

"Yeah. Hook told me to do some rough mowing on the front nine."

"Did you, at any time on Saturday, go onto the back nine?"

"No, sir. Would have been no reason to do that."

"We talked with Gus, who was supervising the back nine, and he said he saw you in the area of the 13th green about the time the man died. How do you account for that?"

"Oh, wait a second. That's right. I was over near the green on 13 in the afternoon."

"Why were you there?"

"Judy Austin said she dropped a bag of ice from her cart and she asked if I would drive over to get it. I did."

"Tell us about that."

"I was taking a break near the kitchen. Judy Austin came back in her cart. She told me she lost a bag of ice back near the 13th green. She asked me to drive my cart over and get it for her. I agreed and took the cart over. I found the bag of ice, picked it up, and brought it back to the kitchen. She thanked me and I went back to my mowing."

"When you got that ice, did you see anything or hear anything out of the ordinary?" Harry asked.

"I don't know if it was out of the ordinary, but when I was driving along the cart path toward the 13th green, I saw a person in knickers driving a cart toward me."

"Coming toward you?"

"Yeah, I was on the cart path going toward the 13th green. He passed me and I guess he joined his friend on the 13th tee."

"How do you know he was playing number 13?"

"Because on my way back to the kitchen, I took the cart path along 13 and I seen the two men in the two carts and a guy in knickers was sitting in one of the carts."

"Would you say that was odd?"

"Not really. He could have driven up to see the green on 13. Sometimes players want to see what the fairway or green area looks like. You know; water, traps, amount of surface behind the green. Stuff like that."

"Does that happen if you've played the course before?"

"Not usually; once you get a picture of the layout, you don't need to refresh your memory unless you take a guest with you and he's playing it for the first time."

"Did you see his face? Was it Dwight Austin?"

"I don't recall seeing his face so I wouldn't know if it was Dwight or not. I probably didn't look at him. I don't like the man and looking at his face is kind of disgusting to me. Sorry, but it is. I think I recall his golf hat being down kinda hidin' his face. He does that sometimes, I think he is kinda embarrassed to have people see him."

"Any other reason he could have been behind you?"

"None that I can think of."

"Another question. When you got the ice, did you see the guy who died?"

"No."

"I know you're being honest with us," Maggie said, "but I find it strange that you would initially say that you were not on the back nine on Saturday when your memory is so clear of the events of which you are sharing."

"I'm sorry, ma'am, I'm always on the go. I work hard and on Saturday, I worked the front nine. I done Judy a favor that took all of three or four minutes. I drove a cart the length of three holes, picked up a bag of ice and returned to the kitchen. It was an insignificant favor in a day full of work. If I'd hit a deer or driven into the lake, then I woulda remembered, but just driving to get a bag of ice near the 13th green, it just didn't stay in my mind."

"Appreciate your candid response. Any more questions, Mr. Searing or Mrs. McMillan?"

"Just one," Lou said. "When did you plan to rough up Mr. Dillon. You didn't do it when you followed the guys back to the rented house. Were you going to do it after their golf round on Saturday?"

"I don't know. I do a lot of threatening. I never carry 'em out. You can ask my friends, my wife, the guys in the Yellowjacket Bar. They'll all tell you I talk tough, but never follow through. I'd had some beers before the Sugar Bowl thing. I was just sounding tough. I had no plans to harm Mr. Dillon."

Harry looked toward Maggie anticipating her set of questions. She surprised him with, "No more questions, Mr. Kennedy."

"Thank you, Mr. Dailey. We appreciate your help in answering our questions. We may be contacting you in the future."

After Dailey left, Harrison, Lou and Maggie looked at each other, raising hands and arms as if to say, "I don't know. He sounded honest." Harrison said, "If we can trust Don, we just caught Dwight in lie number four. He answered that he didn't drive ahead before playing the 13th hole."

"That's right," Maggie said, surprised.

"Wouldn't you, if you were an intelligent being, a millionaire no less who loves to play golf, who plays behind a guy who dies and with whom you had an altercation with forty-eight hours earlier, take the questions and answers of a detective a little more seriously?" Harrison asked, shaking his head in amazement. "Wouldn't you have an attorney at your side? I mean, it really doesn't look too good for the old guy."

Lou and Maggie nodded in agreement. Lou said, "They have weights and basketball in most of the prisons, but he's going to have to buy off a judge to get to a prison where there's a golf course. Usually murderers don't get the posh prisons. It's the white collar criminals who get the good treatment. This guy has me curious."

"He could be very unstable. He accused Bill Wallach of hitting into them four times and he confronts people in anger. He obviously has little respect for authority – just leaving the golf course yesterday and not hanging around to answer questions about the murder of a golfer playing in front of him. He has lied four times if Bob's, Wendy's and Don's stories check out. We may be dealing with a guy who isn't playing with a full deck," Harrison cautioned.

"If that's the case, could he plan and carry out the murder of a man in such a way that we're currently without a weapon, a witness, or a clear motive?" Lou asked.

"Not sure, but it looks like he's our best suspect at the moment," Harrison concluded.

"Phone call for you, sir" said the deputy who entered the conference room.

"Thanks."

"Mr. Kennedy, this is Rick Williams. I have the autopsy results for the victim who died yesterday. The cause of death was cyanide poisoning."

"Thanks, Rick. We'll need a copy of the death certificate and a copy of the autopsy report for our records. Does the medical examiner know of the results?"

"It's my understanding he does. I'll get the copies for you."

"Thanks."

Kennedy turned to Lou and Maggie. "Cause of death was cyanide poisoning just as we predicted. After I talked to you this morning, I got a call from the State Police Forensic Lab and the drops in the cups did contain cyanide. The lemonade in the cooler that was at the tee when I arrived was fine."

"So, we still don't know how the lemonade got into the cup," Lou said. "We can't just presume that the lemonade that Reggie drank came from the cooler. Someone could have driven up to the tee and offered Reggie a cup of the lemonade that was spiked with poison."

"Could've happened that way, Lou," Harrison said. "One fact seems clear, poisoned lemonade appeared at the 14th tee between the time the first group of four teed off and got out past the dogleg, and when Reggie appeared at the 14th tee. This could not have been more than five to ten minutes."

"Right; it also seems unlikely that someone who is not associated with the course, or playing golf, would come all the way out here to carry out this murder."

"I agree," Harrison said. "Whoever did this took quite a risk in having Reggie and only Reggie drink it without others witnessing the whole episode."

"We also don't know for whom the lethal drink was intended," Maggie noted. "Did the murderer want all three to die or did the murderer only want one or two to die?"

"Dillon didn't say any was offered to him," Harrison noted. "Bill was not given any when he left the Port-a-John. My guess is that the killer specifically targeted Reggie and was very lucky to find him alone by the tee, or else the killer wanted one dead and it didn't matter who was poisoned."

۶

Harrison suggested that interviewing Dwight and Don was enough for a Sunday. Lou decided to go home to Grand Haven and Maggie to Battle Creek. Before Lou and Maggie left, Lou asked, "Do you have anything specific that you wish us to do, Harry?"

"When you introduced yourself, you said you could help because of your knowledge of education. So, I would ask you to put that knowledge to work. Since you know these guys, perhaps you could see if there are any circumstances that could provide a motive."

"Sure. Be glad to. In the meantime what will you be doing?"

"I'll be doing more talking. I've got to talk to Billy. I'll be talking with Gus and Hack and the rest of the maintenance crew as well as the kitchen staff to see if they saw or heard anything unusual that day."

"Sure wish we could be there. It's frustrating not to see the big picture," Lou said.

"Before you head home, do you want to conduct another

interview?" Harry asked.

"Sure," Maggie replied. "The more information we can get, the better. Solving this case is a priority."

"Let's call Billy Wingate to see if we can see him," Harrison said, as he picked up the phone and dialed the local number.

"Hello."

"Mr. Wingate?"

"Yes."

"This is Detective Harrison Kennedy of the Otsego Sheriff's Department. How are you today, sir?"

"Doing all right, I guess. I figured you'd be calling sooner or later."

"Mr. Wingate, if it wouldn't inconvenience you too much on a Sunday afternoon, I'd like to ask you a few questions concerning yesterday's death at Marsh Ridge."

"Sure. It isn't an inconvenience. I'd like to help in any way I can."

"Could you come to the sheriff's office, or would you prefer we come to your home?"

"You could come here, but I've got to mail some letters, so I'll come right over."

"Thank you. I'll see you soon."

Harry gave Lou and Maggie a thumbs up. More information was minutes away.

Billy Wingate was a huge man for his height. His skin was weathered, his hair matted where a golf hat would fit snugly, and he moved as if he had some arthritis. Billy appeared nervous as he arrived to talk with the detectives. Lou noticed Billy's hand was cold when he held it in greeting.

"Thanks for coming in on such short notice."

"No problem."

"Mr. Wingate, we'd like you to tell us what you experienced yesterday. No, first go back to the confrontation that Mr. Austin had with a gentleman the other day. Apparently Mr. Austin felt that some guys were hitting into him. Can you shed some light on that?"

"That was pretty ugly. Sad, too. I don't know what is happening to Dwight. Maybe it was the surgery, or drugs related to the surgery. I don't know, but he isn't the Dwight Austin I have known for several years. Anyway, he was telling me that the guys behind were hitting into us. I never really saw a ball or felt there was a problem. He said he was angry and that he was going to confront the guys the first chance he got. Well, we ran into a backup around the 12th tee and the guys caught up with us. After we hit our drives, Dwight confronted the guys and of course they said he was crazy. A shouting match started. We drove away and awhile later one of the guys really did hit into us. Dwight kept his cool, but I knew something would happen later. He just boiled inside."

"Did he threaten those guys?"

"In a sense. He didn't say he was going to get a shotgun and blow them away, but I knew he would do something. I just knew he would."

"Then what happened?"

"When we finished the round, Dwight asked the pro for the names of the group playing behind us. The starter told him that they were a group from Michaywé. So, Dwight called Michaywé and lied about being a friend who wanted to surprise him. The Michaywé operator or one of their employees gave Dwight the address and phone number."

"So now he knew who was behind you guys and he knew they were staying at Michaywé."

"That's right."

"Okay, then what happened?"

"We go into the bar and he seems okay. He didn't say anything else about the confrontation. That evening I think it was, I got a call from Judy Austin and she told me that the Wallach group would be playing Marsh Ridge on Saturday. She thought I should mention it to Dwight so he could get a tee time right behind them. That didn't make much sense to me, but I did what she asked. He said he'd call Bobby and get the tee time. You see, Dwight felt like he could get on any course in Gaylord, at any time he wished, and actually, he did.

He throws his weight around pretty good. He's a multimillionaire you know. He'd just give the pro a fifty or a hundred dollar bill when he'd get the time he asked for. If he didn't get the exact time he'd tip the pro, but only about half or a quarter of what he'd give when he got the exact time he wanted."

"Money talks, huh?"

"I guess it does, I've never had enough of it to find out."

"Me neither." The exchange was lighthearted and everyone in the conference room seemed to relax. "Go ahead, Mr. Wingate."

"So, Dwight told me he'd pick me up at about eight Saturday morning 'cause we had a tee time at eight thirty-seven at Marsh Ridge. We also had a tee time of three-thirty or four o'clock at Black Forest."

"Costs quite a bit to play these courses all the time, doesn't it?" Harrison asked.

"Oh yeah, but like I say, he has all the cash he could ever want. He sued some hospital in Miami for malpractice, and he just drops money like it was free, which for him, it is. He pays for all of my rounds. We play well together and he knows I can't afford it. So, guess I'm pretty lucky. Anyway, this isn't helping you. I'll go on. So, we get to Marsh Ridge, get our carts and warm up. Dwight wants us to stay back from the group in front of us. He pointed out that these were the same guys that hit into us two days before, which I already knew. So, we stay away from the tee till the starter calls us. The guys probably saw Dwight and me. You can't miss Dwight in those knickers with his deformed face."

"Did Dwight say that he planned to get a tee time that would place you guys immediately behind the Wallach group?"

"He just said that we had an eight thirty-seven time."

"Then what happened?"

"Just golf."

"So, you play the front nine?" Harrison asked, trying to lead Billy to talk some more.

"Yeah. We stopped at the turn for food. The play was not fast so we had a hamburger even though it was late morning. I was too hot.

Dwight and I were going to play later in the afternoon at Black Forest. I told him I was going to Jac's to play some cards. He played on and I guess some guy asked to join him. Then the two of them started the back nine."

"The next thing you know –" Harrison was interrupted.

"Well, we got word that there was some problem out on 14. I immediately thought it was the murder mystery weekend folks kicking up a production. The ambulance came and headed out there. A few minutes later Dwight appeared and said he quit 'cause of some problem on 14, and with it being so hot, he needed a rest before we play Black Forest. He was in a pretty good mood and ordered drinks for all. I never did understand the reason for his celebration."

"Did he say who died or anything about the death scene?"

"No, he didn't seem to know a guy died. He said play would be backed up and they may not let him play from 14 so he just got out of the heat. I knew you wanted to talk to him, but Dwight said we had a three-thirty or four o'clock tee time and we needed to go. I told him he shouldn't run from the cops. He said we weren't running. We'd be available to talk, but he wanted to play, so we left."

"No one thought to leave names and phone numbers?"

"Guess not."

"How do you think the guy died?"

"Don't know."

"Do you think Dwight had a part in this, based on the confrontation?"

"Naw. He couldn't do anything like that. If this was a murder, it had to be planned and carefully executed. Dwight is getting old like me, he isn't sharp anymore. He gets upset and angry, and it's embarrassing, but he wouldn't kill anyone. He certainly wouldn't do it 'cause he thought someone hit into him on a golf course. If he had any reason to kill anyone, it would be the people involved in the malpractice problem down in Miami. No, Dwight fights with his mouth and goes after people with lawyers. He'd rather have their money than their life. The money puts him on a golf course everyday. A murder puts him in prison. It wasn't Dwight. I don't have a lot of money, but I'd be a fool not to bet every dollar I have that Dwight is innocent, completely innocent."

Harrison thanked Mr. Wingate for answering their questions. After Billy left, the three briefly discussed what he had to say. They realized that they were no closer to solving the murder than they were when Billy arrived several minutes ago.

Lou decided it was time to leave for Grand Haven. He and Carol would be getting in around midnight. Maggie and Tom had an equally long trip ahead of them. They thanked Harrison and the three briefly discussed their next steps. For Harrison it would be more interviews. He would talk to the ranger and continue to investigate where leads took him. Lou and Maggie planned to look into motives by talking further with Reggie's golfing friends.

The three clasped hands in farewell. Each felt they knew one another better and respected each other for their unique talents. They decided to call and report findings regularly. The Searings and McMillans pointed their vehicles south on I-75.

CHAPTER 8

Monday, July 11
Gaylord, Michigan
Two Days After the Murder

The next morning, Harrison was out at Marsh Ridge talking with Bob and Wendy. He said that he needed to talk with the ranger who was in the vicinity of the 14th tee last Saturday. Bob checked his list of ranger assignments and said that it was Mark Thompson. Mark was a part-time ranger who helped out on weekends. He lived in Vanderbilt, about ten miles north of Gaylord. Bob gave Harrison his phone number and his address from the employees' roster.

At about ten o'clock Harrison turned right onto Summit and pulled into the driveway of Mark Thompson. He knocked and a white-haired, overweight, well-tanned man opened the door. "Yes?"

"Good morning. I'm Detective Harrison Kennedy of the Otsego Sheriff's Department. Could I have a few moments of your time?"

"What's the problem?"

"I want to talk with you about what you may have seen or heard last Saturday around the 14th tee of Marsh Ridge."

Mark's face flushed from the anxiety that came over him. "You can come in, sure, but I don't understand what you're talking about."

"You didn't hear about the guy who died on the golf course last Saturday?"

"Yeah, I heard about that, but why are you talking to me?"

"Because you were on the course when it happened."

"I'm not sure where I was when he died."

"As a ranger, what part of the course do you work?"

"There are two of us, one works the front nine, and the other works the back nine."

"Last Saturday, which nine did you work?"

"I don't remember for sure. I think it was the back nine."

"Is it all right if I come in and ask a few questions?"

"Oh, sure. Come on in. Want some coffee?"

"No thanks, I'll probably only be here a few minutes. I'll also be taping our conversation for review later."

"Have I got any rights? I'm a little nervous about this. I've never had a detective from the sheriff's department in my home before. Should I have a lawyer with me?"

"You are not a suspect. I just wanted to ask a few questions, but if you're comfortable with an attorney, we can wait if you want to see if your lawyer can meet with us."

Mark excused himself, went to his kitchen and called someone. When he returned, he said that his lawyer was coming right over and that he was not to say another word till she arrived. In about five minutes a woman in a red, late-model Buick pulled into the drive. Her name was Kara Ingram. Kara was a recent graduate of the University of Michigan College of Law and a native of Vanderbilt. She had been the valedictorian of her high school class, gone off to the prestigious school, and unlike others who got a taste of the big world and wouldn't think of coming home, Kara had come home to use her talents and knowledge to help her friends and neighbors.

After the customary handshakes and formal greetings, Mark invited Harrison and Kara to sit down at the dining room table. Kara turned to Harrison, "Now, what's the problem?"

"Last Saturday a man was poisoned on the 14th tee of the Marsh Ridge Golf Resort south of Gaylord. I'm talking to anyone who might have seen or heard anything that I can tie to this crime. Mr. Thompson was a ranger on the course that day and may have been in the area of the 14th tee when this happened. So, I'm here today to ask Mr. Thompson some questions about that."

"You're suspecting him of murder?" Kara asked.

"No, although if he was in the area he'd have to explain his activity in order to rule him out as a suspect. I didn't come here suspecting him of the crime. I just want to know if Mark saw or heard anything in that area that would help us solve this thing."

"I'd like a word or two with Mr. Thompson," Kara said.

"Fine, I'll go outside. Let me know when you're finished."

A few minutes later, Miss Ingram opened the front door and asked Harrison to return.

"Mr. Thompson has nothing to say at this point, Mr. Harrison," Kara said, after the three of them were seated. "We don't wish to be difficult or uncooperative, but I need more time with my client to understand this situation."

"Could I just ask a few basic questions?"

"As I said, he will not comment at this time."

"So, you think it will be helpful to you, as an attorney, and to me, as a detective to get a judge to issue a subpoena to force Mr. Thompson to answer a few questions about whether or not he saw or heard anything last Saturday afternoon?"

"That's correct."

"Fine. I guess Mr. Thompson is much more of a suspect in this case than I had originally thought. I'm sure I'll be seeing more of you both in the future. I'll be in touch, Miss Ingram."

With that, farewells were exchanged and Harrison Kennedy drove back to Gaylord planning to seek a subpoena. However, on the way to Gaylord, Harrison decided that he wouldn't play that card at this point. He'd wait and see what other information was forthcoming.

ॐ

While Harrison was investigating in Gaylord, Lou was getting a haircut at the Head Shed Barber Shop in Grand Haven. Sue, the owner and his barber, had been cutting his hair for years. Lou always thought it ironic that she kept getting more money while the number of hairs on his head were steadily decreasing. Sooner or later, he'd be paying big bucks and Sue would have nothing to do. But Sue was good. She was not a hair stylist mind you, she was a barber and a darn good one.

"Well, what case are you working on now, Lou?" Sue asked.

"Just got back from Gaylord. Maggie and I are helping a sheriff's detective who is investigating the death of a golfer at Marsh Ridge."

"Heard about that in the news. An education administrator may have been poisoned while playing golf. That the one?"

"Yeah, that's it."

"Man, I tell you, administration can be murder. I've got some customers in education administration and from what they tell me, that's one stressful occupation."

"Can be. Not a whole lot different than any other occupation. Talk about stress, I think teachers have a lot more stress dealing with children; each a unique learner, each coming to school with a host of joys and conflicts. The teachers are the ones with the stress. But yeah, the administrator has his or her own set of stresses. No question about that."

"Well, you and Maggie got it all wrapped up?"

"Oh, no, just starting. This one will be complicated. Lots of subplots and characters involved. This investigation will be my next book – should have Hollywood producers knocking on my door like shoppers waiting for the doors to open at Dollar Days in the mall. It'll make a good movie. I'll be sure and get a haircut before going to the Academy Awards," Lou said, with a chuckle.

"Well, if anyone can get to the bottom of it, you and Maggie will crack it. Of that, I have no doubt."

"This one won't be easy, Sue, you got any advice for me?"

"Well, I have little information on the case, but from what I've read in the paper, and the hundreds of mysteries I've read over the years, my guess is that this murder is about revenge. I see revenge written all over this one and I'll be watching the paper and waiting for you to come back in a month to tell me I'm right."

"Well, revenge figures into most murders, Sue. So, you've given yourself a wide birth of possibility."

"If you want me to be specific, keep looking at that beverage woman," Sue advised.

"Sounds like you've been investigating?"

"Only know what I read in the paper and that's not much. But, just remember today in this barber shop. The solution to the case involves the beverage girl and revenge."

"Okay. If you're right, I'm going to have to bring all of my cases in here for your psychic reading."

"Well, if you recall, on your last case, I said to check out that principal's life beyond school. Remember?"

"Yeah, I guess I remember that."

The chit-chat turned to Sue's son in school and other topics including the Tigers' struggle to get to five hundred, and Grand Haven in general. Lou paid her along with a two-dollar tip and left to meet Carol for lunch at The Pronto Pup. Two chili dogs often had to be chased by a Rolaids, but it was an occasional treat at a popular Grand Haven eatery.

ﭺ

The evening was perfect for a stroll along the beach behind the Searing home located up on a dune, overlooking Lake Michigan. The moon was full and the lake was relatively calm. With the sun about to set on the horizon, Lou and Carol and their golden retriever Samm walked north where they could see the Grand Haven pier in the distance. They walked barefoot, allowing the cool water to wash over their feet. Their skin enjoyed the caresses of warm air, and the grainy sand beneath their feet provided a welcome massage. Walking hand in hand, Lou recalled buying some minnows, sitting on the pier, and catching countless perch as a little boy growing up in Grand Haven.

"This beach has a lot of memories for you, doesn't it, Lou?" Carol said strolling along hand in hand with her husband.

"You bet. I can recall end of the school year parties out at the beach. It was the beginning of summer and we'd get our report cards. There was always an air of suspense, wondering if I'd get promoted to the next grade. Of course, I always did, but there was a chance that a teacher would think that another year would be helpful. With my hearing loss, I probably only heard half of what was said all year, every year."

"Wasn't this beach where you wished Amanda a great life?"

"Yes, it was; that was an emotional moment for me. She loved the beach and Lake Michigan too. After she graduated from Michigan State University we took a drive over here. Remember? We were living in Haslett at the time. We walked out on the pier and then we stood on the beach together, father and daughter, living a moment in time. We gave each other a hug. It was symbolic for me, kind of a 'have a great life now. I love you,' send-off."

"Didn't you deliver newspapers out at the oval, too?"

"You're tapping all of my boyhood memories, Sweetzie. I remember selling *The Muskegon Chronicle* and *The Grand Rapids Press* to the folks in the trailers and in the cottages up in the dunes. I think papers cost seven cents back then. I used to go to the Bil-Mar Restaurant on my way home and get a coke and play a couple of pin ball games – baseball as I recall."

Samm kept demanding that a stick be thrown and Carol obliged. Lou and Carol turned and headed back to their home. The sun was down at this point. The moon became brighter, stars could be seen twinkling above as Lou and Carol paused to give each other a hug and to share a quiet and romantic moment before returning to the cares and responsibilities of their lives.

"Thanks for being in my life, Sweetzie," Lou said with a firm hug.

"We do have a good time, Lou. We're a couple of fortunate people."

"Very blessed, I'd say."

Samm ran up to the door of the Searing home. She was ready for a good brushing and a long sleep. The fresh summer Michigan air assured Lou and Carol of a restful evening as well.

CHAPTER 9

Tuesday, July 12
Traverse City, Michigan

T he early part of the week was one for grieving in Traverse City, Michigan, Reggie's hometown. Maggie suggested to Lou that the reception following the funeral would provide an opportunity for the golfers to talk about what happened at Marsh Ridge. Lou agreed and further suggested that Maggie attend. He believed four ears taking in thoughts and perceptions were better than two, and especially when his two did not function very well due to an early childhood case of the measles..

The memorial service began at eleven. Lou, Carol, and Maggie attended and sat with Doc, Jeff, and their families. Reggie Macleod was a highly respected leader who cared immensely for people. The most moving portion of the service was a eulogy provided by Nick Deal, an adult with Down Syndrome. He spoke on behalf of Special Olympics. For the past couple of decades Reggie had organized a golf tournament in his community. Not only were the proceeds to go to Special Olympics, but Reggie arranged for a Special Olympian to be a part of each golf foursome. They were great days remembered fondly by members of the community. Thousands of dollars were raised each year.

Next, a member of Reggie's staff at the Sand Dunes Intermediate School District spoke of Reggie's love of children and his joy in doing what he could to see that programs were in place for youngsters with disabilities. Reggie's daughter somehow found the strength to praise her father for all the work he had done for people. She had trouble getting through her list of memories, growing up with her father. She recalled family vacations, Christmas mornings, and his pride in her for being in the National Honor Society.

The golf pro at Reggie's country club spoke. Everyone knew of Reggie's love of golf. It almost consumed him during the eight playable months in Michigan. The pro recalled the hole in one on number 8. He told stories of the joy Reggie gave and received on the golf course. The pro brought some humor to the solemn service by telling of the time Reggie four-putted the final hole of a round when a par would have given him a 69. Most of the mourners groaned - knowing how much a 69 would have meant to Reggie Macleod.

Mrs. Bellingham spoke on behalf of parents of children with disabilities. She noted Reggie's collaborative style of leadership that allowed the parent voice to be heard on matters of policy. Reggie also made it a point to visit parents who had children enrolled in his programs. He took his leadership role seriously.

Jeff Gooch spoke on behalf of the golf group. Jeff shared many memories of Reggie's antics, his love of golf, storytelling, and simply enjoying the fellowship of friends around a sport that each loved.

The luncheon reception, held at Reggie's country club, allowed Lou and Maggie the chance to talk about the day of the murder. Carol was off talking with someone she recognized from her days as a consultant for hearing impaired children in the Lansing area. Even though each mourner wanted to talk with friends and relatives, Lou and Maggie reserved a table in a corner of the reception hall. If Reggie's friends could handle a discussion of that fateful day, Lou figured each speaking and listening to one another would provide an excellent forum for ideas and memories of the circumstances of the day to be shared.

One at a time, the men arrived, sat down, and joined in the conversation while picking at their buffet luncheon. Lou said, "Art, can you tell me what's on your mind about Reggie's death last Saturday?"

"Yeah, I want to know if the ranger is behind bars yet?"

"What do you mean by that?"

"I'm sure that the old man killed Reggie, but now I think the old man had an accomplice and that would be the ranger."

"Tell me more."

"I never thought about it till early this morning to be honest. I closed my eyes and tried to remember every detail. I almost wanted to be hypnotized so that I could relive the activities. I knew I would see you today, and I wanted to be as accurate with my memory as possible."

"Thanks. Talk to me about the ranger."

"Well, number 14 is a dogleg to the right. It cuts right at about two hundred yards out. I tried to cut the corner. If I was successful, I had only a six or seven iron into the green and my chances for a birdie were good. Well, I didn't quite make it; I had a slight slice and I was a little short. So, I was in the woods, but didn't expect to have any trouble finding my ball. All the others went to the left side thinking they would have a longer second shot to the green, but they wouldn't have the trees to worry about. One has to respect them for playing it safe, but I deserve credit for taking the risk to cut the corner."

"You're my kind of player, Art. Proud of you," Lou added.

"Thank you," Art said, smiling. "Anyway, I took Walt to his ball and then drove the cart toward the woods. While I was driving across the fairway I glanced to my right, or back toward the tee, and I saw the ranger sitting in his cart. I thought nothing of it. The sight of a ranger on the course is typical. They're all over, usually on the cart paths, but they often go across fairways or sit up on hills looking at two or three groups. In fact, like I say, I didn't even recall that glance until this morning when I concentrated and went through every motion I could recall last Saturday."

"What was he doing?"

"Nothing. He was just sitting in the cart. He was looking in our direction and his cart was facing us. It was like he was looking for us to finish our second shots to the 14th green."

"He was sitting in his cart on the 14th tee?"

"No, not on the tee, in front of the tee about twenty or thirty yards I'd say."

"Can you describe him?"

"Not from that distance, but we had spoken with him earlier in the day and it was the same guy. He was overweight. He had a baseball type hat and white hair. I remember that."

"Do you remember anything about his cart?"

"It had a small red flag sticking up high in the air. He had a cooler with him; I razed him earlier asking if any of his refreshments were for sale thinking they were probably spiked with some booze. It was a small personal cooler."

Lou thanked Art for his comments, turned to Jeff and said, "If it wouldn't be too emotional, I'd like to hear your story about what happened."

"Good, 'cause I've been waiting to tell it. I thought we'd be interviewed by the Gaylord detective, though."

"We're working together, Jeff. Your telling me is as good as telling him. I'm recording this and I'll give him a copy. If Harrison needs more information, he'll probably call you."

"All right, that's great. I feel more comfortable talking to you and Maggie, anyway."

"Anything you'd like to start with?"

"Yeah. I've been trying to go over the activities of last weekend myself, looking for some tip or event that would help. In addition to what we mentioned at the course, I think the whole thing is a conspiracy."

"A conspiracy?" Lou asked surprised.

"Yeah. There were three people on that course last Saturday who had reason to kill. If the three people I'm thinking of put their anger together, they could work together to kill at least three of us."

"Talk about the three," Maggie said, pen ready to record.

"The most obvious was the old man with the deformed face and knickers. He had the altercation with Bill Wallach on Thursday. We all knew that something would happen. Some revenge would be offered. So, that old man could be one player. If people think it's a coincidence that the old guy was playing right behind Bill's group on Saturday, they're very naive."

"Okay, and the second?"

"The second would be Judy Austin. When Walt got back from his gambling in St. Ignace, he told all of us that he had met Judy at the casino. He said that she was angry with Reggie over his dismissing her from her teaching job. She thought that he had ruined her career. So, on the course, we had Judy, and what does she do, she's the beverage girl who takes the coolers out around the course. How did Reggie die? Poisoned lemonade. It doesn't take a lot of grey cells to figure out that she's a major suspect."

"Two down and one to go," Lou remarked taking copious notes.

"My last suspect is a guy, I don't recall his name, but...."

"Don Dailey?"

"Yeah, maybe. He had a run-in with Dan a week ago Friday night in the Sugar Bowl. According to Dan, when he got back to the table, that family was angry with him for some decisions they didn't like regarding programming for their disabled daughter. I heard that Dailey has a job at Marsh Ridge and travels around the course. There you have it – three people who are angry with three of us. If any one of them knew that the others were also angry, they could have put their heads together and figured out some way to make them all satisfied."

"Sure does make sense. Thanks, Jeff," Lou said. "Oh, one more question, Did you guys drink the lemonade at the 14th tee?"

"Yeah. It was a hot day and it was free."

"Did you see anyone else in that area when you were playing 13 or 14?"

"I don't remember. Those holes are out on the perimeter of the course. I don't recall seeing anyone."

"You didn't see that old man, Judy, or Don at any time you were playing those two holes?"

"Can't say that I did. Maybe there was some activity, but I don't remember anything out of the ordinary."

"Jeff, do you know of any other people in Reggie's life who would want him dead?" Maggie asked.

"No, I don't. Reggie has always been a likeable guy."

⌇

Maggie turned to her right, "Matt, have you anything to offer?"

"Well, for what it's worth, when we were playing the front nine, I banana sliced the ball on number 5. It went clear over into the next fairway. Because I was so far out of the way, I left on my own to find the ball. Walt said he'd walk to his ball as he needed the exercise. When I got to my ball in the middle of the fairway, I noticed some people and a few carts near the 8th hole. I didn't realize it at the time, but the three people were the ranger, the maintenance worker named Don something or other, and Judy. They looked serious, and the girl handed something to the ranger. I was too far away to know what it was, but it was small, like a medicine bottle or a small envelope of some kind. As I said, nothing to concern me, but once Reggie was poisoned I got to thinking back to that meeting and wondering if there was a connection between his death and those three. Know what I mean?"

"Good eyes, Matt. We don't know what it means yet, but all of these observations help and will eventually add up to solving this thing. Did the group continue talking?" Maggie asked, taking careful notes.

"The meeting took a few seconds. They came together, got out of their carts, and exchanged some words. Judy handed the ranger the item, whatever it was, and they turned toward the far backside of the course. The girl pointed at something in the direction of the 13th green or 14th tee. A few seconds later, each got into a cart and drove away."

"That's helpful. Was anything else out of the ordinary?"

"Not that I can think of, Maggie."

"If you do think of anything that might help us with this, would you please give one of us a call?"

"Absolutely. Thanks for getting involved. I'm sure you'll find out who killed Reggie."

"Thanks for your confidence. It may take a little work to convict the murderer, but we'll get to the bottom of this, bet your next hole in one on it."

On Maggie's right sat Doc Lewis. "Doc, is it too soon to ask you to share your thoughts about Reggie's death?"

"No. I want to help. As you know I wasn't there, but I do have my theory for what it's worth. Wish I could give you some magic information that would make the light go on and lead to what you're looking for."

"What's your theory, Doc?" Maggie asked while the others listened intently.

Doc adjusted the volume on his hearing aids so he could hear Maggie's questions. And after thinking for a few seconds said, "When I look to the obvious, I see Reggie being murdered by that girl, Judy. She was angry at Reggie and she told Walt her father was very upset as well. Too obvious though. Then there was the guy who confronted Dan in the Sugar Bowl. He's a maintenance worker at the course. Also too obvious. And the old man in knickers playing right behind Bill and Reggie two days later. Again, too obvious. If you look to two or more of them working together, you get a conspiracy theory. Too obvious."

"How about the ranger? Is that too obvious, too?" Maggie asked.

"The ranger? What about the ranger? I haven't heard about that."

"Art just told us that he had seen the ranger back near the 14th tee after the rest of his group had gotten to their drives."

"I didn't hear that. Too much noise in this hall for me to follow a conversation. Sorry. But the ranger wasn't an obvious suspect. I don't think he did it."

"Why do you say he didn't do it?"

"I just know he didn't do it. He was a friend of Reggie's. He wouldn't have a reason for murdering a friend."

"How do you know he was a friend of Reggie's?"

"I recall one of the guys telling me that Reggie and that ranger were on the Western Michigan University Golf Team back in the early

'60s. I don't think golf teammates would kill one another, especially for no apparent reason years later."

"Okay, so back to looking beyond the obvious. What do you think?" Maggie asked.

"I've no clue, no evidence, and no proof, but I think the guy who killed them was the pro, Bob Sanders."

"Talk to me about it," Lou said, intrigued by Doc's theory.

"Stay with my theory of its not being the obvious. The pro placed all the golfers on the course. He controlled who played and the order of play. He also controlled his staff's moves. He's the logical person for no one to suspect. That's why I think he's guilty."

"Why would he want Reggie dead?"

"Oh, I didn't say he wanted Reggie dead. I said he killed him."

"You're suggesting that someone else, like Dwight Austin for example, paid him to kill Reggie?"

"Precisely. I heard that the old man had a lot of money. Why wouldn't a young golf pro want thirty to fifty thousand dollars of pocket cash? Why wouldn't he want to please a fine customer? Seems like a perfect setting for a murder. No witnesses. The pro's back at the clubhouse shortly after it actually happens. If he was at the scene, it's normal for him to be out and about in a cart checking on things, meeting with the players and easily manipulating the scene so that poison is given to Reggie or maybe it would have been given to others, too. He could have even been at the tee talking with them. Who's going to question why the head pro is out on his own course?"

"Does make sense," Maggie said, tilting her head and jotting down Doc's thoughts.

"Of course it does," Doc continued. "Judy, Don, and Dwight all say they didn't do it and they're right. No one thinks to question the pro. There's no motive for him to have done it. He wouldn't kill his customers, especially since he has no obvious grudge against any of them. But maybe he did it to make a good customer happy, the father of his best beverage girl at that."

Doc continued, "Speaking of the beverage girl. You might look into a possible relationship between Bob Sanders and Judy Austin. I don't know anything, believe me I don't, but wouldn't you think a beautiful beverage girl and a handsome young pro might make a couple? The plot thickens even more if you imagine that he wants to make her happy by getting rid of her problem, the one guy who ruined her life by ruining her career, and, the one guy who can block her being hired in another district with a poor recommendation, which he would surely give."

"You sure are making a lot of sense, Doc," Lou said while everyone seemed to nod in agreement.

"Of course I am. Now I'm no detective. You two are. I can't prove a thing. But, when the courtroom gets quiet and the judge says, 'Have you reached a verdict,' and the jury foreman answers, 'Yes, your Honor. We find the defendant guilty,' you'll see Bob Sanders hang his head, because he'll realize that he's played his last round of golf. And all for Dwight Austin's money and the love of a pretty girl he hired to smile and sell beer and pop. Count on it, Lou and Maggie. Count on it."

"Gotta admit, you make a good case. I'll let Harrison know about your theory and we'll check it out," Lou said.

Several people wanted to talk with Reggie's friends but didn't interrupt because it was obvious that the six were having a serious conversation. Satisfied that they had given Lou and Maggie all they could, they got up and began to mingle with the others.

The two detectives were comparing notes when Bill Wallach joined them.

"You two look deep in thought."

"I guess we are, Bill. Good investigators are always working on a case," Lou said.

"Can't figure you folks out."

"What do you mean?"

"The old man killed Reggie. I told you the guy in knickers was at the 14th tee. A guy in knickers was playing right behind us. How much clearer can this case be? I'm beginning to really understand how some folks were feeling about the O.J. case as it dragged on and on."

"Gotta cover all the bases, Bill," Maggie replied.

Walt joined them for a moment. Lou and Maggie asked if he had any theories or thoughts to share about Reggie's death.

"Bill and I've been talking about it since it happened. The old man got his revenge. Open and shut case. Put him in the slammer and get this thing over with."

"Thanks for your thoughts, men," Maggie said, continuing to take notes. "I'm really sorry about the death of your good friend. Lots of folks want to talk with you two. Don't let me be in your way."

کرے

Having talked with the six golfers, Lou and Maggie now had additional information to share with each other and with Harrison. When Lou and Carol returned to Grand Haven, several messages were on their answering machine. First he called Harry.

"Hi, Harry. Lou here, What's up?"

"Can't seem to get my mind away from that mystery weekend happening when Reggie died. It's ironic. People walking around trying to solve a fictitious mystery while I'm pulling up to discover a dead golfer."

"Yeah, I've got to admit that it's strange."

"I wonder if this was a coincidence or if the mystery weekend was a deliberate part of the killer's plan," Harry asked.

"It could be a deliberate attempt to confuse us."

"Why would we be confused?"

"By that I mean, if everyone at the course tied incidents on the course to the murder mystery weekend, they weren't sure if the activities they saw were related to the real murder or to the play."

"For example?"

"I was talking to Matt Maloney. He sliced the ball over into another fairway and while he was over there he saw Judy, Don, and the ranger talking. She handed the ranger something. Matt originally may have assumed it was a meeting related to the play for the guests, or it could be a clue in our investigation."

"What you're saying, Lou, is that we could be investigating two murders, the fantasy one at the resort and the real one on the 14th tee."

"Correct. Furthermore, the killer may have planned it that way. The killer could have arranged to have Reggie killed at Marsh Ridge because the weekend murder mystery play was going on. The play created an added confusion. Many people at the resort were thinking the drama was associated with the play, when in fact, a real murder was taking place."

"Got it. Remember, the victim's group got a call on Thursday night to inform them that they had to switch their tee time to Marsh Ridge," Harrison said. "That may not have been a coincidence to be blamed on a bus full of golf writers. It may have been a plan set by the killer to get the victims to the course where a murder mystery was all set to be played out. The killer gave them the real thing, which they and everyone at the course thought was just a part of the weekend fun."

"Could be. Maybe Judy, Dwight, and Don got together and decided to put on their own version of a murder mystery weekend. We talked to Doc Lewis at the memorial service for Reggie today in Traverse City. Doc's convinced that the pro, Bob Sanders, is the murderer. He thinks Bob was having a relationship with Judy and that he's helping her get back at Reggie for ruining her career. He says the pro knows the course and is in charge of all staff. Doc's betting that when the verdict is read in court, Bob Sanders will be guilty of first degree murder."

"Sure. He's a likely suspect. He seems to be the outsider so far, but Doc could have a point. We're looking for someone who dropped poison in a cup of lemonade. Could be anyone. Could be someone coming onto the course from a nearby farm or road. Bottom line is, someone put poison in a cup and we've got to not only find out who did it, but to present the case beyond circumstantial evidence. We've got enough circumstantial evidence to put three people in prison for life at the moment. We've added Mark Thompson to the list; let's look closer at the pro as a suspect. Lou, we've got to have more than

'I think... We need at least one, 'I know...' You understand?"

"Yeah. I do."

"Well, I'll let you go. Thanks for the good information."

"I appreciate it, Harry. The more I think about this, the more I'm convinced that I've found another job for retirement."

"What's that?"

"Carol and I can go around to famous resorts and put on mystery weekends. What a life!"

"Nice work, if you can get it."

"Sounds relatively simple. The writing would be fairly easy. All I'd need is a victim like the golf pro, the bartender, or the reservations manager. Then I need a murderer, some guy who didn't get a tee time to his liking, or a chef who didn't get a promotion. Then I confuse the guests. I'll lead them to various characters and then give 'em that one clue that will lead them to solving the case."

"Why wait, Lou? Go on the circuit now. You'd be great at that!"

"I mean, can you imagine? Golf in the morning. Dine in the evening. Introduce the characters, give the clues, sit back and let people have fun. Carol and I could get paid for simply using our imaginations. Life couldn't be better, could it?"

"Sounds like a winner to me."

"Then when we get tired of working the big resorts on land, we can go to the big resorts on water, cruise ships."

"Lou! Wake up, pal. Get out of dreamland and get your mind back to Marsh Ridge and a murder we've got to solve."

"I'm with ya, Harry. I'm going to send you the tape recordings of the interviews at Reggie's memorial reception."

"Sounds good. I talked to a lot of people, but got nothing new that will help us."

CHAPTER 10

Wednesday, July 13
Gaylord, Michigan

On Wednesday, Harrison called Lou. "Lou, I've made arrangements for you, Carol, if she'd like to join us and help out, and Maggie and her husband to come to Marsh Ridge. I think if you are on-site, we could collaborate on solving this crime. I've talked with the resort's general manager, Mr. Workman, and he has agreed to accommodate us. He wants this thing solved as much as we do."

"A weekend at Marsh Ridge sounds like a great idea. I'll talk to Carol and Maggie to see if it's in the cards."

"Great. It seems to me that we might have it solved by Sunday if we all concentrate our energy on this thing."

"I agree. I'll be back with you soon."

Lou contacted Maggie. She thought that the idea was a good one. She didn't know if the resort could accommodate her disability so she called and talked to Mr. Workman.

After identifying herself, she stated the purpose of her call. "Mr. Workman, I'm calling to ask what I might expect in terms of the accessibility of your resort. I'm a wheelchair user and I always call ahead to help me prepare for what I might find."

"I'm glad you called, Mrs. McMillan. We are proud of our accessibility and I'm hoping you'll find everything to your liking."

"I'd like to ask a few questions if you don't mind."

"Please ask."

"Is the room I will have free of steps of any kind, like to get into the shower? Does the bathroom have a handrail? Is there a seat in the shower? Are the sinks lowered? Are the doors sufficiently wide to comfortably get my powerchair through them?"

"I can proudly say 'yes' to every question. We may be a bit different than most resorts in that the owner of our resort, Mr. Bryan Birch is a chair user as well. Our accessible rooms meet his specifications, and I'm certain you will be pleased."

"That's wonderful! Are ramps available at the restaurant, the administration building and other places I may need to go for our investigation?"

"Yes and no. There isn't a ramp to every building, but there is one to each of the most commonly used buildings."

"It sounds like I'll have little difficulty while I'm at Marsh Ridge. I can't wait to experience your resort. Michigan has a good reputation for accessibility, but I usually have some difficulty. Accessibility doesn't always mean the same to everyone. Perhaps your resort will be the epitome of accessibility."

"Mr. Birch makes sure that his resort goes the extra mile when it comes to making chair users and others with disabilities feel welcome and comfortable."

Satisfied that she would be able to be independent, she brought the conversation to a close. "I've enjoyed talking with you. I'll see you soon. Friday evening, I believe."

"The pleasure will be mine."

Maggie looked forward to getting to the scene of the crime. Unfortunately, Maggie's husband couldn't make the trip. He had paid for a spot on two charity scrambles in the next week and people were counting on him to play and support their causes.

Carol thought the idea a great one. A weekend at a premier northern Michigan resort in the middle of summer sounded too good to be true. She typed in www.marshridge.com and within a few seconds was looking into paradise. She found a full-service resort with Jacuzzi lodging which would be delightful, especially after her gardening muscles had been put to the test recently. Lou called Harrison back and gave the okay. Lou, Carol, and Maggie would meet him at the resort four days later, around six o'clock Friday evening.

Chapter 11

Saturday, July 16
Gaylord, Michigan
Marsh Ridge Resort

Lou, Carol, and Maggie arrived the night before and were assigned to their rooms in the Scandinavian Lodge. Before retiring for the night, Maggie, using her powerchair, and Lou and Carol walking hand in hand, toured the grounds. They thoroughly enjoyed the ambience of the premier resort. The Inns were magnificent two story buildings with large porches. Rocking chairs were plentiful, and pots of geraniums adorned the porch. Hanging baskets of flowers were everywhere attracting hummingbirds.

With a little imagination one would feel like he or she was visiting a botanical garden with flower beds throughout the resort. Cedar bark paths linked the attractive Inns that housed guests throughout the expansive resort. Birch and pine trees were everywhere. A creek snaked its way through the complex with water tumbling over rocks and caressing the banks. Gardens were full of annuals providing splashes of red, yellow, and blue for all to enjoy, including the bees and insects of all kinds.

Early in the morning on Saturday, Harrison, Lou, Carol, and Maggie had an appointment to meet with the manager of the resort, Dan Workman. Mr. Workman was a young looking forty-two. Handsome, stylish dresser, and always with a smile for his staff or a customer. The four received his warm greeting. "Welcome to Marsh Ridge."

"You've got one beautiful place here, Mr. Workman," Lou said.

"Well, thank you. We are quite proud of it. Our goal is to give people a chance to escape from their daily stresses and enjoy a beautiful setting."

"Thanks for making your resort accessible to people with disabilities," Maggie said sincerely. "It allows us to enjoy a beautiful part of Michigan. I appreciate your resort making me feel comfortable."

"You're welcome. We're committed to quality service for all of our guests. I know you will find our staff's mission is to serve you and others who stay at Marsh Ridge. I know you'd expect any manager to say that about his resort, but it is not a cliche here. You'll see what I mean."

Harrison set the tone. "Lou, Carol, Maggie and I are here this weekend to continue our investigation into the murder of the golfer a week ago today."

"We continue to be shocked and upset that such a tragedy could have occurred here at Marsh Ridge. You only need tell us how we can assist you."

"We appreciate your cooperation," Harrison said. "One of the pieces of information we'll need is the names, phone numbers and addresses of the guests who were registered here for the weekend of July 9 and 10. Our main interest is the guests who attended the murder mystery weekend, but we'd like to have the names of all the registered guests for Friday and Saturday nights."

Dan picked up the phone and said, "Jill, please bring me a computer printout of all of our guests the weekend of July 9 and 10, and please identify all who were here for the mystery weekend."

"We'd also like to be able to talk to some members of your staff," Maggie said. "We know that Harrison has talked to kitchen and maintenance staff. We'd like to know who the bag drop workers were that Saturday morning and the name of the supervisor for those young men or women."

Once again, Dan picked up the phone. "Jill, in addition to our guest list, please bring me the roster of the weekend employees we hired to work in the bag drop area, driving range, and golf cart retrieval."

Lou added, "I guess my request is to talk with the bartender or bartenders who were working the afternoon of Saturday, July 9."

Dan picked up the receiver, "One final request, Jill. I need the names of the bartenders assigned to Jac's on Saturday afternoon, July 9."

"We appreciate your providing this information for us," Harrison said. "We believe it will make our weekend productive."

"We want this solved as soon as possible. Not having the crime settled is bothering our workers. They're all wondering if anyone on the staff is involved. So, your successful investigation is our goal."

Jill entered Dan Workman's office with computer printouts of the information requested a moment ago. She gave the papers to Dan who immediately handed them to Harrison.

"I also want to apologize for an error by our desk clerk when you arrived. She failed to inform you that you are our guests this weekend. Marsh Ridge is yours to enjoy as much as possible as you continue your investigation. All expenses are handled. If you can find the time for some golf, the staff will arrange for your play. I have alerted my resort administrators, including our golf pro, Bob Sanders, and my supervisors of all operations that you folks are here. They and their staffs will cooperate fully with any requests you have. I've made it very clear to every one of my employees that solving this murder is our highest priority."

"Once again, as Detective Kennedy has said, we appreciate your support," Lou said to Mr. Workman. "I doubt we'll have the time for enjoying your beautiful course, but we sincerely appreciate your offer."

"Can't thank you enough, Mr. Workman," Harrison said sincerely. "Your spirit of cooperation is beyond our expectations and we hope to solve this as soon as possible. The three of us have much work to do. Guess we'll be about our business. Since this is Saturday morning and the murder occurred a week ago today, is it safe to assume that the employees here today are the ones who were here a week ago?"

"Yes, that's a safe assumption. Of course, as you can imagine, substitutes may be working because of sickness, but in general, employees have a regular schedule and the ones here today are those assigned weekend work."

Maggie replied, "We'll be making phone calls during the weekend. How do we access an outside line?"

"All calls will be paid for by Marsh Ridge. You can call from your rooms or from any phone on the complex. I'll give you the credit card number that our administrators use."

"Once again you're most gracious, but we'd be calling most of the eighty mystery weekend guests and the bill could be quite high," Lou said.

"Mr. Searing. I said earlier that solving this murder is our highest priority. If you need to call Paris and talk for six hours, the cost will be nothing compared to the peace of mind of my staff and the reestablished reputation of our world famous resort once this murder is solved. Money is no object in getting to the bottom of this tragedy."

"Once again, the four of us thank you very much for your cooperation. I'm quite confident that we'll have this solved when we leave," Harrison offered.

"That would make me a very happy man."

Harrison, Carol, Maggie and Lou shook hands with their host. Outside, they found a beautiful and warm Michigan summer day. The place was theirs. They had a feeling they would know who put the poison in the lemonade by the end of the weekend.

Lou and Maggie returned to their rooms. Harrison suggested that they all meet at Jac's for breakfast and a planning and strategy session. During breakfast Carol volunteered to call each of the guests who were at the resort for the murder mystery weekend. She would ask basic questions to see if she could find anyone with information about the murder.

While Carol was calling, Lou and Maggie decided to retrace the activity of the dead golfer from the time the golfers arrived at Marsh Ridge to Reggie's death. They wanted to talk to the bag drop boys. Later in the day, Harrison planned to talk to the bartender. In the meantime, Harrison worked with Lou and Maggie.

Lou felt strange not getting a bill for their breakfasts. He felt more generous than ever about leaving a tip. Before they got out of the door however, the waitress approached Lou and gave him back his money. "Thank you for your generous tip, Mr. Searing, but Mr. Workman insists that you not pay a dime during your stay with us. He personally has taken care of gratuities for all staff who have the privilege of serving you this weekend."

"That's kind of him," Lou said. "Thank you for the excellent service this morning." She smiled and shook his hand. Lou felt some paper compressed into the palm of his hand. He closed it so that the item would not drop to the floor. He put it in is pocket. The four of them walked out to go back to their rooms. They had decided to make Maggie's suite their headquarters.

While they were making their way to the Scandinavian Lodge, Lou reached into his pocket and took out the folded piece of paper. He opened it and read, "I'd like to talk to you while you're here. I have some information that may help you. I get off work at three o'clock. I'll meet you at the bench facing the pond, just east of the Bergen Lodge."

Once in their room, Carol said, "Okay, show me what you want me to do."

"Let me do the first one and you can do the same for the rest of the calls," Lou instructed. "Just take them one at a time." He dialed the first number.

"Hello."

"Is this Mr. Trap?"

"Yes."

"Mr. Trap, my name is Lou Searing. I'm assisting the Otsego

Sheriff's Department in the investigation of a murder that occurred last week at the Marsh Ridge Resort. The management of the resort is cooperating with us in this investigation. Their records show that you were at Marsh Ridge last weekend for the murder mystery weekend. Is that correct?"

"Yes. We were there."

"Mr. Trap, during your stay at the resort, did you witness or hear anything that might be associated with the real murder?"

"No. It's kind of hard to separate fact from fiction in this case. My wife and I pretty much stayed in our rooms or at the center of the mystery activity. We didn't talk with strangers or employees. We didn't even hear any rumors or comments about the murder until after we left when we heard it on the news. In fact, you'll find that everyone in our group thought that the real murder was a part of the drama and no one died. I'll bet that's what you'll learn from everyone."

"Thanks. Will you please take down my number and if you think of something after we finish, I'd appreciate it if you'd give me a call. I'm at the resort this weekend working on the investigation the number is 1-800-555-3324. After this weekend, you can reach Detective Harrison Kennedy at the sheriff's office, that number is area code (616) 555-9898."

"I'll call if I think of anything."

"Thank you, Mr. Trap."

Carol listened carefully and then began the process of calling the forty couples. She had a large, yellow legal pad to write down any comments she found interesting.

Harrison took the time to listen to the tape recordings of some of the earlier interviews. He thought that he might have missed some important comment that would give a clue to the mystery.

Lou and Maggie went to the pro shop to retrace the steps of the golfers and the others who had arrived a week ago.

じ

While Lou, Carol, Maggie, and Harrison were trying to find the clue that would solve the mystery, Larry and Courtney Rogers were visiting with a good friend in Battle Creek. They had been invited to Don Collins' apartment to celebrate Don's decision to head to New York for a career in the theater. The decision was a gutsy one. Don didn't have a connection or even a lead for work and every actor dreams of being discovered. Courtney and Don had been friends for many years while attending Kalamazoo College and studying drama.

Larry and Courtney knocked on Don's door about eleven-thirty. Don planned a celebration lunch. In addition to his acting talents he was quite a chef. In fact, if an off-Broadway opportunity didn't surface, he felt sure he could find work cooking. If the Waldorf Astoria didn't have an opening, there are McDonald's on most corners in need of a dependable young man. As long as Don was around food, he figured he would live. He planned to keep enough money in the bank to get back to Battle Creek if his dream fell on bad times.

Hot coffee and chit-chat about activities in their lives over the past several days flowed easily as the three were seated comfortably on the deck of Don's apartment, set off the 7th green of the Battle Creek Country Club. Don liked to spend time on the deck watching all of the city's rich and influential people having fun with the little white ball.

"Nice view here, Don," Larry said.

"Yeah, it is. This is nothing like the place I was a week ago."

"Where was that, Pebble Beach or Augusta?"

"No," Don said, chuckling. "I was at Marsh Ridge Resort up in Gaylord. I've played a lot of courses, but those folks did a great job of blending a golf course into nature. Anyway, I got a call from a guy who said they needed an actor for the weekend."

Courtney chimed in, "How could you drive up there and be in a play. You were always good at memorizing lines, but give me a break!"

"Well, it wasn't your typical community play. It was a murder mystery weekend at this golf resort. People pay a couple of hundred bucks a piece to be at this resort. The entertainment was trying to solve the mystery. The guests all find a victim and get some clues and then the group that solves it gets prizes. There's a lot of good food. It's kind of a neat idea. Lots of fun."

"What did you do there?" Larry asked.

"Actually this will probably sound strange, but I was the confuser."

"The confuser?" Courtney asked.

"Yeah. I had to appear in my golf outfit. My job was to interact with the guests and talk in ways that would throw them off their thinking about the murder."

"Doesn't sound like you had any script to learn," Larry said.

"No, I didn't. I was just to appear at the course and begin fooling people. All the participating guests wore name tags, so I knew who was trying to solve the thing."

"Give us an example of what you did," Courtney asked.

"Well, for example, this couple was driving a golf cart and they came in my direction. I stopped them, and of course they thought I was a golfer and not an actor in the murder drama. I said, 'You folks having fun?' They answered that they were. Then I said that I was talking to a couple of other guests and - 'Probably shouldn't tell you this, but they said that the bartender probably did it' knowing full well that he didn't. So, I was out there looking like a part of the scenery. I'd putt on the practice putting green. I'd hang around the pro shop. I'd have a drink in the bar. I'd knock some balls out on the driving range. You know, kind of always be around, but not in the way."

"For this they paid you?"

"Yeah. Easiest work I've ever encountered."

"Did you ask if you could tour with them?" Larry asked with a laugh.

"Would be nice for about a month and then it would get kind of old hat. I'd want to challenge my acting skills a bit more than hanging around a golf course confusing people."

"Isn't that where a golfer was murdered recently?" Larry asked.

"Don't know. I haven't heard about that. I don't get a newspaper and except for picking up a USA Today a couple of times a week, I don't hear much of what's going on."

"Yeah. A guy was poisoned on a golf course up north, and I think it was in Gaylord. In fact, I think I've heard of the man who died. He was in special education, and being a special education teacher, I think I've heard his name."

"You're mistaken my friend, I was there a week ago today and there was no murder. As part of the play, an ambulance came out to the resort, siren blaring and all. They went out to a tee on the back side and picked up a guy, but he wasn't dead. That was all part of the play. Listen, this acting company really does things up big. They even had a helicopter brought in on one of their productions."

"This wasn't a play, Don. A man was murdered!" Larry said with conviction.

"As I said, you've got to be mistaken. They were actors."

"Well, one man didn't do a good job of acting, 'cause he died. No sense arguing all night. At any rate, you had a pretty fancy weekend up there."

"Yeah. Nice work if you can get it, and it just happened to fall into my lap. Excuse me; I'll get the meat for the grill."

༈

Carol estimated that each call took about five to seven minutes and so far, after about seven calls, she noticed that there was a pattern developing. Each couple remembered the weekend well. Each had fun, but they didn't see or hear anything out of the ordinary. Carol heard glowing comments about the production, and most looked forward to the next event. Luckily, she felt like she had awakened only one man from sleep. The next couple on the list was Tony and Crystal Ebaugh of Kalamazoo. The phone rang six times with no answer and not even an answering machine. She moved to the next couple of names on the list.

Lou and Maggie went to the parking lot where golfers were arriving. The bag drop boys assisted the guests by taking clubs from cars and putting them onto a cart. The players then put on their golf shoes and began to put away their wallets, car keys, and other personal items from their pockets. They replaced those items with a ball marker, a golf ball or two, a golf glove, and a couple of tees.

They approached the supervisor. "Hi. I'm Lou Searing and this is Maggie McMillan. I believe Mr. Workman has informed you of our work here this weekend."

"Absolutely. My name is Ben Armstrong. How can I help you?"

"We'd like to talk to the workers who interacted with the golfers when they arrived last Saturday and before they teed off, if possible."

"Not going to be a problem. There are seven high school kids that we employ for this job. Six of them are here today and the other kid, Jimmy Shekleford quit almost a week ago. If you need to see him, he lives in town. Do you want to speak to the guys individually or together?"

"Together is fine."

"The only thing I'd ask is that if a customer comes up, one of the guys will need to assist them. Mr. Workman wants you to get everything you need, but he also expects our customers to be treated like royalty. So, I trust you'll understand if one of them needs to greet a guest."

"Oh, absolutely. Not a problem. We don't want to interfere with your operation."

The supervisor called the guys over and introduced them to Lou and Maggie. He told them to answer any questions and to be as helpful as possible. The supervisor asked if he could listen and possibly participate. Lou indicated that it would be fine.

After the boys had gathered, Lou began, "Thanks for meeting with us for a few minutes. We understand that one or more of you may need to leave for a few minutes to help a customer. First of all, this is Maggie McMillan and I'm Lou Searing. We're working together to figure out how the guy died at the 14th tee a week ago."

Maggie smiled and said, "Good morning. It isn't everyday I get to meet such good-looking young men. Thanks for helping us."

"As you know, last Saturday, a golfer was killed out on the 14th tee," Lou began. "You may have already talked with Mr. Kennedy of the sheriff's department. Maggie and I want to ask you if you saw or heard anything out of the ordinary either in the morning when the golfers arrived or at anytime during the day."

At first there was silence. It didn't appear that anyone was hiding anything. It was just that no one felt comfortable speaking. Then Robby Johnson spoke up, "Um, I don't recall anything being different in the morning. I can't remember the guy who died 'cause I never saw his picture so he could have been anybody. In the morning, we put a lot of people on the course and we move quickly 'cause the golfers want fast service and sometimes people are late and the starter wants the tee times to be right on the money."

Mike Rivera spoke next, "I agree. Nothing was out of the ordinary. If anything had been strange, we'd have known it. We work well together, covering for each other to make sure everyone is getting excellent service. We need the tips and we don't need Mr. Armstrong getting on our case for not hustling. So, there isn't time, especially in the morning."

Maggie interjected, "I imagine that you guys have thought a lot about last Saturday morning since learning that the golfer was killed. I'd like to ask you to take a few quiet minutes now, and in your minds, go back a week and think about how the morning unfolded. Try to remember what you were wearing. See the cars coming in and try to see it all happening again. You can close your eyes if you wish. Would you do that for us?"

"We'll try anything that might help," Walt Dudock said.

"Good idea, Maggie," Lou replied. "Let's just be quiet for a few seconds and try to relive last Saturday morning."

It looked like a bag drop prayer meeting. The guys lowered their heads and concentrated, thinking carefully. The adults did their best to be still so as not to interrupt their thinking. After several seconds Lou spoke. "Did that help?"

Anthony Willin, who had not spoken yet, came up from his concentrated thought and said, "I wouldn't say this is out of the ordinary but Jimmy, the guy who quit, was talking to one of the maintenance workers, Don something or other. He seemed to be spending too much time talking to him. I remember Brandon and Mike calling him over because cars were pulling in faster than we could get to them."

"Yeah, that's right, Tony. He wasn't pulling his weight and we got kind of pissed at him. Sorry, ma'am. Wasn't thinking," said Andy, a bit embarrassed. Maggie smiled slightly and nodded her forgiveness.

Andy added, "I remember now. It wasn't a problem, he came back and got to work. I agree with Tony – it isn't out of the ordinary."

Just then a car pulled in and Walt excused himself. He quickly went over to help four golfers who were getting out of a car with Indiana license plates.

Ben Armstrong added, "Kids are kids. They get distracted, don't pay attention like they should. We had a high school girls' tournament out here last summer. I never saw golfers getting so much attention in my life." All smiled and chuckled. "But, yeah, last Saturday morning, Jimmy was talking to that maintenance worker for longer than his coworkers appreciated."

Brandon Goines, the quiet one, listened to what they said. He finally added a comment. "I don't want to get anyone in any trouble. Jimmy didn't do nothing that any of us wouldn't do. He only talked to the maintenance guy for a few minutes. Let's not be too quick to point the finger at Jimmy. He's a good kid."

"Brandon, trying to solve this murder is like putting a five-hundred piece puzzle together," Lou said. "We look at hundreds of little pieces of information and we try to see patterns or groups of clues. The only difference, and it is a big difference, is that we can't look at the box to see the picture we're trying to put together. Nobody's ratting on anyone. We just need to reconstruct that day as much as we can."

"I know," Brandon said.

"Is there anything else anyone remembers?" Lou asked.

No one offered anything. Lou and Maggie expressed their thanks to the boys for giving them some time. The young men left and got back to their jobs.

"I just thought of something that hit me while we were talking about Jimmy," Ben said.

"What's that?" Maggie asked.

"Last Sunday Jimmy came out here to quit. I had to give the kid credit for coming out in person to say he was quitting. Most guys tell another to give me a message or they'll call and tell me over the phone or call in the middle of the night and leave a message on the answering machine. But, Jimmy came out. He was polite. He thanked me for giving him a job. He's a nice kid."

"Did he say something that you want to share?" Maggie asked.

"It isn't what he said. He drove away in a Jeep Cherokee. An SUV is the envy of any kid sixteen to twenty. I didn't think of it at the time, but it just hit me, how could Jimmy get that vehicle? I mean, he could have borrowed it from a friend. He undoubtedly did. I know his parents and they're just scraping by. Jimmy doesn't have money to spend on a vehicle like that. I guess now I'm really wondering why he quit. I didn't ask, but he didn't say he got a better job. He must have borrowed that Jeep from a friend. The strange thing for me isn't what happened Saturday morning. The strange thing is Jimmy's quitting and driving that Jeep last Sunday."

"Thanks for your thoughts, Ben. Maggie and I are staying in the Summit Lodge if you have any other thoughts."

༄

By now, the bartender, Stacy Hammonds, had arrived for work. She was tall and blonde, attractive, and domineering. When she walked in, Harrison offered a greeting, "Good morning."

"Don't tell me I've got a customer already!"

"I'm not looking for a drink. I'm looking for information."

"As long as it isn't my phone number, address, or real name, I can probably help," Stacy said with a smile.

"It's none of those. I'm Harrison Kennedy, a detective with the Otsego Sheriff's Department. We're continuing our investigation of the murder here a week ago. I talked with the other bartender a day or two ago, but I understand that you were working last Saturday."

"Yeah, usually Tom can handle the bar, but we had a lot of golfers and our mystery weekend was that weekend, so they asked if I could do a little overtime. Hey, when you add tips to overtime, I'm smiling all the way to the bank."

"Imagine you are. Just going to ask a couple of questions."

"Shoot. Probably shouldn't say 'shoot' to a detective investigating a murder," Stacy said, smiling and feeling kind of proud of her sly humor.

Adding to the lightness of the interview, Harrison said, "My first shot is, did you hear or see anything out of the ordinary last Saturday?"

"Nothing happens in here that I'd call ordinary. Guys are telling stories, talking loud, drinking more than they should. A ball game is usually on TV, glasses are clinking, money is exchanged, bets are placed here and there, and obscenity or two fly through the air. This place is the last place you'll find anything ordinary. Actually, all that I just said is typical, but then you throw in that murder mystery weekend, it gets worse. The place was full of frustrated amateur detectives wanting to impress each other about who did what, where, and why and I'm telling you when I walked outta here at the end of my shift, I couldn't see or think straight for all the noise and confusion I had to put up with."

"My sympathies, Stacy. Doesn't sound like fun."

"Oh, it's a fun place all right. I just said nothing ordinary happens here. I love it!"

"Maybe I should ask if anything ordinary happened here last Saturday."

"Now you're getting somewhere."

"The ordinary thing that often happens is that Dwight Austin comes in and flashes his money; and if he's had a good round or he's elated about something, like a couple of birdies or he wants to celebrate some big event, he buys everyone a drink. That happened last Saturday afternoon. He comes in like some big feared outlaw in the old western movies. He comes through the door, smiling, and shouting,' a drink for everyone!' Tom and I just do a head count, multiply times six or seven bucks and if he's still sober enough to understand what's going on, we tell him what he owes. If he isn't, we tell Billy what he owes and then we mail him a bill at the end of the month. So, it was ordinary for Dwight to come in happy, but now that I think about it, it was not ordinary in that he seemed overly joyful. For all I know he got a hole in one."

"He didn't say why he was happy or you didn't hear anyone say why he may have been overjoyed?"

"I try to stay away from the sick SOB. He harasses me but sooner or later I'll get even. I should say something, but I want to keep working here, money's good, and the boss likes his customers happy, so I put up with it."

"You don't talk to him?"

"No more than I have to. He is ugly, literally. He's always complaining about this or that. He gets people mad at him and then he invariably does something vengeful to get back at them. It's like a hobby. It's like a guy who finds sport in hunting other men. You know, get a head start and then see if you can escape me. He doesn't really do it, but he seems like the kind of guy who would."

"Not a very pleasant guy."

"His daughter won't have anything to do with him."

"His daughter?"

"Yeah. Judy Austin, one of our beverage girls."

"Dwight is her father?"

"Yeah. He'll often deny it, but he's her father. Judy and I hung together for awhile and she shared a few personal stories. Treats his daughter like dirt. I mean, this is a sick guy, Mr. Kennedy, a very sick guy."

"Did Dwight get her a job out here at Marsh Ridge?"

"Oh, yeah. His money gets him whatever he wants here. He gets his tee times. He gets whatever he wants to eat or drink. The pro, Bob Sanders, you might as well put a ring in his nose with a rope tied to Dwight Austin's golf cart. It's kinda sad to see grown men bow down to a guy the way this place does to Dwight Austin. I don't play those games, but I pay a price and that's where the harassment comes in. If I report him, I'll pay for it. So, as long as I want to work here, I just make the best of it. Gotta tell you, Harrison, you can't believe how happy I would have been if Dwight had drunk that cup of lemonade a week ago. Dwight Austin lying on the 14th tee, dead, would have caused me to celebrate big time. There would have been drinks for everyone and I'd have gone into debt just to celebrate his demise."

"Do any others here feel the same way?"

"Judy hates his guts."

"Judy, his daughter?"

"Oh, yeah, she's only here because it's a job and she needs the money. In fact, when Judy gets drinking, she gets a little free with her tongue like anyone else, and she's talked of putting him to sleep."

"Are they talking to each other?"

"No way. She won't be in his presence if she can help it. Kinda sad to see a father and daughter having such dislike, even hatred for one another, but that happens, I guess."

"Anybody else out here or even in town with similar feelings about him?"

"Don't know about town, but at this resort, you won't find much respect or anyone liking the guy."

ᘓ

The phone rang three times. "Sheklefords."

"Mrs. Shekleford?"

"Yes."

"My name is Lou Searing. I'm investigating the murder at Marsh Ridge a week ago. We're talking to people who were working at the course that day. May I talk to your son?"

"Jimmy had nothing to do with that."

"Oh, he's not a suspect. We just want to know if he saw or heard anything that might give us a clue."

"I guess it would be all right. Just a minute."

"Thank you."

A few seconds later, Jimmy came on the line. "Hello."

"Jimmy? My name is Lou Searing. I'd like to ask you some questions about your job at Marsh Ridge."

"I don't work there anymore."

"I know. I talked to Mr. Armstrong. He said you did good work. I've got some questions I'd like to ask. Could you meet me at McDonald's in about 20 minutes? You can bring your parents if you want."

"Yeah."

"I'll be with a woman named Maggie. We're easy to spot. Maggie uses a wheelchair and I'm bald. See you in a few minutes."

"OK."

Jimmy told his mother he was going to town.

⤳

Carol was making her nineteenth phone call. She still hadn't talked with anyone who had anything that would help in the investigation. At least not until she dialed the number of Tom and Sally Quest. A man answered and Carol went through her spiel, expecting the usual, 'Sorry can't help.' This time she heard, "Yes, as a matter of fact something did happen that might help you."

Carol interrupted. "Do you mind if I record what you say. I want the detectives to hear exactly what you say."

"I'd rather you didn't."

"Not a problem. I'll relay what you have to say. Go ahead."

"Sally and I have found that we can get a jump on the mystery weekend by talking to a lot of people in a variety of settings throughout the resort complex. We've been coming to the Marsh Ridge mystery weekends since they began several years ago. We love the good food, fun, and it's such a beautiful resort to enjoy a weekend. You meet people from throughout the country, actually. Anyway, Sally was on the putting green early in the morning. She told me she approached this guy and asked, 'Got a clue to the murder?' She said he seemed surprised at her question and he didn't quite know what to say. So, she asked it again, 'Got a clue to the murder?' He apparently said, 'Gonna happen on the 14th tee.'

"Sally said, 'Thanks for the tip. Good luck on your round!' Well, as you know, in the mystery weekend murder, the lifeguard at the pool was killed by the jealous sunbather. There was no murder at the 14th tee in the weekend program. We found out later that there was a real murder. So, whoever Sally talked with, knew about six hours in advance that a murder was going to take place."

"Did you report this to anyone?" Carol asked.

"No. We just found out about the real murder. We were told that that was not real, you know, part of the production. In past productions, the writer and the actors threw red herrings at you, and we'd come to expect it."

"How can Sally be sure that the guy she talked to on the putting green was not trying to deceive her?"

"You don't fool Sal. She reads people, know what I mean?"

"Who did she talk to? What did he look like?"

"You'll have to talk with her about that. I didn't ask her those questions. In fact, I'm not so sure we want to get involved. I guess by sharing what I've said, we're involved."

"We can start by saying she talked to a man who was on the putting green getting ready to play golf at around eight o'clock in the morning. Correct?"

"Yes. If you want more detail, you'll have to talk with her. She's gone to town to get groceries. Should be back in an hour."

"Thanks much, Mr. Quest. You've been very helpful."

"You're welcome, I guess. Sally probably won't be very happy about my getting her involved. If she decides to clam up, that's her choice."

"Detective Kennedy or I will call in a few hours. Thank you, again."

జా

Lou and Maggie were in McDonald's sipping hot coffee. Jimmy came in, looked around, spotted the wheelchair and a bald head, and approached them. Jimmy was a handsome lad. He was wearing baggy pants, a T-shirt, a necklace, and his hair was bleached in streaks.

"Jimmy Shekleford?" Lou asked.

"Yeah. You the guy that called?"

"Yes. I'm Lou Searing and this is Maggie McMillan."

"Hi, Jimmy. Thanks for meeting with us. Want something to drink?"

"No, thanks."

"We want to talk to you about your job at Marsh Ridge. Mr. Armstrong said you did a good job working for him."

"Thanks. I liked it there."

"We asked to meet you because we're looking into the murder of a golfer there a week ago."

"I don't know anything about that," Jimmy said, showing some anxiety in his response. Maggie watched him like an eagle eyeing its prey. She wanted to record all his body language. She suspected from the start that Jimmy was involved.

"We talked with the six guys who were working with you last Saturday. We asked them if they saw or heard anything out of the ordinary. We'd like to ask you the same thing, " Lou said.

"I didn't see or hear anything. Did they say they saw or heard anything?"

"We're collecting information, Jimmy. Just as you would want us to keep anything you told us to ourselves, we choose to not share what they said. You understand don't you?"

"They probably said that I spent too much time talking to Don Dailey. They were kinda mad at me that morning 'cause I wasn't pulling my weight."

"Who's Don Dailey?" Lou asked.

"He's on one of the maintenance crews."

"You were talking to him that morning?"

"Yeah. He called me over and wanted to talk."

"What did you two talk about?"

There was a sustained pause before Jimmy continued, "Don't remember."

"Did it have anything to do with the mystery weekend?"

"No."

"Did it have anything to do with the murder of the golfer?"

Once more there was a pause as Jimmy looked at the floor. Maggie would have given anything to have him hooked up to a galvanic skin response for his answer. "No."

"Okay. If you recall anything in the days ahead, will you call Mr. Kennedy at the Otsego Sheriff's Department?"

"Yeah."

"Oh, Mr. Armstrong said you came out to say you were going to quit. He said that was a very mature thing for a young man to do. Most call him and quit or have a friend tell him."

"Felt I should tell him. He gave me the job and I felt it fair that I tell him in person."

"Good for you, young man," Lou said. "Maggie do you have any questions for Jimmy?"

Jimmy, did you quit at Marsh Ridge for a better job?"

"No. I don't have a job. I didn't want to work for awhile. I need to work on my summer school classes. I'm gettin' behind."

Maggie continued, "Mr. Armstrong said you came out to see him in a good looking Jeep Cherokee. I really like those vehicles. My husband's been thinking of getting one someday. Do you like yours?"

"Yeah. They're fun to drive."

"Surprised your dad would get a car like that."

"It isn't my dad's."

"Oh, it belongs to a friend?"

"No. It's mine."

"It's yours, and you've got no job for payments, gasoline, insurance? None of my business, but it takes a lot of money to own a car."

"It was a gift. I've got a rich friend."

"You're a lucky kid. Very lucky," Maggie said. "Jimmy, do you want to tell us what you know? I get a feeling that you know something about this that you're keeping to yourself. When you quit your job, get a new car, and don't have another job, it looks suspicious. I'm sure you understand."

"I didn't do anything wrong. I gotta go now."

"Sure, Jimmy," Lou said. "Thanks for meeting with us."

As Jimmy left, Lou and Maggie compared notes and both concluded that they hadn't gotten much. "He said more by what he didn't say than by what he said," Maggie said. "One of our biggest clues to what really happened last Saturday is resting in that kid's head. I'm pretty sure of that."

෴

It was noon and Carol met the three detectives at Jac's Place for lunch and a debriefing. One quarter of the weekend visit to solve the murder was complete. They sat down and looked at the menu. Carol said, "What a dilemma. I can have anything on this menu, since the resort is picking up the tab, and still I'll probably get a tossed salad and a bowl of soup."

"Not a dilemma for me. I'm having soup and salad," Harrison remarked.

Maggie decided to be conservative and join Carol in her choice. Lou's head was very much on the job at hand. He wasn't even thinking about food, but to be social he ordered a chicken salad sandwich with chips.

After coffee and water arrived at the table, the talk immediately turned to what they had learned that morning. Carol reported on her twenty-six calls. She told the group about talking with Tom Quest. "His wife Sally had talked with someone at the practice putting area. This person told her the murder would take place on the 14th tee."

"Who did she talk to?" Lou asked.

"She was out shopping. Mr. Quest said that she would be back this afternoon. I told him that Harrison or I would call back."

"I'll call her," Harrison offered.

Harrison briefed everyone on what he had learned. "I talked with the bartender. Her name is Stacy Hammonds. She said that Dwight came into the bar after his round and was in a very jovial mood. He offered to buy drinks for all. She didn't know what could've made him so happy. He often bursts into the bar and buys a round for everyone, so that behavior is not atypical for him. But, I learned a new twist in this. Stacy said that she hates the old guy. He sexually harasses her. She said she has talked with Judy, who, according to her, is Dwight's daughter. Judy has very strong feelings against her father, too, and has talked to Stacy about killing him. So, we have two women who hate this guy. I know Dwight didn't die out there, but the poison could have been meant for him, and drunk a little early by our victim. His celebration in the bar could have been because he's still alive."

"Very interesting, Harry," Lou said. "I hadn't thought of that possibility."

Maggie spoke next. "Lou and I talked with the bag drop guys. The only thing they found out of the ordinary was that a kid, Jimmy Shekleford, was not pulling his weight and was talking to Don Dailey quite a bit that morning. This was at the pro shop, parking lot area."

Lou added, "Maggie and I met and also talked with Jimmy. He, as Maggie said, quit his job and suddenly has a brand new Jeep Cherokee. Jimmy's parents just get by and here he is driving a new car with no way to pay for it. He said he had a rich friend. Maggie was watching his body language like a hawk. It looks suspicious."

"The way he answered, or didn't answer questions let us know that information is in him, but he won't share it," Maggie said.

"Theory?" Harrison asked hoping for Maggie to point them in a positive direction.

Maggie responded, "I've always got a theory. The car came from Dwight. He's the only one in this drama with any money, and a new car takes money. Dwight is paying off Jimmy for doing something. I've got some thoughts on the 'doing something,' but I'm not ready to elaborate. I think that Jimmy is definitely in this drama, and he's driving around in his payoff for the part he played. Dwight is also in this drama some way. His way of thanking a young kid for very significant help is to give the kid what he doesn't have, a vehicle, which is every teenager's dream come true. To get the car comes the promise that nothing gets said, and Jimmy is, so far, holding true to that promise. He's an honest and good kid. So, if we can't get what he knows before trial, it'll come out when he promises to tell the truth, the whole truth, and nothing but the truth."

"It seems to me that a key area in this drama surrounds the parking lot, the pro shop, and the putting green," Lou surmised. "This Sally learned something there. Jimmy was working there talking to Don Dailey. So far, all of the characters except Judy were seen there in the morning."

"Let's concentrate on this afternoon for a few minutes," Harrison suggested. "Carol will continue to call people on the murder mystery weekend list. I'll talk to Sally and anyone else that Carol learns might have some information."

Lou stated his plans. "I'll be talking to the waitress who wanted to talk with me at three o'clock by the pond next to the Bergen Lodge. I'll also be organizing what we've learned. Maggie and Carol know that I like to write down the details on big sheets of paper. It's my way of putting the various puzzle pieces in groupings."

Maggie said, "I want to talk to Stacy, if that is okay with you, Mr. Kennedy."

"Fine with me."

"I'd like an opportunity for a little woman talk. I think I'll ask Judy to join us. It's time for us to have a little chat."

༄

Jimmy came through the door. "That you, Jimmy?" Mrs. Shekleford asked.

"Yeah."

"Did you talk to the guy who called?"

"Yeah."

"Who was he?"

"They had some questions about the golfer who died at Marsh Ridge."

"What would you know about that?"

"I was working there the day it happened. Remember? I came home and told you about the ambulance coming and everything."

"Yeah, but you said that was all phony and a part of some play going on there."

"That's what I thought, but some guy really died."

"Why would they be talking to you?"

"I don't know. I was working there that day and they talked to the other guys working the parking lot and the driving range."

"What did they want to know?"

"They wondered if I had seen or heard anything out of the ordinary that morning."

"Did you?"

"No. I was talkin' to Don Dailey for longer than I should've. Mr. Armstrong and the other guys got on my case about it."

"What did you talk to this Don about?"

"He wanted me to get into a betting pool on baseball games. He said other guys in the maintenance area saw it as some fun and the more guys got in, the bigger the pot, and the bigger the payoff."

"What did you say?"

"Said I needed every buck I was making and wasn't interested."

"Then what?"

"Oh, he kept trying to sell the idea. Cars were coming into the parking lot and the guys got on me for not working at a heavy time. I told Don I wasn't interested and went back to work."

"Good for you. Proud of you, son."

Harrison called Sally Quest. "Hello. Mr. Quest?"

"Yes."

"This is Detective Kennedy of the Otsego County Sheriff's Department. I understand you talked with Carol Searing this morning concerning the murder here in Gaylord a week ago."

"Yeah. That was late this morning."

"Is Mrs. Quest home?"

"Yeah. She doesn't want to talk with you, though."

"Would she be willing to get on the line for a moment?"

Harrison could hear, "Sal. Mr. Kennedy asks if you'd be willing to talk with him for a minute or two. I think you should, hon." Several seconds later he heard, "Hello."

"Thank you for talking with me, Mrs. Quest."

"You're welcome. I really don't have anything to say. I don't mean to be uncooperative, but I have nothing to help you."

"Your husband said you talked with a man on the putting green who told you a murder would take place on the 14th tee."

"Well, yes, but he was probably a participant in the play that weekend."

"Could you describe the man, Sally?"

"I really don't remember him very well. The conversation was short and I probably wouldn't recognize him if I saw him again."

"Tall?"

"No, actually short."

"Old?"

"No, he looked in his late 20s or early 30s."

"Facial hair?"

"No."

"Bald?"

"No."

"Any scars or deformities?"

"No."

"Any other characteristics? Was he smoking, chewing gum, wearing a golf hat of a specific style?"

"He wasn't smoking or chewing gum. He wore a golf outfit and his hat looked like a baseball cap."

"Is there anything else about him or the words he said that you recall?"

"He had a southern accent. He seemed to hesitate before answering my question, like he shouldn't be saying anything."

"Did you see him at any other time in the day?"

"I can't be absolutely certain, but I could swear he was driving the ambulance that came to the pro shop."

"Anything else?"

"No. I'm taking a risk talking to you. I don't want to be going to a trial or a police lineup. It's easier not to get involved. Probably should've kept my mouth shut."

"You did the right thing by talking to me, Mrs. Quest. There may be absolutely nothing to what you heard, but then again, it might be the tip we need. If it's any consolation, the family of the victim, the Marsh Ridge staff, the community of Gaylord, and sheriff's department are very thankful for your willingness to help us."

The two completed their conversation. Harrison hung up. He couldn't remember the ambulance driver that day. He thought he should sharpen his observation skills, which he thought were quite good to begin with. Harrison picked up the phone, called the dispatcher, and gave his location and phone number. He asked for information about the company that provides emergency service in Gaylord and specifically who to call to ask about staff used on ambulance runs. He was promised a response in a matter of minutes.

Actually, the phone rang in a matter of seconds. "Detective Kennedy?"

"Yes."

"Ambulance service is provided by Otsego County Emergency Services. The person to talk with is Ken Puffer. His number is 555-8976."

"Thank you."

Harry dialed. "Emergency Services."

"Mr. Puffer, please."

"Speaking."

"Mr. Puffer, this is Detective Kennedy of the sheriff's department. Got a few minutes for a few questions?"

"Yes sir, unless a call comes in and I have to leave. I'm short a man this afternoon."

"I understand. Was your company the provider of service a week ago when the golfer was murdered at Marsh Ridge?"

"Yes, sir. I was on that run. You'd probably remember me if you were here in person. I talked with you at the scene."

"Yes. I think I recall."

"Who went on that run with you? Do you have that in your records?"

"It was Shorty Gross. He works all weekend calls. In fact, he's not working today. That's why I'm a man short."

"I take it Shorty is short?"

"Yeah. He's a short guy. He came up here from Mobile, Alabama last winter looking for work. Sight of blood doesn't bother him and he had good references, so I hired him."

"Does he play golf?"

"Actually he's a pretty good golfer. I think he has about a 4 handicap."

"Was he at work last Saturday?"

"Yeah. He rarely misses work."

"What time does he arrive?"

"He gets here about nine in the morning and works till five. He's on call the rest of the time."

"Does he often wear a hat?"

"Yeah. He's a Chicago Cubs fan. He's always got a Cubs baseball cap on. Sometimes I think he sleeps with that cap. Why all the questions, Mr. Kennedy?"

"Oh, we're just checking out every clue and comment made by people who were around Marsh Ridge that morning. One person said that she talked with a guy on the practice putting green. She said he was short and wore a baseball cap and she swore she saw the guy driving the ambulance that afternoon. So, I am checking to see if that would have been possible."

"To be honest with you, Shorty hustles at most of the Gaylord area courses every Saturday and Sunday."

"What do you mean?"

"He'll go to the putting green and, on purpose, putt lousy. Then he approaches guys who are warming up on the putting green and challenges them to bets like 'closest to the hole' for a buck or five bucks or whatever he can get from a guy. The sucker has watched Shorty putt all over the place, and sees some easy money. Shorty then either putts it in or comes very close. The guy sees it as lucky and Shorty asks if he wants to putt for a double or nothing. The guy goes for it and Shorty puts the second one in the cup or pretty close. On some mornings he comes to work here and brags that he took in two to three hundred dollars for a couple hours work."

"So, it's possible that someone could've seen him at the putting green and then driving your ambulance in the afternoon?"

"Absolutely. He tells me he rarely hustles at Marsh Ridge. His friends work there and he doesn't want to ever get reported and embarrass them. But, he has that reputation, and he might have been on the practice putting green that morning. Sure."

"Thanks, Ken. Gonna want to talk to Shorty. You can tell him to expect a call from me when you see him."

"Will do."

Harrison immediately called the police department. He asked for a check on a man named Shorty Gross who once lived in Mobile, Alabama.

Back at Jac's Place, Maggie was about to meet with Stacy and Judy. The three poured decaf coffee and sat down at a table looking out at the beautiful golf course. Maggie set the tone, "Thanks for meeting with me. I'm working with Detective Kennedy and Lou Searing to try and solve this murder. I wanted to talk with you together and I apologize if I ask questions that Mr. Kennedy has already asked, but I want to hear your answers."

"I want to talk with you, Maggie," Judy said. "I fear that I'm a suspect in this thing 'cause I was responsible for the lemonade and I guess it was poisoned lemonade that killed the guy. I also think it's known to most that I had a strong dislike for Mr. Macleod. He ruined my teaching career."

"So, let me begin by asking the obvious question. Judy, did you kill Reggie Macleod?" Maggie asked.

"Absolutely not. I may be bitter, angry, and even revengeful, but give me credit for enough intelligence to keep my body out of a prison for women. I can't imagine life being worse than being cooped up with a bunch of women who got themselves in trouble for one thing or another."

"OK. Second question. Do you know who did it?"

"No. I really don't. If I were a betting woman, I'd say it was Dwight."

"Your father?"

"Yeah. He was very angry at one of the guys in front of him. He could have gotten the poison in that cup of lemonade one way or another. I hope it's not Dwight, but my guess is that it's him."

"Stacy. What have you got to say?"

"The thing to remember is that the key to this murder is money. Money buys whatever people want. The motivator is money. Of that I'm sure. Mark my words. If Dwight Austin didn't do it, he paid to have it done. The murder was a fantastic drama. Should get the academy award! I mean two mystery weekends at a resort. One is for real and one is make believe. Two for the price of one and a lot of confusion. No witnesses and a whole host of motives. You guys got your hands full solving this mess. Money, it's money, honey. Let your crime solving instincts move you toward money. You'll find the murderer wherever there's money. That's all I've got to say."

"I've heard about sexual harassment. Any truth to that?" Maggie asked.

"Maggie, the stories we could tell would give you and your mystery-writing friend enough material for a lifetime of books," Tracy offered. "I told Mr. Harrison that this man is sick. You don't need details, because I won't offer any, but sexual harassment is common, very common."

"Life would be easier if Dwight Austin were out of the picture," Maggie presumed.

"You don't realize how true your words are, Mrs. McMillan," Stacy said, with Judy taking a deep breath and nodding.

༣

It was approaching three o'clock. Lou made sure that he would be at the bench facing the pond near the Bergen Lodge. He strolled over to the bench and sat down. He closed his eyes and tried to relax. The beauty of the resort was intoxicating and a few minutes of quiet time was welcome. He opened his eyes to see the waitress coming toward him. "Hi."

"Hi," said a cute, blond, and slim waitress." My name is Heather. I'm pleased to meet you."

"The pleasure's mine. I'm Lou Searing, as you know. You have some information for me?"

"That's right. I thought long and hard about saying anything. Nobody likes the court scene and the fear of retribution. Know what I mean?"

"Sure do. Takes courage to come forward with information. Thank you for being willing to tell me what you know."

"Well, I was working late at Jac's Friday night. That would have been a week ago last night. The busboy got permission to leave work early. I had to clean tables. The place had cleared out and I was putting the dishes in bins and wiping off each table. I was gathering up the paper placemats and napkins when I noticed a drawing on the back of a placemat. I stopped to look at it. At the time I didn't think anything of it, but after learning that a guy died at on the 14th tee, I remembered the sketch on the back of the placemat."

"Please tell me you kept the placemat."

"Sorry, it didn't mean much to me at the time. I looked at it and threw it away."

"What did you see?"

"The title was 'Murder on the 14th Tee.' Another reason I didn't give it much attention in terms of keeping it was because this was a murder mystery weekend at Marsh Ridge. I thought some guests were putting some clues together. The staff are not briefed concerning the plot unless we have a part in the play. I didn't have a part in this one."

"So, at the top was written, 'Murder on the 14th Tee?'"

"Yeah. Then there was a drawing of the tee, a bench, a cooler with a big X drawn on the tee. There was a name beside the X and it was Wallach. Then, written at the bottom were the words, 'Never cross Dwight Austin!' If that isn't an exact quote, it comes close."

"Here's a sheet of paper and a pen. Would you please draw as close as you can remember it, what you saw?" Lou said, handing her his small pocket notebook and a pen. Heather finished her drawing and handed it to Lou.

"Thanks, Heather. Now, do you have any recollection of who was sitting at this table when this was drawn?"

"Dwight Austin and Mark Thompson."

"When you realized that there was a real murder at the 14th tee, and you recalled the placemat, did you say anything to anyone?"

"No, and I probably wouldn't have even said anything to you, but my uncle is in special education and he said you're a man I could trust to do what's right. So, I decided to talk to you."

"I appreciate your confidence. I'll assure you that I'll do whatever I can to uphold my reputation. I'll share what I've learned with Detective Kennedy and my colleague Maggie McMillan. You saw us at breakfast."

"That's fine. I trust you, Mr. Searing. Good luck with your investigation. I hope my information helps."

෴

Carol resumed her calls once Harrison finished using the phone. None of the remaining people she called had any information that would be helpful. Carol figured that after a day of calls, she talked to thirty-four of the forty registered couples for the mystery weekend. Her success seemed to be finding Sally Quest, who may have provided a vital clue. She thought it came close to a wasted day, but maybe it wasn't. Only time would tell.

The balance of the afternoon was uneventful. A few more interviews took place and much thought went into the case as they prepared for a quiet dinner. Once again they went to Jac's. They hadn't been seated for longer than a minute when Mr. Workman approached.

"Good evening."

"Good evening. Many thanks for the support of your staff," Lou said. "Very much appreciated, Mr. Workman!"

"We're here to assist you in your work. We're very anxious to see this solved and justice brought forth. Are you making any headway?"

"Yes, we are," Harrison said. "It's very helpful for us to be together working on this case."

"Do you expect to have it solved by the time of your planned departure tomorrow?"

"I feel that we'll have it solved," Maggie replied with confidence. "We may not be ready for Harrison to seek a warrant for someone's arrest, but I fully expect that we'll know who did it. I'm not sure my colleagues share my sense of closure, but tomorrow at the latest, we'll have it solved."

"She's the brains in the group, or at least in the group of Searing and McMillan," Lou said. "So, if she thinks it will be solved, I'd have to agree."

"It isn't that obvious to me," Harrison said with some reservation. "But after dinner we'll put it all together and perhaps the plot and murderer will become clear. I sure hope so."

"Well, please remain assured that my staff is committed to serving your needs. Your wish is our command in terms of arranging people to talk to, facilities, records, or anything we can reasonably provide. Enjoy your meal and call if I can help in any way."

"Thank you, Mr. Workman," Harrison said. The two men rose to shake his hand and the women smiled and nodded their appreciation.

"He certainly is a gracious man. I can see why he runs such a successful resort," Carol said sincerely. "He has high standards and expects others to serve the customers in the same way."

"Absolutely," Lou replied.

The waitress knew that this table was to be treated with extra special attention and she looked forward to seeing that Mr. Workman's guests were not disappointed. She presented herself in a cheerful fashion and attempted to be that perfect waitress with all their needs attended to without anyone's realizing that they had been perfectly waited on all evening. "Good evening. My name is Joan. It's my pleasure to see that you have a wonderful dining experience this evening. To help you, could you please tell me if you are in a hurry or do you wish a leisurely meal?"

"Thank you for asking, Joan. We are neither in a hurry nor do we want to be here for more than an hour. We want a relaxing meal, but right afterwards, we have work to do," Lou said, with the others nodding in agreement.

"I understand. Can I get you anything from the bar before your meal?" They ordered water and coffee. Joan began to give the specials, but Harrison interrupted, "I think we can save you that speech, Joan. We're ready to order, aren't we?" The others nodded.

Taking orders was easy because each wanted the broiled whitefish, baked potato with a salad. The salad dressings were also easy as French was the favorite of the men and the women wanted Italian. Joan smiled and excused herself to get the salads and the beverages.

Carol said, "I know the three of you are up here to do very serious thinking and to solve this thing. But, I'd like to suggest that for at least this meal, we talk about something other than murder. I think our brains could use a break from the details of this case. To lighten things up a bit, I suggest we each present something about ourselves. You know, most interesting experience I've ever had, most beautiful scene I've ever seen, biggest thrill in my life, or the one thing no one probably knows about me is...."

"Good idea, Carol," Maggie replied. Maggie told about her trip to Hawaii a couple of years ago. She enjoyed a visit with her cousin Kathy, known as Kitty to most friends. Kathy took Maggie for a glider ride and the view of Diamond Head and the clear water and sandy beach were emblazoned in her memory forever.

Harrison followed with tales about his deer hunting experiences and told an entertaining deer camp story. Carol thought she would tell about the time she won a sweepstakes contest. "Somebody does win those things and I'm a living example that if you put a stamp on enough envelopes, sooner or later, you'll win something."

Finally, Lou told about his hobby of collecting humorous newspaper headlines. "One of my favorites comes from Luckey, Ohio. The headline reads, 'Luckey Trucker Injured in Accident.'" All four enjoyed a good laugh.

"Thanks for sharing; it was fun to hear something other than a whodunit theory," Carol said. "Our conversation for the remainder of the evening will no doubt be devoted to the investigation. I just wanted to hear something else for a change."

"A great idea, Carol," Maggie said. "I get a little tired of the investigation talk, too."

Joan filled water glasses quietly and made sure that everyone was comfortable. She took away empty dishes and when there was a break in the conversation she said, "Mr. Workman would like for you to have a slice of our apple pie. I'm sure you'll not want to turn down this special offer. I only need to know if you wish it with ice cream." The men wanted the topping but the women didn't.

Joan brought the desserts and kept the coffee cups filled. They decided to get back to work. They thanked Joan for exceptional service and headed back to the lodge.

ॐ

Following dinner, Lou made arrangements with Mr. Workman to use one of the meeting rooms in the Fjords Townhouse. Everyone took their materials, notes, and tapes to the room. Carol took responsibility for feeding the computer, clipping various notes together and doing anything that would help.

Maggie asked Harrison, "Did you bring the photographs of the murder scene?"

"Yup. Got them in a folder in my carrying case."

"I'd like to see them when you get a moment."

Harrison immediately went to his case and gave them to Maggie.

Maggie studied them very carefully. She saw something that caused her to be curious but she kept her thoughts to herself for the time being.

Lou continued making lists. He found that his lists helped him organize the major issues. He had a list of suspects, a list of motives, and a list of major clues. He Scotch taped large sheets of paper to the walls of the room. On the suspects sheet he wrote: Dwight Austin, Judy Austin, Don Dailey, Jimmy Shekleford, Bob Sanders, Mark Thompson, Stacy Hammonds, Billy Wingate, and Shorty Gross. Of course there could be many others who were at the course that day, but so far their investigation seemed to point to one or more of these.

On another sheet Lou wrote a list of motives: confrontation between Bill Wallach and Dwight Austin; anger that Judy Austin has for Reggie Macleod; Don Dailey's anger concerning Dan Dillon; possible act to please Judy on the part of the pro Bob Sanders; Dwight's harassment of Stacy Hammonds, and Judy's hatred of her father. As with the suspects, there could be more, but these were the ones that had surfaced.

One more sheet contained major clues. Here Lou wrote: Bill sees a cart leave the 14th tee for the 13th hole and the driver seemed to be wearing knickers and a mask; Sally Quest hears that a murder will take place on the 14th tee and is probably told that by Shorty Gross; Heather Abraham discovers a placemat with the drawing of an X with the name Wallach; Dwight Austin is so happy after the murder that he buys a round of drinks for the people in Jac's; Jimmy Shekleford talks to Don Dailey for a long time the morning of the murder and turns up as the owner of a new car. Jimmy also quits his only job.

The final sheet Lou labeled "Summary." He wrote, Weapon: poison; Place: 14th tee of Marsh Ridge; Time: early afternoon of July 9. Witness: none; Motive: unclear; Murderer: unknown. All that was left to do was match the motive to the murderer and another murder would be solved.

Lou asked, "Will you three take a look at all of this information and tell me if I'm missing something?"

They stopped what they were doing and read the sheets carefully. "I think you've got us up-to-date, Lou," Harrison said.

"I agree," Maggie added, with a nod of her head.

"Looks good to me," Carol replied.

"Time to talk theories, I guess," Harrison suggested. "Seems that we should now be putting the pieces together to see what kind of scenarios we can come up with. Agree?"

"Okay, let's do it. Anyone got a theory?" Lou asked.

"I'll begin," Harrison offered. "Whoever killed Reggie used the mystery weekend at Marsh Ridge to assist in their plot. I believe this person, or persons, devised a plot involving more than a few people. This would explain Shorty saying it would happen on the 14th tee. I believe that Judy was the mind behind the murder. She hated her father and she hated Macleod. She tried to frame Don by asking him to go get the ice, which I am predicting she pushed off the cart. This would put him in that area about the time of the murder. We know from talking to Walt that Judy knew Macleod was golfing in the area. She was able to find out where he was scheduled to play on Saturday. Then she orchestrated his move to Marsh Ridge where she could place her father behind Macleod. I believe she planned the whole thing. The people who helped her were Shorty Gross and other friends. So, my theory is out there for your consideration. Since the test results show that the ground was not contaminated, someone drove up to the tee when Reggie was there and offered him a cool drink from a thermos or small cooler."

"Makes sense," Lou said.

"Let me take a crack at it," Carol said, ready to offer her opinion for what it was worth. "I've thought all along that Dwight Austin is the most obvious murderer. I believe he was behind the golfers being transferred to Marsh Ridge. I think he made sure he was behind the group so he could signal whoever was to do the poisoning when the group got to the 14th tee. He knew the cooler of lemonade was at 14. He has the money to buy off people to do things for him. We'll find that he engineered the whole plot. He simply found someone to offer Reggie the cup of poison." Carol continued, "I think Dwight wanted to kill the man who ruined his daughter's career."

"Good thinking, Carol! Maggie, got any thoughts?" Lou asked.

"If intuition has a part to play, I'd say Stacy is a strong suspect. She is a friend of Judy's. She hates Dwight for the crimes committed against her and she would have a reason to kill Macleod because he damaged her friend's career. She is an employee of the resort, knows the people, procedures, activities and she was probably in Jac's on Friday night. She could have written the diagram on the placemat. I don't have all the details you have, but I think Stacy will in some way figure into the murder."

"Seems that a major hole in all of this to date is not knowing who drove up with the poison." Harrison stated.

Maggie said, "Well, Lou, what is your theory?"

"I don't mean to be uncooperative, but I'm going to ask for more time before I put forth my theory. I will say that I tend to think that Judy is definitely involved and my guess is that Maggie is right when she thinks that Stacy is involved. I also think Shorty plays a part. I don't think Dwight is the murderer. He came near death with his facial cancer and he loves golf too much to give it up for the rest of his life. Judy, on the other hand, had a strong reason to kill Macleod since he really upset her applecart with the firing. Those are a few of my thoughts."

"Tomorrow is another day," Harrison said yawning. "We'll talk to Shorty Gross in the morning. Carol, do you have any follow up phone calls to make?"

"I think I've got six couples who weren't home when I called today."

"Okay. Maggie, what plans do you have?"

"I want to visit some of the places where the suspects work. I want to go to the kitchen, the maintenance department, and the bar. Finally, I want to visit the pro shop."

"Lou, what are you going to do?"

"I think I'd like to listen when you talk with Shorty, and I'd also like to go with Maggie when she visits several work sites."

"Looks like we'll all be busy. Shall we meet for breakfast at seven-thirty?"

"Sounds fine with me," Lou said. "We've a lot to do tomorrow if we want to wrap this up."

"Harry, do you mind if I keep the crime scene photos overnight?" Maggie asked.

"Not at all."

Before Maggie went to bed, she called Tom to report on her activities and to see how he scored at the golf scramble in Battle Creek. Following her phone call, she decided to hook up her laptop computer to read any e-mail and more importantly to go onto the internet and visit a website to stay current with software and information that she can use to accommodate her disability. Maggie has found that technology is a good friend, a friend that has allowed her to maintain her independence. She believed that knowledge is power and by frequently going to the internet, she felt up-to-date.

She independently, with the help of her accessible room, prepared for bed and closed her eyes believing that the crime would be solved the next day.

CHAPTER 12

Sunday, July 17
Gaylord, Michigan
Marsh Ridge Resort

At seven-thirty the group was seated in Jac's for breakfast. While a light rain fell causing the golfers to use their umbrellas, the detectives and Carol ordered the buffet thinking they could eat quickly and get on with their agreed-upon tasks. While they were eating, Lou said, "I talked to Mr. Workman last evening when we finished our work. I wanted to contact the head of the mystery weekend and ask him some questions. His name is Mr. Growe. We found him at a resort in Miami. I asked him about his production and what I learned was quite interesting.

"They set up for the mystery weekend in advance of their guests' arrival. The plot is the same one used at a variety of resorts. Their procedures are quite simple. He and his wife arrived on Thursday. They met with the resort manager, and based on the plot, a meeting was held Friday afternoon with the actors and those few staff who were involved. They met with the golf pro, bartender, hostess in the restaurant, and the locker room attendant. When the guests arrived, a reception was held and the weekend was explained to the guests. Each guest was given, via a short drama, the murder plot. At Marsh Ridge, the plot consisted of the lifeguard found dead in the swimming pool.

Guests were given a sheet with some basic information and clues. The guests were organized into groups and sent out to solve the murder in the course of the weekend. He said that they often purposefully dreamt up phony situations to divert attention away from the real plot."

"Did you ask him about the real murder?" Harrison asked.

"Yeah, I did. He said he heard about it and that it was most unfortunate. He was concerned for the family, but also for the resort and somewhat concerned about his reputation. This is understandable. But, he didn't know anything about events leading to the real murder, nor did he see or hear anything out of the ordinary. I don't think he had anything to do with our case."

"Good, Lou," Harrison replied. "I'm glad you contacted him. That's a piece we hadn't touched on to date."

The four finished their breakfasts and prepared for a purposeful day. Carol returned to her room to try to reach the remaining six couples. Maggie was waiting for Lou and Harrison to finish interviewing Shorty Gross before taking her tour of the various work sites of the suspects.

꒜

Harrison and Lou waited for Shorty to arrive for work at about nine o'clock. He was right on time. Ken provided a meeting space for the interview. "Good morning, Mr. Gross. My name is Harrison Kennedy of the Otsego Sheriff's Department and this is Mr. Searing who is assisting me. We'd like to ask you a few questions. I trust that would be all right with you?"

"Yes, sir. I don't think I can help much. But, if you've got questions, I'll try to answer 'em."

"Thank you. We'd like to go over the day, a week ago yesterday. You arrive for work here about when?"

"I get here about nine o'clock. That's when I'm to report."

"You come here from home?"

"Yeah. That's right."

"Might you come here from some other place, you know, pay

some bills in the morning, get in a few holes of golf before work, anything like that?"

"No time for golf that early in the morning. I get up, have some breakfast, shower, dress and come in to work."

"Do you know Judy Austin?"

"Yeah. She's a beverage gal at Marsh Ridge."

"What is your relationship with Judy?"

"I know who she is. I've dated her."

"Do you know Stacy Hammonds?"

"Yeah. Know her, too. In fact, I know Stacy better than Judy. We dated for several weeks about six months ago."

"Where were you a week ago last Friday night?"

"Oh, man. I don't know where I was a few days ago, let alone a week ago."

"Give it a try. Friday night, a week ago. That was the evening before the murder."

"I was playing pool in town with some guys. On my way home I stopped at Marsh Ridge and had a few drinks at Jac's. Yeah, that's it. I stopped for a drink at Jac's."

"Sit at a table or at the bar or what?"

"I think I was at a table."

"Who was with you?"

"Lotsa people. I mean this was Friday night at a popular bar. The place was packed and especially that night because the resort was having its mystery weekend."

"Try to remember, Mr. Gross. Who were you with?"

"Well, I know I spent some time with Stacy 'cause she works there, and I like being around her even though we don't date regularly anymore. She's a fun gal."

"Who else was with you besides Stacy?"

"Dwight and Judy Austin were there. I also remember that Dwight Austin and one of the rangers were at a table next to us. I think it was Mark Thompson. Yeah, it was."

"Was Judy at your table with you and Stacy?"

"Yeah, for awhile. Others stopped by, but the three of us were at the table for a stretch."

"And at another table you said you saw Dwight Austin and Mark Thompson. Anyone else there?"

"I didn't pay much attention. The vibes aren't too good between those people and my friends. We stuck to ourselves."

"While you were there, did you, Judy, or Stacy use a placemat to make a drawing on? Do you recall that?"

"Drawing on a placemat?"

"Yeah, you know, turn one over and sketch something out?"

"This ain't school, man. We were drinking and listening to music and having a good time. Gotta be pretty bored to be drawing pictures at a bar during high tide."

"Shorty, if I may call you that?"

"Sure, everyone calls me Shorty."

"Were you at the Marsh Ridge putting green on Saturday morning before coming to work?"

"I told you guys, I came here from home. Some days I stop at golf courses and do a little putting. Sometimes I even challenge some guys for petty cash."

"We've learned that you were at Marsh Ridge that morning, that you were on the putting green, that you talked to a woman there and that you told her the murder would be at the 14th tee. Do you recall that?"

"Oh, wait a minute. Yeah. I was there. I'm sorry, guys. Yeah. I did stop at the golf course before coming here."

"Do you recall talking to this woman?"

"Yeah. A woman did ask me about a murder. I guess she was with the murder mystery weekend."

"Did you say, 'The murder will be at the 14th tee?'"

"Yeah."

"How would you know that this was going to happen unless you were involved?"

"I was hoping I wouldn't get drawn into this ugly mess, but I guess that stupid comment to the lady will do me in. I was so shocked by her question, that I just said it. What really happened was that I overheard Dwight Austin say that the murder would happen on the 14th tee."

"Dwight said it to whom?"

"Said it to Mark Thompson, I guess. I don't know, they were sitting next to us and it was noisy and lots of people were around."

"I take it you didn't feel that you should inform the authorities of a possible crime about to be committed?"

"No. Hey, I was in a bar with friends. I overheard a comment. It stuck, and when the lady asked her question, I blurted it out. The next afternoon when we got word that an ambulance was needed at Marsh Ridge and then we learned the body was on the 14th tee, I got real nervous."

"Even at that point or shortly after, you didn't let us know what you had heard the night before?"

"Didn't want to get involved. Going to court, having Dwight Austin as my enemy – was all too horrible to be real. The guy will make your life miserable, and man, I got enough on my plate now."

"Any questions you want to ask, Lou?"

"You said you overheard Dwight say that the murder would occur at the 14th tee. Did you hear anything else?"

"Once I heard that, I tried to see what else I could hear. People came over to our table, the band started up again and Dwight and his friend left a few minutes later. So, I didn't hear anything else."

Lou continued, "Did you tell Judy and/or Stacy what you had heard?"

"I was going to, but didn't."

"Did you tell them after the murder?"

"No."

"Did you tell anybody?"

"No. Just didn't want to get involved. I wouldn't have told you except that the lady told you. It would be her word against mine. She was right, I did say that. That was my big mistake and now Dwight Austin will harass me for the rest of my life. That one-sentence exchange on that putting green that morning will change my life forever. My guess is I'll have to testify in court and Dwight will use his money and his friends to see that I have a miserable life. I'm looking to get out of here now. I'll just pack my bags and go back to Alabama till this dies down."

The three men concluded their discussion. Harrison and Lou drove away believing that if Shorty were telling the truth, it looked like Dwight Austin was the prime suspect in the murder. They knew that he wasn't at the 14th tee when the victim died, but he may have caused the murder to happen and everyone knows that he had an ugly confrontation with Bill Wallach a day or two before the murder. They also knew that Mark Thompson was seen in the vicinity of the tee just before the victim arrived. And, that Mark and Reggie were golf teammates at Western Michigan University and as far as they knew, Mark would have no reason to kill a friend. On the other hand, maybe he did have a reason to kill for a friend.

❧

While Lou and Harrison were talking with Shorty, Carol was calling people she couldn't reach the day before. The phone rang in the kitchen of Tony and Crystal Ebaugh. "Hello."

"Mr. Ebaugh?"

"Speaking."

"Mr. Ebaugh, this is Carol Searing. We're investigating the murder of a golfer in the Gaylord area a week ago. Records show that you were guests for the mystery last weekend at the Marsh Ridge Resort."

"Yes. We attended that event. Lots of fun."

"Good. Glad you had a good time. I'm calling to see if you recall seeing or hearing anything that might give us a clue to the murder."

"Nothing while we were at the mystery weekend, but we have a couple of friends, and strange you should call, but we just talked to them after church. Their names are Larry and Courtney Rogers. They said that they have a friend who was at Marsh Ridge when we were there. Their friend is an actor and he was asked to spend a day there confusing the guests."

"Could you give me the phone number for the Rogers?"

"Oh, they're not involved in any way."

"I know. But the detectives may wish to talk to their friend who was up there during that weekend."

"I guess that would be okay."

Tony Ebaugh assured Carol that he didn't have additional information. He gave her the phone number of their friends. Carol expressed appreciation for his cooperation.

Carol called the Rogers and learned the name and phone number of their actor friend. She waited for Lou and Harrison to return from their interview so she could share what she had learned.

ﾟﾞ

Maggie went to the business office of the resort and asked to speak to the accountant. It was Sunday and the accountant, Mrs. Peters, was not at work. Mr. Workman said that he would call her and ask her to come over to the resort which she did.

"I need to find the requisition requests for supplies for the pro shop, the kitchen staff, Jac's Place, and the maintenance unit," Maggie said. "I'm looking for supply orders and I may have to go back several months."

Joan Peters said that would be no problem. She pushed a few keys on the computer and instantly each supply requested, the date of the order, the arrival date of the order, and the exact location that it was delivered appeared on her screen. ""Is there something specifically I can help you with?" Joan asked.

"No, just all supplies."

"That's pretty simple. It's all right here." Maggie looked at the screen and could see that each unit of the resort had ordered numerous supplies.

"I'd like a printout of supply orders made by all of the departments of the resort," Maggie requested.

"Not a problem," Joan said. A few feet away a long computer printout began to emerge from the machine.

"Is there anything else I can help you with?" Joan asked.

"Yes, does the resort order any poisonous chemicals?"

"I'm sure the fertilizer is toxic and we order tons of fertilizer, plant food, and other material for the maintenance department. We also have a health unit at the resort. This unit is much more active in the ski season, but the nurses usually order supplies and materials for their needs. I would imagine some of the drugs are toxic in large doses, but not being a medical person I can't answer in any detail."

"Would there be any reason for cyanide to be in the health unit?"

"I have no idea."

"Who is the nurse who would have been here the day of the murder?"

"I'd have to check with personnel. Our staff is getting so large with all of the expanded activities at the resort. One moment, please."

Joan called Mr. Workman and asked Maggie's question. A few seconds later she thanked him and hung up. "Mr. Workman said that the nurse on duty at that time was Janice Ketcham."

"Is she here now?"

"I believe so. She's the weekend nurse."

"Do you have a number where I can reach her or better yet, just tell me where the nurse's station is located."

"I've got both. The number is an extension and it's 6650. The nurse's station is located in a cabin next to the Copenhagen Inn. She would be right here," Joan said, pointing to the location on the resort map.

"Thank you very much. Sorry to cut into your Sunday."

"According to Mr. Workman, there are no day's off in our business. We are at his beck and call as our customers must have the finest service. Unless I am on vacation and another staff person can do what I can do, I am always considered to be at work. He has such high standards. I guess that's why Marsh Ridge Resort is consistently rated so high."

In her motorized wheelchair, Maggie made her way to see the nurse. Maggie didn't call first, so she hoped that Janice would be available. With the service ethic at this place being what it is, all she had to do was say to Mr. Workman that she needed to see Nurse Ketcham and she would appear.

It was here that Maggie encountered her first problem with accessibility. There was no ramp to the health unit. Frustrated, Maggie turned off her power chair, took her cell phone from a pocket attached to her chair, and dialed the nurse's extension. She would ask her to come outside. Nurse Ketcham was in and was not attending to anyone. She went out the door and met Maggie.

"Hi, you must be Janice Ketcham?"

"Yes."

"I'm Maggie McMillan. I am assisting in the investigation of the murder that occurred here a week ago."

"Hi, Maggie. How can I help you?"

"I have some questions if you don't mind."

"Okay."

"First of all, I'm surprised that your health unit is not accessible to people with disabilities."

"I'm really embarrassed, Maggie. We usually go to the person needing our services, but I'll talk to Mr. Workman and I'm sure he will respond immediately."

"I don't mean to begin our dialogue on a negative note, but I'm offended by the lack of access into your office."

"Again, I'm sorry. How can I help you?"

"As I said, I'm investigating the murder of a week ago and I'd like to ask a few questions."

"I'll help if I can," Janice said, sitting down on the porch so as to be at eye level with Maggie.

"Did you have any role in responding to the emergency when the victim was discovered?"

"No. As I understand it, one of the golfers who discovered the victim had a cell phone and called 911. Once that occurred, the police and ambulance were summoned. I had no role except to assist if additional medical personnel were needed. I thought it was all phony. You know, a part of the mystery production."

"So, did you go to the 14th tee when you learned that there was an emergency there?"

"No. I was with a golfer who had a sprained ankle at the time and everything seemed to be under control with the EMS team and the police."

"Did you know the victim?"

"No."

"Had you heard anything about him?"

"I think he was a special education director in a school district in Michigan. Judy Austin, a friend of mine, said that he was a director of a program where she used to teach."

"Do you know Dwight Austin?"

"Everyone does. He's obnoxious and a harasser."

"Tell me about that, Janice."

"Several of the women out here have suffered because of his sexual harassment. He gets sexual favors by threatening us with our jobs and revealing secrets from our past. He gets away with it because he has a lot of money and a lot of threats. Reporting him would make life miserable. Money talks and his money gets him what he wants."

"Who specifically is being harassed, Janice?"

"Wendy in the pro shop, Stacy in the lounge, Heather in the restaurant, Liz who is a lifeguard, me, and maybe one or two others who work here. Anyway, I don't want to talk about it, but yes, I know Dwight Austin. Everybody out here does."

"Mr. Workman is so dedicated to his staff that you would think he would take some action," Maggie said.

"Yes. He's a fine boss. If we approached him, I think he would have taken some kind of action to help us. But, the harassment was not from a Marsh Ridge employee nor was the harassment happening at Marsh Ridge, so we took it as our problem and didn't say anything to him."

"So, you didn't go to the 14th tee when the murder took place? You really had no involvement in the episode?"

"That's correct. As I said, I thought it was just a phony activity to throw off the murder mystery weekend guests. This place has a reputation for that. The production people go to great lengths to stage a challenging mystery weekend. It would be typical of them to bring in helicopters, ambulances, and police. So, it wasn't until the next day that I found out that it wasn't a play and a guy really did die out there."

"Thanks, Janice. I may need to see you again for further information."

"I'll be here the rest of the day, and if you need me when I'm not on duty, I'm certain that Mr. Workman will summon me."

※

Lou and Harrison returned to the resort. When they arrived, Carol briefed them on what she had learned from Mr. Ebaugh. Harrison decided to call. "Hello, Mr. Collins?"

"Yes."

"This is Harrison Kennedy of the Otsego County Sheriff's Department. How are you today?"

"Fine."

"Mr. Collins, we're investigating a murder that occurred in Gaylord a week ago. We've learned that you were contracted to work that weekend at the Marsh Ridge Resort. That weekend was their murder mystery weekend. You recall that job?"

"Yes. I'm an actor. I got a call asking me if I'd be willing to assist some people in a murder mystery weekend. I asked what role I'd have and was told that I was to be at the resort and to lead the guests astray with comments and suggestions."

"Who contacted you?"

"You know, to be honest, I really don't know."

"Was it a man or a woman?"

"A man."

"What did he say?"

"Like I said, he asked if I would like to earn some easy money using my acting skills; I asked what he had in mind. He said they were planning a murder mystery weekend and needed someone to deceive the guests or to plant suggestions that were not true so as to complicate the process of solving the mystery."

"For example?"

"For example, I said I heard that a clue in the murder was a gun hidden in a golf bag in the pro shop."

"When did you get the call?"

"The night before."

"That would have been Friday, July 8?"

"Yeah, got the call about eleven Friday night."

"Were you involved in the murder of the golfer that weekend?"

"No way. I thought that was all part of the entertainment for guests."

"What were you contracted to do?"

"I was asked to work Saturday. I arrived mid-morning in golfing attire. I was instructed to go all over the resort talking to the guests and looking like I fit in. I finished at about two-thirty in the afternoon. I was paid and drove home."

"How were you paid?"

"Cash."

"Were you told anything to say about the murder?"

"I was told to tell people that the ambulance and the police arriving in the early afternoon were part of the mystery weekend and not to be alarmed."

"I assume you know that a man really did die that afternoon."

"I just learned it from my friends. I don't read papers and I didn't hear about any murder up there."

"Do you know any of the following - Judy or Dwight Austin, Stacy Hammonds, or Shorty Gross?"

"No."

"Do you know any employees from Marsh Ridge?"

"I went to college with Liz Lake."

"Who is she?"

"She's one of two lifeguards at the resort."

"Was she working that weekend?"

"No, I didn't see her. She starts in a day or two, I think. She's worked there for a couple of summers."

"This man who called you. Was there anything about him that you could describe?"

"No."

"Did you talk to anyone at the resort who was involved in the production?"

"Nope. I had my instructions. I arrived about ten in the morning and went about playing my part."

"So, you didn't talk with anyone in the production company. No one greeted you and explained what you were being paid to do?"

"Nope."

"You didn't find that odd?"

"No. Hey, not a big part, you know, walk around and confuse guests and tell them when appropriate that the big production in the afternoon was phony. I don't need a lot of coaching to pull that off."

"When you got paid, did someone hand you cash?"

"No. At two-thirty I went to the bar and asked for an envelope with my name on it. I did, and there was cash in it. I went to my car and headed home. Easy money."

"You didn't think that odd?"

"No. We actors get jobs and money any way we can. If an employer wants to give me an assignment and pay me without shaking hands or a big warm greeting and a thank you when I leave, fine with me. I do the acting and get paid under their conditions. No, I didn't think it odd."

"Now that you know that a man was murdered, do you think the circumstances under which you were contacted, and that you were to tell people a murder was not occurring when in fact it was, leads you to see that you were involved in a murder plot?"

"No. I was working for the production company that was contracted to put on a murder mystery weekend. I had my assignment to make it difficult for the guests to solve the drama. It all sounded simple and aboveboard to me."

"Thanks for talking with me, Mr. Collins."

"You're welcome."

჻

Lou listened to the conversation between Harrison and Don Collins. He went right to the phone and dialed the number of the production director of the murder mystery weekend. He thought his chances of getting him at this hour on a Sunday morning would be slim, but luck was with him.

"Good morning. Is this Mr. Growe?"

"It is."

"Mr. Growe, this is Lou Searing in Gaylord, Michigan. You'll recall talking with me - yesterday - I think it was. I am investigating the murder of a golfer at Marsh Ridge."

"Oh, yes, Mr. Searing. How can I help you this morning?"

"Just a few more questions, sir."

"Fine."

"Did you contract with a Mr. Collins to assist your company on Saturday, July 9?"

"No. I don't do any contracting."

"You didn't contract with a man to confuse guests so they'd have a difficult time solving your mystery?"

"Absolutely not. That's so foreign to our way of operation. We have our own group of actors and we use employees of the resort, as I mentioned to you before. I never contract with anyone else. It's too messy. I'd need to have records and distribute W-2 forms. It isn't worth it. No, I never employ anyone beyond my small staff."

"Do you ever have anyone with your production try to deceive the guests?"

"Every good mystery has a red herring or two. After all, we writers and actors do need to throw and obstacle or two at the guests. That's what makes it fun, trying to wade through the possible suspects. We are most proud that our mysteries are tried and true. People come to the weekends for relaxation and to have fun putting clues together to solve a fictitious crime on the premises. They don't need people walking around confusing them. I wouldn't have any such behavior as part of our production."

"Did you have any forewarning about the murder that day?"

"None whatsoever. That tragedy had nothing to do with our production. Whoever is at fault may have used our drama to help them with their crime, but my set of actors had nothing to do with it.

Of that I'm absolutely certain."

"Thank you, Mr. Growe."

"You're welcome. Have a good day and please solve that mess as soon as possible."

"We're trying our best, sir."

❧

"I want to talk to Mark Thompson again, "Lou said to Harrison.

"I agree. I think he needs to explain Friday night and his presence at the 14th tee on Saturday."

Mark was working that day and Harrison asked Wendy to page him. Mark drove up in his ranger cart. "Good morning, gentlemen."

"Hi, Mr. Thompson. We've a few questions for you. Last time you wanted your attorney present. I really don't think it necessary, but if you want that, you may wish to give her a call. We'll wait till she gets here."

"I've nothing to hide. I was being cautious before. I'd rather be safe than sorry. Go ahead and ask your questions."

"Were you at Jac's Place on Friday night, the night before the murder?"

"Yeah. I was there with Dwight Austin."

"You usually go there?"

"Not really, but when I do, it's on a Friday night. The place is jumping with people and it's a fun place to be. I'm alone now, don't have many friends, so it's kind of neat to be around younger people having a good time."

"You're a friend of Dwight Austin?"

"Yes. I think I'm one of the few people Dwight would call a friend."

"You just ran into him at Jac's?"

"No. He called and suggested we meet there. He had something he wanted to talk to me about. He had a plan."

"What was the plan he wanted to discuss?"

"Now I need my lawyer. I won't comment about that."

"Did Dwight ever use the back of a placement to sketch something when you were together Friday night at Jac's?"

"Pleading the 5th, men. Won't comment."

"Did you recognize others at Jac's that night?"

"Yeah. Next to our table were some people who work at the resort."

"Who?"

"Let's see. I remember Stacy Hammonds. Dwight's daughter Judy was there. The nurse Janice Ketcham was there for a few minutes and so was Liz Lake."

"Who's Liz Lake?"

"She's one of the lifeguards at Marsh Ridge."

"Was anyone else at your table besides you and Dwight?"

"No. We were there for about an hour. It was just the two of us."

"Okay. Talk to us about your job. We have a general idea of what a ranger does, but tell us in your own words."

"Well, it's my job to move the players along. I try to be friendly and to have something positive to say. If a group is slow and taking too long, I ask them to hurry up play a bit. I position myself around the course where I can see several groups."

"Can you recall any of your movements the day the guy was murdered?"

"I've given that a lot of thought. I remember that I was in the area of the 14th. I tried to replay my moves during that time, and as best as I can reconstruct it, I had finished talking with the victim's friends after they left 14. I stayed near the tee and watched them hit their second shots. Then I left the area and went over to thirteen. I know that I never saw the victim and his friends on the 14th tee."

"When you were still on 14 and looking at the group on 14, did you see anyone moving toward the 14th tee?"

"No."

"When you went to 13, did you talk to Dwight?"

"Yeah. Think I did."

Harrison asked Lou if he had any questions. Lou asked, "Mr. Thompson, did you know the victim?"

"Yeah. I knew Reggie."

"How did you know him?"

"We were teammates on the Western Michigan University golf team back in the late '50s or early '60s."

"So, he was a friend of yours?"

"No, I wouldn't say he was a friend. We played on the same team forty some years ago. He's a nice guy, but I haven't seen him for years. We did recognize each other earlier that day, and we reminisced for a few minutes. He's, as I said, a nice guy, good golfer, but I couldn't call him a friend."

"What did Dwight Austin say to you Friday night about the golfer who died or his friends?"

"That's another lawyer question. Won't answer that without her go ahead. I don't mean to be uncooperative, but I just can't respond to some of these questions without her approval."

"We understand. Thanks for helping us. We'll be in touch." With that, Mark left to speed up the slow golfers.

Lou and Harrison found Thompson's responses intriguing. "Thompson seemed very helpful with most of the questions, but he wouldn't say anything about Dwight, the placemat, the plan, or anything Dwight had said about the victim or his friends," Lou summarized.

Harrison added, "There's obviously something we need to hear and it could be pivotal to this mystery."

It was lunchtime and the day was going much too quickly. All four agreed to meet for lunch at Jac's Place. Lou almost dreaded going back into the real world after all of the good food along with incredible service they had received. Once again, they ordered the buffet so that they could eat and talk and use every moment for solving the murder. After everyone had filled their plates and sat down, Lou began, "Well, we're nearing the last few hours of the weekend that we've dedicated to solving this crime. We've gotten a lot of information, but we're not ready to suggest that you arrest anyone, Harrison. Or, have I misjudged someone's thinking?"

"I'm beginning to feel pretty comfortable that the murderer is one of two people," Maggie said. "Dwight Austin or Judy Austin. In both cases they needed people to assist them. We have substantiated that neither one was at the 14th tee when the victim drank the poison and died. I can build a good case for either of them and my guess is that when all is said and done, one will be found guilty of the murder."

Harrison added, "I tend to agree, but what's risky is that we only have circumstantial evidence concerning both suspects. Neither was at the scene of the murder. We have no fingerprints, no witnesses to the murder, nothing but theory. This will be settled in a court with people giving testimony under oath. It may be the only way to get the truth."

"I think the circumstantial evidence is most damaging to Dwight," Lou said. "I say this because of his placemat, the statement given by Shorty that Dwight said that the murder would be at the 14th tee, and his leaving the scene and not being cooperative following the murder."

Maggie chimed in, "The major damaging circumstantial evidence may be with Dwight, but follow this line of reasoning. Dwight is not liked by the women of Marsh Ridge. I'm hearing stories of harassment involving relatively young and attractive women who won't turn him in for fear of their lives or of being fired. Judy hates her father and she hates Reggie Macleod who fired her from her special education teaching job. She could have planned her own murder mystery weekend here at Marsh Ridge. She could have planned it with the help of friends, many of whom were at Jac's Friday night. She could have asked Don Collins to come up to help with her play. The placemat map could have been drawn by Judy. She might have placed it at her father's table after he left and she may have had the waitress on her side. Maybe she asked the waitress to meet with us to share what she found. Judy sees Macleod done in and they frame dear old dad who gets convicted and sent off to prison where he is incapable of sexually harassing the women of Marsh Ridge. Judy and her friends kill Reggie and thereby win on both scores."

"Very interesting, Maggie. Very interesting," Harrison said. "Good thinking. But, if Dwight Austin did it, who gave the victim the drink?"

"It could be Mark Thompson. Mark, as we know, will not answer any questions about being with Dwight on Friday night," Maggie recalled.

Lou looked to Maggie, "What did you find when you visited the work sites?"

"I met with the resort accountant and she gave me a printout of all supplies ordered here for the past couple of months. None of what I found has helped to date."

Lou added, "I wonder if the kid, Jimmy Shekleford, was the one who did this?"

"A high school kid?" Carol questioned.

Lou defended his observation, "Well, he was there that day, he quit a day later, he drives a new Jeep Cherokee but doesn't have a source of money to pay for it. Jimmy could have done what Mr. Austin asked him to do for that goodly sum of money or even for the promise of a car. All he'd have to do is go to the 14th tee and give the golfer a prepared drink. Pretty simple act for a new car and a man who could buy you freedom if ever questioned by the authorities."

"It's a good theory and may have happened," Harrison said. "But, I don't think Dwight did it. Stop and think for a minute. As Billy said earlier, he loves golf, plays it almost everyday up north in late spring, summer, and early fall, and then plays all winter in Florida. This is his life. Why would he risk all of that because a foursome hit into him and he had an argument with a golfer?"

"Anger leads people to do irrational things," Lou said.

"Yeah, but somebody messed up his face with botched cancer surgery and he didn't end that person's life," Harrison offered.

"No, he ended the doctor's career with a suit that gave him millions of dollars. He got even in court and he won enough money to assure him the land of milk and honey for the rest of his life. No man of normal intelligence would ever risk losing this gold mine because some guy hit a golf ball or two into his area of play," Lou reasoned.

"Yes, but anybody who angers this man pays. You hear fear in all the people we've interviewed. No one will confront Dwight because he gets even. He got even with the hospital in Florida and he always makes people pay for their poor judgment. We may think hitting a golf ball or two into another foursome is nothing, but to Dwight Austin it comes close to an international event. Bill Wallach didn't know who he was tangling with that afternoon. Dwight probably figured he couldn't get defeated in court. How could he? He wasn't at the 14th tee when the murder took place. In court, he'd have the finest lawyers and they would have little trouble convincing a jury that there's reasonable doubt that he killed that man. He'd be off free and ready to bring his revenge on all who worked to put him behind bars."

"Seems to me that we're back to point zero once again," Carol concluded.

Lou responded, "There's just one minor clue that we're missing and then this case is closed. Agree, Maggie?"

"Absolutely. We're close. We'll have it locked up by this afternoon. You'll be ready for your arrest by five o'clock, Harrison."

As they finished a chocolate chip cookie and coffee, they planned their last four hours at Marsh Ridge.

Maggie wanted to visit a couple of work sites she'd missed earlier. She was going on, as she called it, "a scavenger hunt." Harrison was going to Vanderbilt to talk with the attorney for Mark Thompson. Lou decided to pour over the evidence to date and look for that one remaining clue. Carol continued to try to contact a few of the guests who were not reachable since she began calling all of the mystery weekend guests yesterday.

꒳

Harrison pulled up at the home of Kara Ingram in Vanderbilt. Luckily for Harrison, she was at home. "Mr. Harrison. Good to see you again."

"Thank you, Miss Ingram. Got a few minutes to meet with me?"

"Am I billing you by the minute?" Kara asked with a chuckle.

"I'm afraid you'll be billing your client, Mr. Thompson."

"Not that murder again. Mark had nothing to do with that, Harry."

"Hasn't been ruled out in our mind. He keeps coming up as a possible suspect. The one who poisoned the golfer. He was at the

14th tee just before the three golfers arrived. He's a friend of Dwight Austin, and he was with Dwight the night before at Jac's where the details of the murder could have been finalized."

"I've talked to Mark and I'm convinced he's innocent."

"What else would I expect a man's lawyer to say?"

"Yes, I know. But, I believe it, and I know I can prove it if he's brought to court."

"Lou Searing and I talked with him late this morning and he was helpful."

"He talked with you without my permission?"

"I offered him the opportunity to call you, but he said he would risk your reprisal."

"What did he say?"

"He answered our questions, but when we asked him about his meeting with Dwight the night before to discuss a plan, he wouldn't talk without your advice. He wouldn't tell us anything that Dwight had said about any of the golfers in front of him or if Dwight actually wrote on the back of a placemat. So, he leaves us suspicious by not answering our questions."

"Mark and I have talked several times since the murder and I understand his reluctance to speak, but he didn't kill anybody, Harrison."

"Is the prosecution going to have to put him on the stand to get the truth out of him? He's a prime suspect. He was closest to the victim, he's a friend of Dwight's, and those two factors, circumstantial as they are, make him a man who'll have to explain to a jury why he wasn't the one to offer the fateful drink."

Kara listened to Harrison's thoughts and repeated her belief in her client's innocence. Harrison thanked her for her time and returned to the Scandinavian Lodge to keep working on the case.

Maggie drove her motorized wheelchair to the first aid station next to the Copenhagen Inn. Once again she called Janice on her cell phone. She learned that Nurse Ketcham was assisting a young boy so she waited outside. The rain had stopped and the sun was shining through wispy clouds. In about five minutes the young boy left. Janice came outside and said, "Can I help you?"

"I think so. I'd like to ask you a question or two, if you don't...." Maggie started to cough and gag a bit. She was able to ask for some water and Janice instinctively went into her cabin, got a cup from the dispenser, filled it with water and took it to Maggie. Maggie drank it slowly and continued to cough, but recovered.

"Swallowed wrong or something. Thanks."

"That's my job. Glad I could help. You have a question or two?"

"Yes, I do. The day of the murder you said you didn't go to the 14th tee. But, what were you doing before the sirens and the commotion began?"

"I had gotten a call that a golfer had a sprained ankle. I think he said he was in the woods looking for a lost ball and stepped on a rock or large branch which moved suddenly. So, I drove out to get him."

"Drove out where?"

"It was about the 16th green."

"So, you would have driven past the 14th tee or that approximate area shortly before the murder?"

"Yes."

"Did you see anyone or hear anything in the area of the 14th tee that you would characterize as suspicious?"

"No. It was a simple out and back trip. Didn't stop going or coming back, didn't talk to anyone. I remember thinking it important to get the ankle iced and immobile."

"What was the golfer's name?"

"Let me look in my log. Let's see that was a week ago yesterday, right?"

"Yes, July 9."

Janice went inside the health unit to get her log. She returned and said, "Here it is. John Rollins, sprained ankle, treated and released."

Maggie noted her response and said, "What happened when he was released?"

"What do you mean, what happened?"

"I mean did he walk away, did you take him back to his cart and friends, did you take him to his car, did you take him to the clubhouse? If he had a sprained ankle and you treated him, he had to get from this first aid station to someplace. Did a friend pick him up?"

Janice was having trouble explaining what had happened. Either she had forgotten or the man had been able to walk out on his own. "You know, I don't remember. I just don't remember." Janice was looking like she was beginning to break down. The stress of it all seemed to be taking its toll.

"Thanks for answering my questions and for helping me with some water."

"Sure. Want me to take the cup and dispose of it?"

"No, in fact, I'd like a little more water. My throat is still a bit scratchy." Janice got some more water and the two women parted.

Maggie called Wendy in the pro shop while she drove her chair back to the Scandinavian Lodge. She entered the room where they had set up headquarters, got everyone's attention and said, "I told you we'd solve this crime by the end of the day. The clock on the wall says three-thirty and I'm ready to draw my conclusions. Anyone want to beat me to the punch?"

Lou said, "You could use some glory. Tell us how you think it happened."

"I just came from Nurse Ketcham's station, which is where I went when I said I'd be back soon. I went there to test a gut feeling about Janice Ketcham being involved in the murders."

Maggie continued, "I asked for the name of the golfer she was treating for a sprained ankle. She looked into her log and told me he was John Rollins. I called Wendy and learned there was no John Rollins registered to play."

Maggie held up a patterned Dixie cup and continued with the others concentrating fully on her every word, "When I was talking with Janice I faked a coughing jag and asked for a cup of water. This is the cup that she gave me. Does this mean anything to anyone?"

Neither Lou, Harrison, nor Carol said a word. Maggie took an envelope from the table and removed the police photos at the scene of the death. Look at the paper cup on the ground near the victim. Notice the patterned Dixie cup. I looked in my notes and saw that Mrs. Battles told us that Judy takes out lemonade as well as styrofoam cups. Bill said that he saw the masked driver in knickers leaving the bench area where the lemonade and cups were located. I believe that the driver pushed some Dixie cups up into the styrofoam cup dispenser so as not to bring attention to the different cups. So, the Dixie cup is, for me, the mistake the murderer made. Since the Dixie cup was only requisitioned to the nurse's station and since the nurse told me she drove out to pick up a golfer about the time the murder took place, I'm ready to say the murderer is Janice Ketcham."

"Very good, Maggie! Very good!" Harrison said, hearing a solid theory with some evidence to back it up.

"It's the women of Marsh Ridge, isn't it, Maggie?" Lou said, feeling certain that Maggie had solved another one.

Maggie nodded, "Yes, I believe so. My theory is that Judy and the other women here at the resort wanted to kill Reggie Macleod to get her revenge for firing her and to keep Reggie quiet should anyone call asking about how she did working for him. To accomplish this, they used the confusion of the murder mystery weekend and devised a plot to assure the investigators that Dwight Austin did it. Once Dwight was the obvious murderer, the women of Marsh Ridge could watch him rot in prison and be free of his harassment. So, for the price of a privately delivered cold drink, on a very hot July afternoon, Reggie and Daddy would be out of their lives for good. It was simply an opportunity that these women couldn't pass up."

"Sounds good to me. But, the patterned Dixie cup could have come from any work site at the resort," Harrison suggested.

"You're right, it could have, but I checked the supply orders from each unit here at Marsh Ridge and the medical unit is the only one that orders this style of Dixie cup. The model number matches the patterned cup. Granted, someone could have brought these cups from home, but we've got the cup tied to the person in that cart, and I believe that person was the nurse.

"One final observation. I stopped at Jac's Place before seeing Janice. I went over to the window on the east side of the bar. With binoculars you can see the 13th hole. You could identify the golfers playing that hole. I suspect that someone, probably Stacy Hammonds, tracked their progress, and called Nurse Ketcham so she could drive to the 14th tee to offer the poisoned drink."

"Who do you think was involved?" Carol asked of Maggie.

"I think the group at Jac's on Friday night did the major planning. So, that would be Judy, Stacy, Janice and Shorty. I think Shorty called Collins who was a friend of Liz Lake, the lifeguard. My guess is that when we get all the details, Wendy and some other waitresses were also a party to this."

Harrison said, "You think we can arrest Janice Ketcham on suspicion of murder?"

Maggie said, "I'm quite certain that the prosecutor could convince the judge that there is probable cause to suspect Janice Ketcham for the murder of Reggie Macleod."

↭

The phone rang in the kitchen area. "Kitchen."

"Is Judy Austin there?"

"No, she's out on the course with the beverage cart."

"Would you please ask her to call or come over to the health unit?"

"Sure."

"Thanks."

When Judy returned to get more beverages, she saw the note. She called Janice Ketcham. "Health unit."

"Hi, Janice, this is Judy returning your call."

"Thanks. I think we're in trouble."

"What happened?"

"The lady in the wheelchair is asking questions that are getting too close for comfort."

"Like what?"

"Well, she asked about my whereabouts when the murder took

place. I told her I went out to get the golfer with the sprained ankle. She asked for the guy's name so I made up something that sounded like Don Collins. Several minutes later I thought to call Wendy to find out if she had asked her any questions. Wendy said that she asked if a John Rollins had registered for golf that day and of course, he hadn't."

"That's no big deal. You just say you forgot the name, thought it was John Rollins. We'll get a real name and you can insert that when you see her again."

"They'll just contact that person and he'll say he never had a sprained ankle and we'll be in deeper."

"What else did she ask?"

"It isn't what she asked, she started coughing. I'm a nurse and I know a real cough and she wasn't coughing because of anything in her throat. She asked for water and I gave her a cup. The cup was identical to the cup we used to give the guy the poisoned drink. I know there are police photos of the victim and the cup is lying on the ground. She could trace the cups to my office."

"There are all kinds of Dixie cups in the world. Anyone could have used that kind of a cup."

"Not out here. I special ordered that style of cup. When I requested it from accounting, I was told to get another type cup because they can bulk order. It isn't cost-effective to get a few boxes of one type of cup when the other sections of the resort are all ordering plain cups or styrofoam cups. I persisted. I wanted those cups. I could kick myself for it now."

"We're okay, Janice. The evidence is clearly behind Dwight. We've planted it all so perfectly. We don't have anything to worry about."

"I think we do. I stumbled and stammered. I just couldn't come up with the lie on the spot. She picked up on that. She's good. I think we're cooked, Judy. I really do."

"Maybe we should get together and talk a bit. Don't worry, Janice. They have no witnesses, no fingerprints, nothing but circumstantial evidence. We're okay. Thanks for calling and telling me about this."

ADMINISTRATION CAN BE MURDER

Harrison walked over to the phone and dialed the sheriff. "This is Harrison. I think we've got the murder at Marsh Ridge solved. As you know, I've been working all weekend with Lou and Carol Searing and Maggie McMillan. We've got it cracked and I'm comfortable with seeking a warrant to arrest Janice Ketcham, the nurse at Marsh Ridge for the murder of the golfer on the 14th tee."

"Good work, Kennedy. The whole community will be glad to have this behind them. Peace will follow the fear that some killer is on the loose."

"Yes. I plan to inform Mr. Workman and to tell him that additional arrests may be forthcoming as there could be a conspiracy involving other persons at the resort. But, I'm comfortable advising the prosecutor that we have the evidence to convince a judge in a preliminary hearing that there is probable cause to believe that Janice Ketcham did indeed give a poisoned drink to the golfer."

"Yes, tell Workman. Good idea."

"I'll talk to Mr. Workman, arrest Janice Ketcham, and bring her downtown. You'll deal with the media, I trust."

"Correct. We'll release a statement indicating that we have arrested Miss Ketcham and charged her with murder. I'll release no details except to say that the conclusion is substantiated by evidence uncovered by you and your colleagues. Does she have any family?"

"I don't know. If she does, this is going to be disturbing news."

"Okay, Harrison. Good work. Give my congratulations to Mr. and Mrs. Searing and Mrs. McMillan."

"Yes, sir."

Harrison told Lou and Maggie of the sheriff's acceptance to seeking an arrest warrant and of his congratulatory statement. Harrison then left to seek the necessary warrant, stating that he would return shortly. He figured to be gone less than an hour. He would have to ask the prosecutor to issue the warrant, have the judge validate it, so he could have it in hand when he arrested Janice. He suggested that Maggie contact Mr. Workman and ask him to meet with them in about an hour.

Maggie called Dan Workman. It was about four-thirty on Sunday afternoon when Dan Workman entered the room where the detectives had been unraveling the crime.

"Thanks for coming over, Mr. Workman," Harrison said.

"Not a problem. It's the end of the weekend and you were hoping to have this crime solved. Have you been successful in reaching your goal?"

"Yes, sir, we have. I have talked with Sheriff Patterson and he has asked me to brief you before we make the arrest."

"I appreciate the courtesy."

"Mr. Workman, I regret to inform you that we are about to arrest Janice Ketcham for the murder of the golfer at your resort a week ago."

"Janice Ketcham? You've got to be kidding. There must be some mistake. Are you sure?" Mr. Workman asked, as surprised as one could be.

"We're sure we can convince a judge that there's reasonable cause to believe that Miss Ketcham committed the crime and that the case should go to trial where we also believe we have the evidence to convict her of the murder."

"I just can't accept this. Of all the people, I never would have guessed that Janice could have done this. She is such a caring and compassionate person. There must be some mistake."

"We don't think so. No one is immune from taking another's life," Harrison explained.

"I must also tell you that there could be additional charges, related to some of your employees, in this case. We suspect, and I repeat, we only suspect that others may be involved, but we don't have the evidence at this time to justify arrests."

"This is a nightmare. I can see the whole resort suffering greatly from this tragedy. We may never recover, financially or emotionally."

"The media will find out when we get Janice downtown. You may want to think about how you will handle your staff as the news is released. By the way, does she have any family?"

"Her mother lives with her. You do need to be compassionate here, Mr. Kennedy. Janice's mother will need medical attention when she hears this. It could bring on a fatal heart attack. She isn't well anyway and this news would be devastating."

"We'll see that medical and emotional support is available. Thanks for telling us."

"Well, I thank each of you for your work this weekend. I still can't believe what you're about to do. We'll continue to provide whatever support you need as this goes to court. I was hoping that the murderer would not be one of our employees, but if you're right, my worst fears have been realized."

"Thank you again for all of your support," Lou said. "Your staff has been very polite, respectful, and kind. We're sorry that we have to disturb the Marsh Ridge family, but a murder has been committed and we have the evidence to suspect, and we think, to convict Miss Ketcham."

"Thanks again for briefing me."

کم

Harrison and Lou went to the nurse's station. Janice Ketcham was alone and welcomed Harrison and Lou into her office. Maggie waited outside. "Still working on the investigation?"

Harrison was direct and to the point. "I have a warrant and am here to arrest you for the murder of Reggie Macleod." Harrison went through the Miranda rights while putting handcuffs on her wrists. He also said that he had learned that Janice's mother may need some medical attention upon hearing the news. He promised it would be provided.

Janice sat as if in a stupor. She didn't show any emotion and stared into space.

Harrison continued, "We'll need to take you with us to the sheriff's office in Gaylord. You will need your attorney if you have one, and, if you don't, the court will assign one to help you."

Janice continued to sit as if in a trance. Harrison had seen this reaction before. Some people go into a rage when they hear the charge of murder. Others seem to crawl into themselves as if in a state of denial or shock.

"You'll need to come with us now," Harrison said. "Can we help you with any of your belongings?"

Janice got up from her chair and started to walk toward the door with Harrison on her elbow. "My purse is in that closet there," Janice said nodding toward a closet next to her white medical supply case. "You could get that for me, I guess."

When Lou opened the closet to get her purse, he noticed a pair of knickers hanging on a hook. When he lifted the knickers off the hook, a black hood fell to the floor. He quickly recalled Bill Wallach stating that he had seen the driver in the cart wearing knickers and that it looked like he had a black covering over his head.

They got in Harrison's car and drove from the resort to the station. Janice was photographed, fingerprinted, and placed in a jail cell. Harrison began the long process of filling out reports.

Janice had no attorney so the court appointed Mr. Ben Hall to represent her. Ben got a call at home in the middle of Sunday dinner with his family. He excused himself and headed to the Otsego County Courthouse for his first opportunity to bring justice to a respected community member.

⌒

Sunday evening, cars began to arrive at Judy Austin's apartment complex in Gaylord. They arrived individually. Shorty Gross arrived first, followed by Stacy Hammonds. Then Liz Lake and Wendy Blackman pulled in. Finally Heather Abraham appeared, apologizing for being a few minutes late. Judy offered beer and soft drinks from her refrigerator.

They gathered in the living room and it became quiet. The air was thick with tension - something had gone terribly wrong. "Thanks for coming over on such short notice," Judy said. "Janice called me this afternoon and told me some things that may, I repeat, may, be putting us out there as suspects in the murder a week ago. I don't know why she isn't here yet, but I'll tell you what she told me." Judy repeated what Janice had told her to quiet the nerves of the group.

"Oh, NO!" Stacy exclaimed.

"This was a sealed and tight plan. The set-up was perfect!" offered

Liz Lake. "I took a big risk by involving my friend, Don Collins."

"Once they can prove that Janice gave the drink to the golfer and not Dwight, we're dead meat," Wendy said.

"It's all circumstantial," Judy said. "Nobody saw Janice give him the drink. There are no fingerprints, nothing."

Shorty was deep in thought, then interrupted, "Seems like we need to add something to this to make it more obvious that Dwight did it. You know, take some of Janice's cups and plant them in Dwight's home. Judy could do that."

"Let's just kill him!" Heather exclaimed.

"Haven't we done enough killing already?" Wendy asked.

"Precisely my point. If we're going to take the hit for one golfer as Janice seems to think, then let's get one more and at least we'll have accomplished our goals. We already got Macleod for Judy, let's get Dwight for all of us."

"Hey, I've got a life ahead of me. I don't want to spend it in some women's prison with a bunch of losers!" Liz exclaimed.

"If this thing gets pinned on us, we're going to the pen so what difference does it make?" Stacy said.

"I'm out of this. I didn't give the guy the drink," Liz said emphatically.

"Whoa, whoa. We all agreed to do this. There isn't any getting out now," Judy said with emotion.

"That was when it was the perfect plan and we couldn't go wrong. Well, somebody screwed up and it isn't going to mess up my life or the life of my friend who came up here to help." With that, Liz got up and left. She knew she was betraying the rest of the women, but getting discovered was not in her plan. She felt that leaving would make her no longer a party to this ugly mess. She knew she could pay a price for the life lost. She was in the planning group, but she didn't pull the trigger.

"Relax, relax, let's get our heads cool and think this out," Judy said, obviously playing a leadership role. "I still say we're okay. Remember, there are no witnesses and no evidence of our being at the scene. Let's just think for a moment."

"I think we should just blow Dwight's brains out and take the case to court. There are other cases where sexually harassed women have killed a guy and the jury sympathizes under the circumstances," Stacy suggested.

"No, no, no. Hold on. We would probably win on the Dwight murder, but no jury or judge is going to accept our killing a guy as a set-up to get Dwight." Heather said, shaking her head.

"I agree that we need to put him out of circulation, otherwise we get big prison terms and he's out on the course everyday free as a bird for all of his wrongdoings," Shorty explained.

"Are we all in agreement that we need to take Dwight's actions into our own hands before we get accused of murdering Macleod?" Judy asked, wanting to take a poll.

Everyone's head nodded affirmatively.

"The next question is how do we do that?" Judy asked.

"Seems like we've got lots of choices. We can shoot him, send a MACK truck at him, poison him, drown him...." Wendy suggested.

"Drown him. That sounds like a good idea. We could plan a late evening pool party. We'd want to thank him for all he has done for Marsh Ridge. We'd have food and pool time. We all get him in the pool and then we just hold him under long enough to do the job and then panic, call 911 and explain that we were all in the pool playing around and we discovered him on the bottom. No one sees us hold him under and we accomplish our mission," Stacy said.

"Can we be assured he'll come, and come alone?" Heather asked.

"Booze and food usually brings him and if we say this is a special party just for him, no one else is invited, we'll be all right. If he brings someone with him, like Billy, for example, or others are in the area when the accident is to happen, we just won't pull him down. Simple as that. We'll just plan a pool party and send him an invitation signed, 'The Women of Marsh Ridge,'" Stacy suggested.

"I don't vote for drowning him," Shorty said. "We should be able to knock him off in some other way. We'd be with him when he dies and that doesn't look good for us. We botched the last one. I think we need something clean where we're nowhere around."

The phone rang. Judy answered. It was clear to the others that she was upset.

"Janice has been arrested for the murder of Reggie Macleod," Judy said, looking angry and solemn at the same time.

"Oh, my God!" Stacy shouted.

"Oh, no," Wendy moaned. "Where is she?"

"She's downtown in jail. She's got a court-appointed lawyer."

"We've got to get down there and be with her!"

"Are you kidding, Wendy? We'll just reinforce our own guilt," Judy said.

"But she's a friend and she's in trouble. We can't leave her out there hanging by herself!" Heather exclaimed.

"She can't take this rap alone. We're in this together," Wendy said.

"Calm down," Judy pleaded. "There are no witnesses, no fingerprints, it's all circumstantial evidence. It'll get thrown out and she'll be free. You'll see that I'm right. Sure, it's lonely, but the lawyer will get her bail and she'll be out and back to us real soon. I suggest that we stay calm and leave the procedures up to the lawyers and the judge. We just have to hope that she doesn't implicate us in this thing."

"What do we do now?" Heather asked.

"This is a time to stay low, quiet, and see what develops," Stacy said. "Let's continue to plan Dwight's demise. We've got time for this. We can't act now. We need to settle and let cool heads prevail. We'll end his life, of that I'm sure. But, we need to relax and stay quiet, yet committed."

"Is Liz okay? Have we lost her?" Heather asked.

"She'll be alright. I'll talk to her tomorrow," Judy replied, confident she could bring the group together again.

The phone rang in Don Collin's apartment. "Hello."

"Don. This is Liz Lake in Gaylord."

"Hi, Liz. How ya doin'?"

"Things are bad, Don. Real bad."

"What's the problem?"

"The police have been investigating the murder up here and probably have arrested Janice Ketcham, the nurse at the resort. They no doubt know you were up here with us and that makes you involved."

"Murder?" Don stated, immediately recalling Roger's comments. "I was told this was just a phony deceitful act to throw off some resort guests."

"You'll never forgive me for getting you involved, and I'll probably never forgive myself. I'm sorry."

"What happened?"

"Some of the women who work here at Marsh Ridge have been sexually harassed by Dwight Austin for a few years. We didn't feel we could bring charges against him. We'd lose our jobs and he'd be vengeful. We feared for our safety. We decided to set up a plan that would make it obvious that Dwight killed the golfer. If our plan worked, Dwight would be arrested and sent to prison for life. We'd be free of his harassment. It seemed so simple. We needed someone who was not well-known up here to get involved by deceiving the mystery guests into thinking this was all a part of the mystery weekend. We didn't want the guests to be curious over our actions. I told them you were an actor and could do this very well. That's when we asked you to help us."

"When I heard the sirens and stuff I thought it was all a part of the production and the deception I was being paid to provide. You lied to me."

"You were at the wrong place at the wrong time, Don. You're innocent, and the detectives will see that. You aren't a co-conspirator in this murder. So, you need to get a lawyer and get in touch with the police, before you get arrested and find yourself in court, or maybe in prison."

"I don't have a lawyer, and don't have money for a lawyer, and I'm about to leave for New York to get lost in Manhattan with an alias."

"Do what you think you need to do, but you'll be hunted down. Running from it only gives the impression of guilt. I mean we're talking about a man murdered, an upstanding citizen, a man who made a career out of helping children with disabilities and their families. This will be followed to the end. I think they already know that a man named Don Collins from Battle Creek was with us plotting to kill these men, and that puts you at the scene of the crime."

"Yeah, I've already been interviewed by a couple of detectives."

"What did you tell 'em?"

"The truth: that I got a call to come up and deceive folks."

"Do the right thing, Don. Get a lawyer, call the detectives, and tell them the truth."

"I'll think about it. This is all I need right now."

"I'm sorry, Don. I'll forever be sorry for getting you involved. I'll do whatever I can to get you cleared of this. I really will. I'm in it, too. We need to support each other and get clean."

"Thanks for your call, I guess. I could be arrested any minute now; is this what you're saying?"

"Yes. I can't be certain, but I think you're known and if they have enough evidence to arrest Janice, they may know you were with us, contracted to help us. As I said, ask friends for the name of a lawyer, give him or her a call and explain the situation. Tell the lawyer that you don't have the money to pay, but you need some help."

"Guess I will. I can't ruin my whole life."

"Good. I'll be in touch."

⸙

In the meantime, there was much activity around the Otsego County Courthouse. The media had learned that Janice Ketcham had been arrested for the murder of the golfer. The editor of the *Gaylord Herald Times* was already planning for a front page headline in the morning, "Suspect Arrested for Golfer's Murder." The staff writer assigned to the story was probing and getting as much information as she could.

There was an interruption on television in the Gaylord area to present the news. By 7 p.m. it was on the radio. Those watching channel 7 at 7:10 p.m. heard, "We interrupt this program for a news bulletin. A nurse at Marsh Ridge has been arrested in the murder of the golfer who died of poisoning a week ago. Details at eleven."

Lawyer Hall asked for and was granted private time with his client. He slowly unraveled the bizarre set of circumstances and events that could lead him to prominence in Gaylord, give him a name that was recognizable in the community, and pave the way for him to run for the state senate in a couple of years. This case looked like a godsend.

As Hall saw it, he could help a desperate woman – a victim of sexual harassment – accused of murder. She acted in a way that she thought would bring justice for a couple of real bad situations. Helping her friend, Judy, who was devastated after her firing from helping disabled children, and framing a man who harassed her and abused her daughter. She hoped the truth would get Dwight out of society to a place where he could no longer hurt women. Hall decided to put all of his energy into the case and he knew he would prevail. He would be up against the county's most prestigious lawyer, the county prosecutor, Victor Balance.

Ben Hall had learned early that the little guy needed help and that's why he had entered the law profession. He was disturbed by the justice that money could buy. The underdog had no chance to get good and fair treatment. Good lawyers come for a fee and good and rich lawyers know anyone who is anybody. They live by the rule that it never hurts to use contacts in high places to get what your client needs. Ben had a strong compulsion to be there for the little guy. He made it clear to Gaylord officials that he wanted to represent those without the resources to hire a lawyer.

His firm knew Ben's desire and supported him. Even though the energy he invested took away from the one hundred and ten percent he was already giving the clients who could afford the high fees of Williams, Walters, and Lewis.

Ben knew how to get Janice bail and he was sure that the judge wouldn't find her a threat to society. He just needed a little time to plead his case.

Ben was paged while at the courthouse talking with Janice. He couldn't imagine who it could be unless his wife needed to tell him some very important news.

"Mr. Hall?"

"Speaking."

"Mr. Hall, this is Dwight Austin. I've learned that Janice Ketcham has been arrested and charged in the murder at Marsh Ridge a week ago."

"That's correct."

"I want you to know that I'll pay for her bail and all of her legal expenses. I've heard that you are a bright young attorney, and I feel certain that she's going to get good legal care, but I want it understood that money is no object in seeing that Miss Ketcham receives every opportunity to be cleared of this accusation."

"Thank you, Mr. Austin. I will pass along your kind offer to my client. Thank you for calling."

"My number in case you ever need any money to represent her is 555-6788. Do not hesitate to call at any time. Am I making myself clear?"

"Yes, Mr. Austin. Thank you for calling."

ॐ

Because it was Sunday, nothing would happen until morning when the Honorable Judge Byrd would convene his court for the arraignment. Ben Hall and Janice Ketcham would be present along with the prosecutor, Victor Ballance. The proceedings would undoubtedly be short. The prosecutor would set forth the evidence sufficient to suspect Janice of murder. The judge would ask Janice how she pleads and her attorney will say, "My client will stand mute." The judge will enter a plea of not guilty.

Judge Byrd knew Janice's mother and he also knew Janice. Gaylord is a relatively small town and most people who live in the community knew the Ketcham family. Judge Byrd would probably believe Janice to be safe in the community, would set a reasonable bail, and release her.

⤺

Ben met with Janice before he left. "I forgot to tell you that when I was paged for a phone call, the caller was Dwight Austin."

"What did he want?" Janice asked.

"He offered to pay your bail and to pay any legal fees so that you would get the finest service possible."

"I wouldn't take a nickel from him!" Janice replied with venom. "This whole thing is because of him. My life is ruined because of that sick man, and he has the gall to call and use his almighty dollars to help. It's no different than shoving someone down a long flight of concrete steps and then saying here is some money for your medical care. It's filthy money and not one penny will be used to defend me. I would have no lawyer before I would stoop so low as to take a penny that belongs to Dwight Austin."

"I understand. I'll call and indicate that as your attorney, we do not wish to receive any compensation from him for your defense."

"Thank you. I like you. We're going to get through this just fine."

"You bet we are, Janice. Be patient and follow my advice and a bright tomorrow will await you."

⤺

Harrison, Lou, Carol, and Maggie met in Harrison's office. They all clasped hands and shared congratulations. The weekend had been most productive. "We'll be on our way back to our homes," Lou said.

"Sure. Can't thank you enough for your help in solving this case," Harrison replied.

"You're welcome. As usual, Maggie saw the pattern. She found that one mistake you were looking for, the Dixie cups."

"She sure did. Let's talk for a moment about next steps. I'm definitely of the opinion that this was not the plan of one woman. I think we need to question Mr. Collins in greater detail. I also suspect that other women at Marsh Ridge are involved."

"I agree with everything you've said. I'm hopeful that we'll get more information when we talk to Don Collins. I also think Shorty may be involved and the Friday night gathering at Jac's seems to be a focal point of their plan. I also have to conclude that Judy is involved in this. She knew about the golfers being in the area," Lou offered.

"Absolutely."

"Is there anything you want Maggie and me to do from Battle Creek and Grand Haven?"

"I'd like you to find Mr. Collins and see what you can learn from him. I'll talk to Shorty again and continue to follow any leads I get up here."

"Okay, sounds good. If that's all, you know where you can reach us. We'll head south and hope that this rain doesn't cause much delay."

"Have a safe trip. I'm sure you'll be up this way again soon, as more develops."

"We're just a call away. See you, Harry."

Maggie excused herself to call her husband to let him know when he could expect her to be home.

"Hi, dear, we're finished up here in Gaylord, at least we're finished for the weekend."

"Did you solve it, Maggie?" Tom asked.

"I think so. I feel sorry for the young lady, actually. I think she got caught up in a lot of anger and misdirected her energy into believing she could make things okay, when in fact, she simply ruined her life. But, yes, dear, we solved it and I'll be coming on home."

"I've missed you. You sure you want to try to drive all the way tonight? Maybe you should spend one more night up there and be rested for the long drive," Tom advised.

"I feel okay and I want to get home."

"I'll bet you enjoyed Marsh Ridge."

"What a place, Tom. It was almost totally accessible, all of our meals were taken care of, it was the perfect setting to investigate a murder. You could have played thirty-six holes of golf each day and all for free."

"Sounds too good to be true."

"You know, Tom. I think I've adjusted quite well to this disability over the past few years, but when I saw the people in the pool and the golfers on the course, I miss doing those things. I'm thankful for my mind, my memories, and my imagination. With these I can still swim and play golf. But, the thought occurred to me on more than one occasion, I miss my limbs and all they did for me, Tom. I really do."

"There was an article in the paper yesterday about an adaptive golf clinic. Sounded like something you might like to try."

"Interesting. Save the article for me. It might be just what I need to get back on the golf course."

"I love you, Maggie. Come on home. I'll wait up for you, my dear."

Maggie drove her chair to her van, said farewell to Lou and Carol, and left Gaylord a very satisfied investigator. She had figured it out once again. There was much satisfaction in solving a mystery; if it weren't for the lives that get changed forever, the work could become fun.

CHAPTER 13

Monday, July 18
Gaylord, Michigan

As predicted, Judge Byrd convened his court. A trial date was set, bail was agreed upon by Mr. Hall and the prosecutor. Janice was free to go. Her bail did have a provision restricting her to the state of Michigan.

At 10 a.m. Dwight went to the mailbox, took out his mail, and came upon a business envelope addressed to him with a Gaylord postmark. He went into his house, sat down at the dining room table, opened the envelope and read,

> *Mr. Austin. I am writing to you to save your life. I have learned that a plan is in place to kill you. The murder will be by drowning. You will be invited to a party. I choose not to make myself known at this time, but if you are able to avoid this threat on your life, I will identify myself to you. I'll expect to be financially rewarded at a price equal to the value you place on your life – at least five million dollars. Failure to provide these dollars will be cause for me not to warn you of future threats. Believe me, I am the only one who is willing to tell you of your*

*fate. By the way, the invitation to the party will be signed,
"The Marsh Ridge Recognition Committee."*

Dwight took a deep breath and got up from the dining room table. He walked outside and paced on the sidewalk in front of his home. He did some of his best thinking when he was by himself, quiet, and walking.

ॐ

Lou Searing called Don Collins. He left a message on Don's voice mail asking him to call. At about seven-thirty that night, the phone rang at the Searing residence. Carol answered.

"Lou Searing, please."

"Just a moment please; Lou, I think this is Mr. Collins returning your call."

"Lou Searing. May I help you?"

"Mr. Searing. This is Don Collins. You called earlier."

"Yes, I did. Thanks for returning my call. I called to ask you more questions about your time at Marsh Ridge Resort a week ago."

"I've talked with an attorney in Kalamazoo. He advised that I should only talk to people in his presence."

"I understand. How can we work this out? I can come to Kalamazoo in the morning if that's convenient, or we could have a conference call."

"If you could come to Kalamazoo, that would be preferable."

"Where shall I meet you?"

"My lawyer's office is in the Old Kent Bank Building. It's downtown. You can't miss it."

"Is nine in the morning all right with you and your attorney?"

"It's fine with me and I'm certain it will be with my lawyer."

"What's his name so I can find his office when I get to the bank building in the morning?"

"Steven Anderson."

"Thanks. I'll be bringing Maggie McMillan who's working on this investigation with me."

"Fine. See you in the morning then?"

"Yes. Thanks for calling back."

$\mathcal{L}$

Ben Hall and Janice Ketcham met Monday afternoon. Ben needed to know what Janice knew so he could defend her. He wanted to win this trial so he devoted time and energy to getting the facts straight. Ben asked, "I need you to tell me exactly what happened. I can't do the job we need to do unless I have all the information you have. I, as I trust you know, work under very stringent ethics of confidentiality. You can tell me what you know and trust that I'll keep that in confidence. I don't need surprises from the prosecution and I don't want you to tell me later that you knew something and chose not to share it with me. Understand?"

"Yes. I want to tell you what I know. I don't want to spend years in jail. My mother needs me and I have a life to live."

"What happened, Janice?"

"It began last spring. A group of us were becoming friends."

"Who's in the group?"

"Judy Austin, who is Dwight's daughter; Wendy Blackman, the assistant golf pro; Stacy Hammonds, the bartender; Liz Lake, the lifeguard; Heather Abraham, a waitress; and Shorty Gross who is an ambulance driver in Gaylord."

"Were all of these people involved in planning of the murder?"

"Yes."

"Okay, go on."

"We liked to party and we enjoyed each other's company. We were all single or divorced and became a good group of friends. Anyway, as we got to know each other, we found out about each other's lives. One thing we all had in common was that we were sexually harassed by Dwight Austin, I mean the women were. Not his daughter as far as I know, but the rest of us were."

"What type of harassment?"

"Well, with Heather it was sex or he'd see that she'd be fired.

Heather needed the job to support herself. He threatened her so she didn't have the option of turning him in to the police. You see, Dwight has a very controlling personality. He is very powerful. His money gives him the power. You'd think he owns the Marsh Ridge Resort the way he throws his power around there. Wendy was in a difficult situation. Dwight learned something very personal about her past life, which I won't tell you, but Dwight demanded sexual favors for keeping this very private secret from getting out and destroying her career and reputation in the community. Also, I have a daughter. She lives with her father. Most don't know that I have a daughter from a previous marriage. I learned that Dwight was abusing her as a young teenager, so rather than bring it to the police, I arranged for her to live with my ex-husband over in Cheboygan. She'll be okay, but I wanted him dead. We've all had our lives torn up by this sick man."

"Nobody was willing to report this sexual harassment?"

"No. We'd lose our jobs for one thing and we needed the money to live. Most of us looked for other jobs, but Marsh Ridge pays well and we needed every dollar to pay our bills and to get along. The second reason we didn't say anything was because we feared his revenge. If one of us made our story known, he would make life very difficult for us. His money and his threats were such that we'd pay a heavy price. A year ago, an employee on another course where Dwight plays filed some charges against him and life has been horrible for her ever since. So, we all took the harassment and tried to support each other."

"So, am I jumping ahead by concluding that the women of Marsh Ridge wanted to somehow get Dwight Austin out of circulation?"

"We sure did. We'd spend time just talking about how we could do that."

"Well, then, how did Reggie Macleod become involved?"

"Dwight's best friend is Billy Wingate. They golf together all the time. Billy called Judy and told her that Dwight had an altercation with a Bill Wallach at the course called The Natural. It was a serious confrontation and he was afraid Dwight was going to do something he would regret. Billy said that he had seen Dwight get mad, but this was real ugly and he was wondering if Judy would check on her father to see if he was all right."

"What type of altercation?"

"Apparently Dwight accused Mr. Wallach and others in his party of hitting into them four times. Mr. Wallach claimed that it never happened. Sounds pretty simple but tempers flared. Several holes later, Mr. Wallach really did hit into Dwight's party and while Dwight didn't respond, he was furious and Billy knew that revenge was imminent."

"Okay, then what happened?"

"That night Judy went to gamble in St. Ignace. While there she met a guy named Walt Wilcox who was up north playing golf with seven of his friends. Well, in that group were Reggie Macleod and Bill Wallach."

"Who is Reggie Macleod?"

"He's a special education director in a district where Judy used to teach. In fact, Reggie Macleod fired her and that revenge attitude kind of runs in the Austin family. She found out from this Wilcox guy that they were scheduled to play Marsh Ridge on Saturday morning. So Judy called her father and told him that Bill Wallach was scheduled to play at Marsh Ridge on Saturday and that he had an eight-thirty tee time. She learned this from calling and talking to Wendy Blackman, the assistant pro."

"So, Judy set up the opportunity for a confrontation at Marsh Ridge between her father and Mr. Wallach."

"That's right. She called Billy Wingate and suggested a tee time right behind Wallach's foursome. So, when Dwight called, Wendy was quick to oblige him."

"Okay, then what happened?"

"On Friday night, all of us met at Jac's Place and got this idea. We could kill two birds with one stone so to speak. Judy was the mastermind. She figured that we would set up Dwight. He and this Wallach guy would be on the same course. There was a mystery weekend scheduled for that weekend."

"Explain, please."

"People come to the resort for food, entertainment, and the chance to try and solve a murder mystery. It is billed as 'Mystery at the Marsh.' It's very popular. People come from all over to enjoy this fun weekend."

"Go on."

"She told us that we could poison some lemonade and give it to Macleod who would be playing in the group ahead of Dwight. He would definitely be a suspect. Mr. Macleod would die as the price for firing Judy from her job and also, I forgot, he was about to be contacted by a school district to see how she did at her last teaching job. Judy couldn't afford to have Reggie talk to this school district. Our plan was perfect. Dwight would get accused of the murder and be sent to prison for life and we'd be free of harassment."

"What was the plan?"

"Well, lemonade was being served on the 14th tee. The plan was for Stacy to monitor the progress of the players. She could see number 13 from the bar. If it was a go, she would call me. I took a thermos of poisoned lemonade and some cups to the 14th tee. We got the idea to give Reggie a note saying I, with knickers and a mask, was the weekend mystery murderer. The note asked Reggie to drink my lemonade as a thank you for his help on this very hot day."

"Where did you get the cyanide?"

"My grandfather is a jeweler in Petoskey. Jewelers have been known to use cyanide for cleaning. Not so much lately, but in the past. I stole some cyanide from my grandfather's work area at his jewelry shop. I used to work there part-time to help him in the holiday season."

"Go ahead."

"I was really quite lucky when I got to the tee. I didn't know what I would find. Sounds like lousy planning, but it's what happened. I waited a bit back in a grove of birch trees until I thought I had a good opportunity. One guy was on a cell phone and was in front of us, facing straight ahead. He didn't see anything. The other guy was in the Port-a-John. He came out as I was pulling away and he may have seen the cart, knickers, and mask. I don't know. If he did, it was what we wanted because once again, Dwight would be suspect."

"You did this alone?"

"Yes, I put on the knickers, Wendy was to notice the color of Dwight's knickers and socks when he arrived at the course. She then got me an identical outfit from the pro shop. We thought that if anyone saw a person in knickers around the 14th tee it would further implicate Dwight. So, yes, I gave him the poison."

"Was anybody else involved?"

"Yeah, a guy named Don Collins from Battle Creek. We needed somebody to be on the resort grounds who could deceive the guests and to help people believe that the sirens and ambulances were all a part of the murder mystery weekend. We wanted everyone to think that the golfer did not die, but was a part of the fun at the resort. So, Liz Lake knew this actor in Battle Creek. Shorty called him and said we'd pay him a fee if he would come up for about five hours. He was told to talk to the guests, confuse them, and to get the rumor around that nobody was hurt. It was all part of the production."

"So, he was in on it with you?"

"Yeah. He didn't know we were going to kill Reggie, but he was helping us."

"Did anybody else see you at the 14th tee?"

"Nobody as far as I know."

"Then what happened?"

"I took a few cups and pushed them up into the cup holder so the cops wouldn't be suspicious of my Dixie cup by the body and the styrofoam cups normally in the cup dispenser."

"Why didn't you use the styrofoam cup?"

"Just didn't occur to me. I took the cups from my office. Thankfully, at the last minute I saw the different cup at the cooler and, as I said, stuffed a few up the cup dispenser. I was sure that would satisfy a good detective."

"Okay, then what happened?"

"I went back to my office. Judy went to the tee after I gave the guy the drink, but before the police and ambulance arrived. She was there. Her job was to change coolers. She threw out the old lemonade and took the cooler back to the kitchen so the authorities would not discover that the lemonade in the cooler was not poisoned."

"Was anything else in the plan?"

"Yeah. When we were at Jac's Place on Friday night, we saw Dwight and his friend Mark Thompson writing on the back of a placemat, so we made up the story to tell the people investigating the murder that Heather, the waitress, saw a placemat where Dwight was sitting. On the placement was drawn a picture of the 14th tee with a big x on it with the name Wallach next to it. A reference to his wanting to get even. So, Heather told the detectives she saw this. This was to further implicate Dwight. Also, Shorty was to tell somebody, hopefully a mystery guest, that he had heard that the murder would take place on the 14th tee. Then when the real murder was discovered, this person would remember hearing it and recall Shorty's saying that he heard that the old man said it. Once again, Dwight would have another strike against him."

"Got to give the group credit for coming up with a fairly complicated plot," Ben said, continuing to note all aspects of the conspiracy.

"Lotta bright people in the group. We have such collected hatred for Dwight Austin that we couldn't leave any stone unturned."

"What happened that led to the arrest? I heard the prosecutor state his evidence, but what's your story?"

"He was right on. The investigators cracked it. I screwed up with the Dixie cups. The police photos of the guy on the ground showed the Dixie cup next to him. The Dixie cups were patterned and were the only ones like that ordered at the resort. The paper cups were only in my office. My having the pair of knickers to make people think it was Dwight if I was seen, and the black hood was in my closet. That evidence really hung me. I should've gotten rid of that stuff. I wasn't planning on getting caught. The cups from my office, the mask, and the knickers are what put me in court with you. Yes, I did kill him. That's the truth."

"Did you volunteer to give him the drink or were you coerced into doing this?" Ben asked, looking for a defense for his client.

"I volunteered. I was a part of the plan and it made sense. There was no pressure. I wanted to be the one who freed Judy from all of her pain in being so unjustly fired by that special education director. I also wanted her to get that next job and I knew that if Reggie lived, he'd give her a bad evaluation. Judy is a close friend. We've been through a lot together. And, I wanted to frame Dwight. I wanted to do what I could to make sure he'd rot in some cell for the rest of his life. When someone abuses your child, you never forget it. I mean, a child, Mr. Hall. My child."

Janice began to break down. Ben did what he could to console her. "Killing the guy isn't enough punishment. Rotting in a jail cell away from children and women and golf for the rest of his life, that is the hell I wanted for this evil man," Janice said, wiping a tear slowing moving down her cheek.

"I think this is enough for today, Janice. Thanks for being so cooperative. It'll really pay off when we get to court."

"I trust you and hope that I'll be okay."

CHAPTER 14

Tuesday, July 19
Kalamazoo, Michigan

The next morning, Lou and Maggie were right on time, on the eighth floor in front of the law offices of Anderson and Lorimer. They asked the receptionist to announce their arrival. The receptionist was gracious and invited them into a conference room furnished with leather chairs and a solid walnut table. "Mr. Anderson and Mr. Collins will be with you in a minute."

"Thank you."

A couple of minutes later the two men entered the room. After greetings, the guests were offered coffee. Lou began, "Thank you for meeting with Mrs. McMillan and me."

"Good morning, Mr. Anderson and Mr. Collins," Maggie said. "I am pleased to meet you." Both gentlemen nodded and mumbled something like, "Thank you. Nice to meet you."

"Mr. Anderson, do you mind if I tape record this meeting?" Lou asked. "I want to share the information we discuss with Detective Harrison Kennedy of the Otsego Sheriff's Department."

"I don't think it would be in the best interests of my client to record this meeting. We're not trying to be secretive, nor do we want to be uncooperative, but at this point we'd like to answer your questions without being recorded. I trust you understand."

"It's your call. Thank you for considering our request."

"I wish to state at the outset of our discussion, and your questions, that my client, Mr. Collins, is innocent of any wrongdoing and I'll have no problem defending him against any accusations to the contrary."

"Likewise, I'll state at the outset that, we're not accusing Mr. Collins of murder in this case. But, we do have a few questions that we need to ask in light of our investigation and the evidence we've obtained in the last couple of days."

"Go ahead with your questions."

"At any time during your stay at Marsh Ridge, were you at the 14th tee?"

"I could have been. I don't recall. I was all over the course."

"Did you know there would be some activity at the 14th tee?"

"I was told that the production company would be bringing an ambulance to the golf course to add to the drama of the mystery weekend and to throw off the guests. I was told that no one was in trouble at the 14th tee, that it was all a part of the show. In fact, I didn't know that anyone had died until I was talking with friends a couple of days ago."

"Did you meet with anybody about your role for that day?" Maggie asked.

"No. As I said earlier, I just arrived and got about my work. I met lots of people, but I didn't meet with anyone who said they were a part of the weekend production."

"Did you see Liz on that day?"

"No. I didn't see anyone I knew. You will recall that I even got paid by picking up an envelope at the bar that had been addressed to me."

"When you talked with Mr. Kennedy a couple of days ago, you didn't recall anything unique about the man who called you about doing this work. Is that still your response? Was there anything about his voice, personality, the way he talked, used swear words, husky voice, soft voice, anything that would help us try to identify who called you?"

"I really don't remember. Wait, it's coming back. It seemed to me that the voice had a tint of a southern accent. Yes, it did, because I recall thinking it odd that someone with a southern accent would be calling me from northern Michigan."

"Please recall that conversation for us?"

"It went something like this: 'Don Collins? A friend of yours, Liz Lake said that you might like to earn a little money for doing what you do for a living. We need someone for about five hours tomorrow to be at the Marsh Ridge Resort. This weekend is what is called 'Mystery at the Marsh.' We have many return guests and we need a new person to interact with a lot of people and just give them phony clues about the mystery. Could you come up tomorrow morning and work till around two-thirty in the afternoon? We'll pay you an hourly fee plus meals and mileage.' I asked who I would meet. He said there would be no need to meet anyone. I was just to arrive and begin interacting with people. He said that in the afternoon there would be sirens and ambulances coming to the 14th tee on the golf course, but that was all part of the production for the murder mystery weekend, no one would be hurt or killed. It was all phony, to help me deceive guests from solving the real mystery."

"What time did you get the call?"

"It was late and that surprised me, but I was up so it didn't bother me."

"Did you hear anything in the background?"

"There was some noise, like the call came from a party or from a place where several people were gathered."

Lou asked Maggie, who was taking copious notes and studying the body language of both men, if she had any questions she would like to ask.

"Thank you, Lou. Yes, I have a few. Mr. Collins what can you tell me about Miss Lake?"

"She's a friend of mine. I met her at Kalamazoo College. We were both drama majors. She's quite intelligent. She works hard. She's very attractive. She has some trouble controlling her emotions. She goes along with the crowd and then when something doesn't go her way, she bolts from the group. I saw this a lot in the college plays. If something didn't go Liz's way, she wouldn't have anything to do with it."

"Have you talked with her in the last few days?"

Mr. Anderson interrupted, "I'd like a few moments with my client."

"Sure. Would you like us to leave the room?"

"We can go to my office. Please excuse us."

"Certainly."

A few minutes later the two men returned and sat down. Mr. Anderson said, "Thank you for understanding our need to dialogue. Mr. Collins will respond to your question."

"Yes. She called Sunday evening. She heard that Janice Ketcham was arrested and charged with the murder. She feared for me and apologized for suggesting that I come up to Marsh Ridge. She said that working with them would make me an accomplice to the crime and that I should seek legal counsel."

"And did you?"

"Yes. I called my friends, ironically, the ones who told me about the man dying on Saturday and they suggested Mr. Anderson. I called Mr. Anderson first thing Monday morning and he agreed to listen to my situation and to counsel me."

"Did Miss Lake mention any other names to you in her conversation?"

"I only remember Janice's name."

"I'm going to mention some names and you tell me if you have ever heard any of them either at Marsh Ridge or from Liz Lake or Janice Ketcham."

"Okay."

"Judy Austin?"

"No."

"Stacy Hammonds?"

"Yes. In making the rounds that day I did go into the bar and while there I met a woman by that name. I drank a beer and she chatted with the customers."

"Again, did she say or do anything that you found strange or out of the ordinary?"

"Only one thing, but maybe it was typical. She had a pair of binoculars near the end of the bar. She went over to the window and kind of surveyed the course, or at least the part of the course that she could see from that vantage point. She did this about every five to ten minutes."

"Heather Abraham?"

"No."

"Shorty Gross?"

"No."

"Dwight Austin."

"Yes. I think I heard Stacy mention his name to somebody on the phone or someone at the bar. She seemed upset by what she had heard. I don't know who Dwight is, but his name was mentioned by this Stacy and she wasn't happy."

"What did she do after the phone call?"

"I don't recall."

"I mean, did she call someone else, storm out of the bar, say something under her breath? Do you recall anything?"

"No. Sorry, I don't."

"Just one more name. Wendy Blackman?"

"Yes. I think she's in the pro shop. I heard several golfers referring to her as Wendy. I didn't talk with her. I talked with the pro whose name was Bob something or other."

"Please tell me what happened after the ambulance came and left the course."

"I continued to do what I was being paid to do. Some people were talking about the death out on 14, but I assured them that it was all phony and just a part of the production to add atmosphere to the mystery weekend and that no one was hurt in anyway. When it turned two-thirty, I went to the bar and asked for an envelope for Don Collins. I opened it and found the money that we agreed upon. I went out to my car to begin the long drive back to Battle Creek."

"Were you paid by check or cash?"

"Cash."

Mr. Anderson said, "I think that my client has shared all the information he has about this case. I do have another client waiting for me. Do you have any remaining questions?"

"No. This has been very helpful and we appreciate the way you both are cooperating with us."

Mr. Anderson replied, "Mr. Collins is prepared to proclaim his innocence. I have counseled many clients over the years, Mr. Searing and Mrs. McMillan, and I assure you that Mr. Collins is telling the truth and we have no hesitation in doing whatever it takes to clear his name of any overt action with the person or persons responsible for this hideous crime."

"Thank you, gentlemen," Lou said.

"My thanks as well," Maggie added.

As Lou and Maggie drove out of town, they talked about the interview. Both agreed that they believed Don Collins. But, each had a strong feeling that the murder was the result of a conspiracy and the people involved seemed to be Judy Austin, Liz Lake, Shorty Gross, Janice Ketcham, and Stacy Hammonds. There could be more, but these four were probably behind the murder. Right now, the only person arrested and taking a media hit for the murder was Janice Ketcham. Lou and Maggie wondered if Janice had volunteered to give the drink or had been coerced into doing it.

"I think we should talk to Liz Lake," Maggie said.

"Agree."

⫤

That evening Lou contacted Liz Lake. He called the Marsh Ridge Resort and asked for the pool. As luck would have it, Liz answered, "Pool. Lifeguard Lake speaking."

"Miss Lake, this is Lou Searing in Grand Haven. I'm assisting Mr. Kennedy of the Otsego Sheriff's Department in investigating the murder which occurred at your resort several days ago."

"I'm on duty and there are several children in the pool. I can't talk now and I don't think I want to talk to anyone about that."

"I know that you need to give all of your attention to your job, but it's very important that I talk with you and soon."

"I said, I don't want to discuss anything with anyone."

"I've talked to Mr. Collins earlier today and he was very helpful. I believe him and think that you could help us solve this tragic crime. I really think it to be in your best interest to talk with me, Miss Lake."

"You talked with Don Collins?"

"Yes, my colleague and I talked with him and his attorney in Kalamazoo this morning."

"Okay. I'll talk with you, but not now. All of my attention needs to be on the kids in the pool."

"I understand."

"I'll call you later. What is your number? Just a minute I need to get my clipboard. Okay. Go ahead."

"My number is area code 616-555-5689."

⌇

Later, at Stacy's, Liz remembered that she was to call Mr. Searing. She gave him a call when she got home at ten-thirty.

"Mr. Searing. I'm sorry I forgot to call. This is Liz Lake. I hope I'm not calling too late?"

"No. We're just returning from an ice cream cone trip. Thanks for calling."

"How do you think I can help you?" Liz asked.

"As I said earlier today, I talked with Mr. Collins and his attorney this morning in Kalamazoo. They were most cooperative. We now have conclusive information about the murder of the golfer on the 14th tee. However, I suspect that the killer didn't act alone. Since Don said that he got a call from you, I'm thinking that you might know something about a plot to kill the golfer."

"I really don't want to talk about this."

"No, I imagine you don't. Let me say that if you're involved in the murder, your future is kind of bleak. If you agree to cooperate with the authorities, you'll be treated in a much more positive fashion by the prosecutor and the judge."

"You mean if I cooperate, assuming I know something, I would not be put in prison?"

"I can't promise that, but I do know that your cooperation will be viewed as a turning point in solving this murder and the prosecution will look favorably on you as a witness who was most cooperative. If you're involved, I advise you to get an attorney, just as you advised Don to get one. An attorney can assist you."

"Mr. Searing, I appreciate your advice and I'll consider it. I'm not admitting to you that I know anything. I want to make that clear."

"Mr. Collin's life is pretty stressed right now. He was just trying to help, and now he's learned that he's linked to people who are suspects in a murder. It would be most helpful to him, if the whole story were to be told so that he could be excused by a judge or at least found innocent by a jury. But, for that to occur we need to know exactly what happened and who was involved."

"Okay. I'll get a lawyer and we'll be in touch."

"I think you're acting wisely, Miss Lake."

"Thank you. Is Don doing okay?"

"I think he'll be all right. Once the truth comes out, he'll be on his way to getting his life back to normal. Again, you can help with this Liz."

"We'll be in touch."

"Thanks for calling and good luck to you."

Liz made a mental note to find a lawyer and discuss her options.

CHAPTER 15

Wednesday, July 20
Gaylord, Michigan

J udy Austin called the women of Marsh Ridge, plus Shorty Gross, to meet at her apartment on Wednesday evening at eight o'clock. When all arrived, they gathered in the living room and resumed their discussion. Liz Lake joined them. She had calmed down. Judy had a talk with her and convinced her that she was in on this so she should use her brains to turn this situation around instead of misusing energy to get upset and run from reality.

"Thanks for coming on such short notice. We may need to meet from time to time at each other's homes or apartments. We need to plan what our next steps will be," Judy suggested.

"What's happening to Janice?" Heather asked.

"She's doing okay, considering what she has been through. I talked with her yesterday and today. She's staying at home with her mother. She saved Mr. Workman the task of releasing her from Marsh Ridge and quit. Mr. Workman was compassionate and offered to do whatever he could to help her and her family.

"Janice is out on bail and working with her attorney to prepare her defense. She didn't say anything about any of us, or at least that's what she says. I told her that we're planning to finish the job that we agreed upon, to see Dwight removed from society so that his harassment will stop. She seemed pleased. I said that all of us are with her. I assured her that the evidence was all circumstantial and that the prosecution can't possibility prove beyond a reasonable doubt that she killed Reggie. Mr. Hall is good and he'll see that she is not punished for trying to defend herself from a very sick man."

"Okay, good. Now, how and when are we going to take care of Dwight?" Heather asked.

Wendy spoke up, "The pool party sounds like a good idea. Accidental drownings occur all the time. People are in a pool and all of a sudden someone is out of sight and it is too late to save them."

Liz reacted, "There's no way that man will die in my pool! I work here and I want to continue to have a job for a long time. I don't want to come to this pool and remember that Dwight Austin was here for his last few seconds on earth. Mr. Workman just might fire me for not doing my job. Bad idea. Bad idea. Come on, at least let's support each other in this murder."

"It doesn't have to be at Marsh Ridge. We can have the party at the county park. Let it happen on public property. Let the lifeguard be the one at the park. We'll just be citizens having a summer picnic," Stacy suggested.

"Who's going to hold him under?" Judy asked.

"I'll do it," Wendy said. "It would give me much satisfaction to remove this evil man from society. If Janice had the guts to volunteer to set him up and to kill the man who fired Judy, the least I can do is serve all of you by keeping oxygen from getting to his lungs."

"Thanks, Wendy. We'll all be indebted to you for life," Judy said. "So, we need a date, time, and an invitation."

"How about a week from Friday," Wendy suggested. "At the county park, eight to ten. We send him the invitation expressing our appreciation for all he has done for the resort. Food and drink on us. No guests. We'll pick him up at seven-thirty and suggest that he prepare himself to swim, boat, eat and drink. Actually, the more we can get him to drink, the more the accident will look alcohol-related and that will help the coroner with the death certificate. Then let's sign it, 'The Women of Marsh Ridge.'"

Shorty spoke up recalling his earlier blackmail note to Dwight, and said, "No, let's sign it, 'The Marsh Ridge Recognition Committee.'"

"I agree," Stacy said.

CHAPTER 16

Friday, July 22
Gaylord, Michigan

When Shorty arrived for work at 9:00 a.m. on Friday morning, Harrison was waiting. "Mornin', Detective," Shorty said with his distinctive accent.

"Good morning, Mr. Gross."

"Here to see me or Mr. Puffer?"

"Here to see you. I've got a few more questions about the murder."

"I've heard you've made an arrest in the case. Got it wrapped up, huh?"

"Not exactly. I'm certain there's more. Gotta be more people involved than one woman killing a man she doesn't know."

"Sounds reasonable."

"I'm talking with you because I'm hoping you can help me with this theory. Did Janice work with the others at Marsh Ridge to kill Reggie?"

"I honestly don't know."

"Was she at Jac's when you, Stacy, and Judy were meeting Friday night before the murder?"

"I don't recall."

"Did you make a phone call that night?"

"No."

"Are you involved, Shorty?"

"No."

"Gonna be a lot easier to come clean now than to hang tough through this and find yourself not back in Alabama but in some prison for murdering a man who dedicated his career to helping kids with disabilities. Not a lot of women to keep you company in prison, Shorty."

"Are you accusing me of murder?"

"I'm saying that we have evidence that Janice gave him the drink and now we know that you were meeting with a group of women at Jac's the night before, and since you've admitted to a woman on Saturday morning that the murder would take place on the 14th tee, it doesn't look real good for you, Shorty. This is an opportunity for you to come clean and work with us. If you're not with us, you're against us and being against a team that has evidence and is close to establishing a conspiracy theory, you're heading down a path that will put you behind bars with a record for life. The choice is up to you."

"You're accusing me of murder."

"I haven't arrested you and I have no plan to do that at this time. I've got more work to do. I'm just saying that it doesn't look good for you and the others at this time. If you're clean, when I finish the investigation, I'll be the first to apologize for suspecting that you're involved."

"I've got nothin' else to say."

"Thanks for your time."

As Harrison pulled away, Shorty could see that the detective was right. It wasn't looking very good. He was in this pretty deep. But, he couldn't give in. He couldn't do it.

Mark Thompson pulled into Dwight's driveway. Dwight had asked him to come over. It was early afternoon on a Friday. Jimmy Shekleford was mowing Dwight's lawn. He did a good job and Dwight paid him well for his work.

"You asked me to come over. Something on your mind, Dwight?"

"Need a good friend. Someone I can trust and you're that person."

"I'll help you if I can. What's on your mind?"

"I'm going to take you into my confidence, Mark. I haven't done that with anyone before now. I couldn't really trust anyone I knew. But, you're different. You can be trusted and I need to trust someone now."

"Sounds pretty serious."

"It is, actually."

"Well, I'm here. Tell me."

"My life's been threatened, Mark. In fact, I'm beginning to think that when the golfer died at Marsh Ridge a couple of weeks ago, the poison may have been meant for me."

"Oh, Dwight. This is called paranoia. Nobody is out to get you."

"Yes , I think so. That Mr. Wallach I told you about was really mad at me, and I think he'll do anything to see me deader than a doornail."

"What could he do to you?"

"I think he and his friends will kill me."

"I don't think so. I can see that this is getting to you. You need to relax."

"Can't. Listen. I got a letter last Monday and it said that my life was in danger. Whoever wrote the letter said that I'd be invited to a party and the invitation would be signed 'The Marsh Ridge Recognition Committee.' They plan to kill me at the party. The writer went on to say that he, or she, expected to be paid at least five million dollars for saving my life. The person said that if I escape the death threat, he or she will return and I am to pay. If I don't, I won't be warned of future threats on my life. I called Mr. Workman and he told me there was no recognition committee at the resort."

"This is nonsense. Why would anyone want you killed?"

"I haven't been a very pleasant person, Mark."

"You're human. None of us deserve sainthood."

Dwight sat solemnly and looked like he was going to get sick.

"What do you want me to do to help you?" Mark asked.

"I wanted to tell you that I had been threatened and if something happens to me I want you to be the executor of my will. I'll pay you for it."

"Hey, man. Nothing is going to happen to you. Snap out of it."

"I hope not. I've made sure that my papers are in order with my lawyer, Lawrence Norwood. I met with him this morning. All you need to do is bury me and see that the house is sold and the contents disposed of. Take what you want and put the rest in a garage sale."

Mark talked with Dwight for quite awhile and then left for an afternoon of work at Marsh Ridge.

Dwight picked up the phone and called Quick and Fast Charters.

"May I speak to Rick, please?"

"This is Rick. How're you, Dwight?"

"Doing okay, I guess. Listen, I'm interested in renting a plane for a trip to Mackinac Island."

"You've come to the right place. Do you want to discuss this over the phone or do you wish to visit with me?"

"I think we can do this over the phone."

"Fine. When do you want to take the trip?"

"Next Tuesday and Wednesday."

"Okay, that would be July 26 and 27. What's your destination?"

"Mackinac Island."

"Number in your party?"

"Six."

"I'll need the names of the passengers."

"Judy Austin, Stacy Hammonds, Heather Abraham, Wendy Blackman, Liz Lake, and Janice Ketcham."

"Will you be going, too?"

"No."

"Length of stay?"

"I'd like you to take these women to Mackinac Island for an overnight stay at the Grand Hotel and shopping. They would be flown up next Tuesday about mid-morning, and they will return late in the afternoon the next day."

"We can accommodate you, Dwight."

"What will I owe you, Rick?"

"Just a minute and I'll give you an estimate."

After several seconds he heard, "Our estimate at this time is one thousand five hundred dollars."

"Fine."

"Where do I tell the young women to meet you or your pilot?"

"At the airport office. We'll take the Cessna, 8484 Uniform. The one you usually take up. Frank will pilot it."

"Thank you, Rick."

"Sure thing, Dwight."

꒜

As predicted, an invitation arrived at the home of Dwight Austin. Dwight opened it and read,

> *You are invited to a beach party on Friday, July 29. This is a special occasion to thank you for all you have done for Marsh Ridge, including the additional business you have brought to our resort. The evening includes food, drink, frolicking in the water and a boat ride. Only swimming suits allowed, no guests, this is our way of thanking you for giving us lots of attention. It's pay-back time. Know you'll have fun. See you on July 29, we'll pick you up at 7:00 p.m.* It was signed, *The Marsh Ridge Recognition Committee.*

Dwight looked at the calendar and noted that the picnic was scheduled for Friday night, two days after his guests would return from their special two days on beautiful Mackinac Island. He sat down at his desk and penned a letter.

> *Thank you so much for your service to me over the years that I've been associated with Marsh Ridge. To show my appreciation for all you've done, I have arranged for you to have a two-day all expenses paid trip to Mackinac Island.*

I've made arrangements for you to be flown to the Island on Tuesday, July 26, at 10:00 a.m. I've made arrangements for you to stay at the Grand Hotel. All shopping, within reason, will be paid for. All you need do at any store is to indicate to the clerk that the purchases are covered by Dwight Austin and no questions will be asked. I'd like to join you for this once in a lifetime treat, but unfortunately I have other plans and you wouldn't want an old man along anyway. All you need do is appear at Quick and Fast Charters at the Gaylord Airport by 10:00 a.m. next Tuesday and you'll enjoy two days of fun on Mackinac Island. I so very much appreciate each of you. I look forward to hearing from you when you return. Janice is invited, too, so please let her know. Sincerely, Dwight Austin.

He addressed it to Marsh Ridge Resort, attention Stacy Hammonds, Heather Abraham, Judy Austin, Wendy Blackman, and Liz Lake. He affixed a stamp and dropped it in the mailbox.

CHAPTER 17

Saturday, July 23
Gaylord, Michigan

On Saturday, Stacy opened the letter addressed to the five women. At first she thought that it was a joke, but upon further reflection she decided that it was legitimate. She called the others and suggested that they meet at her apartment at about eight that evening. Shorty couldn't make this meeting. He was asked to work overtime at the ambulance service. The women arrived and as was their fashion, helped themselves to the refrigerator for a beer or soft drink. "We got a letter today," Stacy said.

"Who from?" Heather asked.

"It's from Dwight."

"What's he writing to us for?" Wendy asked.

"He says that we're to be his guests for an all expense paid, two-day trip to Mackinac Island. He's even going to pay for our shopping. We're invited to stay at the Grand Hotel. He has arranged for us to fly from Gaylord via a chartered plane," Stacy explained. She passed the letter around for all to read.

"I wouldn't go to Pellston on his money let alone Mackinac Island," Liz said.

"Me neither!" Judy offered while she appeared to spit onto the letter.

"Hold on," Heather said. "Why not? I mean, the guy isn't going. Why would we pass up a shopping trip and an all expense paid two-day trip to a premier summer vacation spot?"

"Because of who's offering it," Wendy replied.

"What difference does it make who's offering it. I think we just go to the airport, get in the plane and have some fun," said Heather.

"You know Heather has a point," Stacy said. "We get the last laugh. We take him up on his invitation and then get rid of him two days later. Let's just drop our anger for two days and have the time of our lives!"

"I'm going to have to think about it. Don't count me in yet," Wendy said.

"Listen up, have we ever known a woman on the face of this earth who would turn down an all expense paid vacation which includes shopping at a jewel like Mackinac Island?" Heather said. "We've been this evil man's toys for too long and it doesn't bother me to spend a little of his money. I say let's go and have a good ol' time."

After a little more discussion, all agreed to go. What did they have to lose? They'd request use of their accumulated vacation time. It would surely be granted, especially since the trip was midweek, a time when activity at Marsh Ridge would be less hectic.

ॐ

While the Women of Marsh Ridge were deciding to go to Mackinac Island, Art was watching television in his home in Greenville. The phone rang. He pushed the mute button on his channel selector and lifted the receiver. "Hello."

"Art? This is Butch." Butch was a funeral director in Gaylord. He flew his own plane and hung around at the Otsego County Airport quite a bit. He knew Rick quite well.

"Yeah, Butch. How are ya?"

"Good, good. Listen, I've got some information that I thought you'd like to have."

"What's that?"

"Well, I was at the airport this afternoon and while in the manager's office I glanced down at the appointment calendar on Rick's desk and I saw the name, Dwight Austin opposite ten o'clock on July 26. He's renting the prop plane Tom uses for the midnight mail runs to Lansing."

"Is that right? I heard Dwight was a pilot. I figured he had a plane at the Gaylord airport."

"Yeah he does, but he's got the prop plane at 10 a.m. on the 26th. I'm telling you this 'cause of that conversation we had a couple of days ago when you told me about how this guy's not too high on your list. You said you'd like to know about his coming and goings. Remember?"

"Yeah, I said I'd like to know as much about him as I could. You're right."

"Well, that's why I'm calling you."

"Thanks, Butch. I appreciate your call."

As soon as Art hung up, he had a flash of inspiration. He called Butch back. "Butch, got a question for you."

"What's that?"

"That prop plane out at the airport, what's its schedule?"

"Tom takes it on a midnight trip to Lansing with the mail from this area. He flies it every night like clockwork except if the weather is terrible. He gets back up here around 4 a.m."

"Anyone at the airport when he arrives?"

"Don't think so. I'm never there. There's no tower; he lands, taxies up to the hangar, ties her down and goes home. I mean, I don't know for sure, but nobody in his right mind is goin' to be sitting in the airport only to meet Tom coming in from a routine hop to Lansing and back at four in the morning."

"Thanks, Butch. Just curious. Did you recall seeing anybody else renting the plane before Austin at ten?"

"There wasn't any other name. No one could rent it between the mail run and Dwight's appointment. They wouldn't have time for using it, maintenance, and preparing for Dwight's flight."

"OK, thanks, Butch."
"Later."

❧

Harrison continued to look into various leads over the next couple of days. Lou and Maggie made phone calls and stayed in touch with Harrison. It was one of those short stretches in investigative work when little happens. Lou sensed a lull before the storm. Such was the case in this investigation.

CHAPTER 18

Monday, July 25
Gaylord, Michigan

Late Monday afternoon, Jimmy Shekleford was about to finish trimming the hedge and doing some raking in Dwight Austin's backyard. He looked up from his work and saw Mr. Austin motioning for him to stop and to come into the house. Jimmy did what was asked of him. Mr. Austin had poured him a Classic Coke, his favorite drink. They sat at the kitchen table.

"Jimmy. You're a fine young man."

"Thank you."

"You've taken care of my yard for about six years and you've helped me with many chores. Your parents have been good neighbors and good parents."

Jimmy nodded while wondering why Mr. Austin was so serious.

"Jimmy, I want you to have a good education. I want you to go to Michigan State or the University of Michigan when you finish high school. Maybe you'd rather go to a smaller school like Alma College or Central Michigan University. The place doesn't really matter. What matters is that you have the opportunity for a good education. You do want to go to college don't you?"

"I'd like to go. I'm hoping to get a scholarship. I was hoping that you would be a reference since I've done work for you and you helped me get the job at Marsh Ridge."

"You can always use me for a reference, but you won't be needing a scholarship. I talked to my lawyer this morning, Jimmy. Arrangements have been made for you to have four years of college, all expenses paid. I will talk with your mom and dad this evening, but I wanted to tell you personally."

"Thank you, Mr. Austin."

"You're a fine young man and very deserving. You just go to college and study hard and make a difference in the world, you hear? That's all the thanks I need, your making a difference in people's lives."

"I'll try."

"You'll do just fine."

"Mr. Austin, I feel kinda funny accepting this from you. Your giving me the car and all was more than any other kid could dream of getting."

"I don't want to hear anymore about the car. When I was a young man, neither my parents nor I could afford to have anything like that. We were poor. Kids made fun of me because of our poverty. I made a vow right then as a young man that my son wouldn't have to feel guilty about not having the things other kids had. That's why I gave you the car, so you could drive it and your friends would see you as having something they value. You are the son I never had, and I want you to allow me to keep my promise. I also wanted my son to go to college, and I want you to go and get a good education. Will you do that for me, Jimmy??"

"Yes. You'll be proud."

"I know I will."

Chapter 19

Tuesday July 26
Gaylord, Michigan

Y ou could set your clock by the arrival of the twin engine Cessna at the Otsego County Airport. It was 4 a.m. The plane landed and taxied up to the general aviation ramp. The pilot got out of the plane, locked it, tied it down to the anchors on both sides of the plane, chocked the wheels, and walked with briefcase in hand to his car. He got in, turned on the lights and drove away.

In the deepest darkness of the night with a small flashlight and the help of a mercury light shining high above the small terminal, a man hot wired the fuel truck. Without turning on the truck lights, he drove it out to the plane. He appeared to fill the tank with fuel and returned the truck to its normal parking spot. The entire activity took all of about twenty minutes.

T he women of Marsh Ridge arrived at the airport about nine-thirty. They talked to the owner of the charter service. He explained that they would be whisked to the Island and that the trip would only take about a half-hour. They boarded the plane excitedly and were looking forward to two days of relaxation and fun together.

The pilot, Frank Jackson, was a veteran and a local Vietnam War hero. Frank returned to his hometown of Gaylord for a career in aviation. Because this was a charter flight, Frank was under IFR, instrument flight rules, and would need to file an instrument flight plan. Frank did this and then greeted each of his passengers. He was a charmer and made the young women feel comfortable letting them know that the weather was perfect, the flight would be smooth, and the scenery would be out of this world.

Frank made sure all were securely in their seats with seatbelts fastened. He jokingly said that no coffee would be served and there would be no getting up and moving freely about the aircraft. In truth, the passengers were packed into the Cessna like sardines in a tin can.

The plane taxied down the runway as Frank went quickly through his preflight check list of responsibilities. He made radio contact with Minneapolis Center and was released for takeoff. The plane lifted like steam coming off of a fresh cup of coffee. As the plane gained altitude, the women noticed and pointed to familiar landmarks of the Gaylord area. It was a beautiful view, no matter where the women looked.

Frank heard, "8484 Uniform. This is Minneapolis Center. We have radar contact." Frank responded, "Roger, understand radar contact." He knew that he would be a blip on the screen in Minneapolis until he made his descent into Mackinac Island in a matter of twenty minutes.

Unknown to anyone on board and only one person on land, the sugar added to the fuel was about to gum up the injectors. In a matter of seconds, the flight passed from heaven into hell. The right engine lost power and the plane violently shook as it was still in a climb. Frank knew this was a critical phase and now, with this unexpected loss of power, he instinctively said with underlying panic in his voice, "Minneapolis Center, 8484 Uniform, Mayday, Mayday, Mayday, lost an engine." As Frank was talking, the second engine died. Frank shouted, "Mayday, Mayday, lost second engine." Frank had a flashback to his Vietnam war days when a plane he was piloting was hit. The nightmare was back. The women screamed and shouted in panic and fear.

Frank heard Minneapolis, "8484 Uniform, what is your status?" There was no response. Frank was doing what he could to try to recover from the stall, but it was impossible. The plane spiraled down to earth and crashed into a field. All seven died a violent death.

Minneapolis Center lost 8484 Uniform off its radar screen and of course there was no response to its request for radio contact. Procedures instructed them to call the airport manager where the flight originated and then to call the sheriff's department in the county were they had had their last contact. They followed the procedures.

The sheriff's department took a call a few seconds earlier from a farmer north of Gaylord who saw the plane go down on his property. Instantly, emergency procedures were put in place and vehicles and personnel were rushed to the scene, about three miles north, northeast of Gaylord.

Upon hearing about the crash, the airport manager took the call and instantly knew that Frank Jackson was dead. He knew Frank as a pilot of impeccable credentials and experience. Word went throughout the airport grounds to everyone's shock and disbelief. That a plane that Frank piloted could go down, especially 8484 Uniform, a fairly new plane that Frank personally kept in tip-top condition, was odd. Accidents do happen, but this one totally defied chance. It shouldn't happen to any plane, and anyone who knew Frank would have safely bet that it would never have happened to his Cessna.

۲۰

The Otsego County Ambulance Service received the call for assistance shortly after 10 a.m. Shorty sprang into action, heading north and following the directions from the dispatcher. Once he heard that there was the possibility of seven people killed and most were women he had a sick feeling in his stomach. It was a feeling that he could be on the way to a tragic accident involving people he knew, but then he realized that his friends were probably driving to Mackinac Island. No one had mentioned flying so he felt certain that the premonition of his friends dying in a field north of Gaylord was simply his mind giving him a does of unrealistic fear.

Shorty's ambulance, with sirens blaring and using safe but excessive speed, approached the farm land where the burning carnage lay. A woman, perhaps the farmer's wife, directed the ambulance into her driveway. Shorty stopped long enough to hear the woman give directions even though smoke could still be seen rising into the clear late morning air several hundred yards out in a corn field.

He monitored his radio, and by now the dispatcher had prepared him for what he was about to see. He was expected to find seven people dead, a male pilot and six women who were on a flight to Mackinac Island. There was no longer reason to doubt his worst nightmare, the six women were his friends. It was only by some internal instinct to do his job and assist people in a disaster that Shorty could continue to function, physically or mentally.

At the scene, Shorty assisted other emergency workers in doing all the work that needed to be done. The disaster drills that he had participated in were no longer an exercise, but the real thing. All this time, Shorty couldn't accept that six of the seven body bags contained his dearest friends.

He asked about the identity of the pilot expecting to hear the name, Dwight Austin. Hearing the name, Frank Jackson, made no sense to him. He couldn't understand why his friends were flying with Frank. The plane was reserved for Dwight, or at least that is what a friend had told him.

Shorty transported two of the women to the Otsego County Memorial Hospital and there are not words to describe how one would feel carrying friends, friends who only a few hours ago had been alive and full of energy and hope, to a morgue. It was during the drive to the hospital that Shorty's anger for Dwight escalated. It was almost as if all the grief had channeled itself into revenge.

Shorty realized that everything had gone wrong, everything. The plan began with a set-up to put Dwight behind bars for life, and now, within a short period of time, the women were dead, and Dwight, the man who was the reason for all the planning and for all of the horror, was still walking, a free man.

While driving the ambulance back to the ambulance garage, Shorty entertained a thought. He knew that for his friends, he had to kill this man. It simply wasn't right for Dwight to walk free while the six women he harassed and abused were dead, violently killed in a plane crash. But, he wanted to do it in a way that he couldn't be accused of murder. He didn't want to spend his life in prison.

He thought he'd return to the blackmail. First he'd get some money and that might help him pay for a hit man or to obtain some resources to make the job a bit easier.

Dwight Austin didn't play golf. Instead, he stayed around home. He had his radio tuned to a local station. The eleven o'clock news began in usual fashion, and then he heard, "We've just gotten word that a local plane has crashed a few miles north of Gaylord. The plane was based in Gaylord and belonged to Quick and Fast Charters. The pilot was experienced and the weather was good. It's believed that six passengers were aboard. The pilot's flight plan indicated Mackinac Island as the destination. No names are being released pending notification of relatives. There were no survivors. More details as they become available."

Dwight Austin went into shock after learning about the death of his daughter and the women of Marsh Ridge. He called his doctor because he was feeling light headed, nauseous, and his heart was palpitating. There was no one with whom to share his grief.

Adding to his stress was Dwight's absolute belief that Reggie's friends were plotting his death. After all, there was no party planned at the resort in his honor, the party was not to be held at Marsh Ridge. It made no sense given all of the facilities available. He surmised that the invitation was a ploy to have him picked up, probably in one of those dark limos and taken to his death. His doctor saw him immediately, prescribed Ativan, and suggested the name of a psychologist if he felt he needed some counseling.

∽

Harrison called Lou Searing.

"Lou? This is Harrison in Gaylord."

"Hi. What's up?"

"Lots of action up here today. I don't know if the news has gotten downstate or not."

"Haven't heard anything from the Gaylord area."

"Well, a chartered plane crashed a few miles north of Gaylord late this morning. On board, in addition to the pilot, was Stacy Hammonds, Judy Austin, Wendy Blackman, Heather Abraham, Liz Lake, and Janice Ketcham. We're not releasing the names to the media as yet. We want to notify family members."

"Oh, my God! Very sad. Got any clues?"

"Not a one."

"Where does that leave us?"

"As best I can figure, unless you have some new information, we have two people who may be involved and they are Dwight Austin and Shorty Gross. They are the only two who are still living in this drama. You got any news for me?"

Lou briefed Harrison concerning the meeting with Don Collins and his attorney in Kalamazoo. It led to the conclusions drawn by Lou, Maggie, and Harrison. The conversation ended after Lou said, "Maggie and I will come up and spend a day or two. I think we can wrap this up with some talks with Mark Thompson, Bob Sanders, Dwight, and Shorty. I've got a feeling that the whole thing will come together and we can put this case to rest."

"Great. I enjoy working with both of you and I'll wait for you. When do you expect to arrive?"

"I'll call Maggie right now and brief her of the news you've shared with me. My guess is that we'll be there this evening. How about dinner at the Sugar Bowl at seven-thirty?"

"Sounds good. Have a safe trip. See you soon."

Lou called Maggie and shared what he knew. She agreed that talking to those four plus Billy Wingate, Dwight's golfing buddy, would put the seal on this case. They arrived in Gaylord about seven, checked into the Day's Inn and then arrived at the Sugar Bowl in time to greet Harrison and enjoy the evening meal. The three then took time to extensively discuss these strange and latest developments in the case.

They ordered the special; meat loaf, mashed potatoes and beans with a slice of apple pie for dessert. Coffee cups were filled and they got to work, planning how best to wrap up this investigation.

"I think we need another talk with Shorty. We should do this first," Harrison suggested."

"I agree," Maggie offered.

"Yes, then we need to talk with Mark Thompson," Lou suggested. Both Maggie and Harrison nodded in agreement.

"I'd also like to see Bob Sanders," Lou said to Harrison.

"Why do you think that's important?"

"I've always been intrigued by Don Dailey's comment that he passed a man with knickers in a golf cart coming toward him on the 13th hole. Remember, when he was going after the ice bag?"

"Oh, I can help with that. I learned that there were two or three guys on the course that day in knickers. I talked to Bob about it and he said it was just one of those days. I concluded that Dailey just mistook one of the other guys in knickers for Austin."

"Okay. Thanks, that was one minor detail that I hadn't cleared up."

After dinner they agreed to meet at the sheriff's office at 9 a.m. They would go to see Shorty and then Mark Thompson.

CHAPTER 20

Wednesday, July 27
Gaylord, Michigan

The three were waiting at the Otsego County Ambulance Service when Shorty arrived for work. He was carrying a Dunkin Donuts bag and a large coffee. As he walked through the door and saw Harrison, Lou, and Maggie, he knew he would have an interesting morning. "You folks here to see me or Mr. Puffer?"

"Here to see you, Shorty. Unless you get a 911 call, we'd like to spend some time talking with you about the murder on the 14th tee," Harrison said, leading the questioning.

"I figured that's why you're here. It isn't enough that I have to grieve the loss of my friends, but now I've got the police breathing down my neck."

"I admit the timing isn't good, Shorty, but a golfer, six women and a respected local pilot have died and their families will grieve the rest of their lives."

"You're right. Ask your questions."

"Let me begin with an open-ended question. Do you have anything you wish to share with us? We think you may have information that can explain exactly what happened and we're giving you this opportunity to help us."

"I guess I might as well come clean. I probably need a lawyer, but I could hardly afford these donuts let alone a high-priced attorney."

"We appreciate your wanting to get the facts out, Shorty."

He started his long explanation, "The women of Marsh Ridge wanted Dwight dead because he had been sexually harassing them. The women kept it all to themselves, it was embarrassing and they were scared of Dwight. But, someone leaked something and before long the word got around that he was doing this to others. Janice, Wendy, Stacy, Heather, and Liz developed friendships sharing their terrible experiences. They talked about going to the police or other people who could help them, but they feared Dwight. He would get revenge or even worse, they would lose their jobs. He told them that if they ever said a word about this he would see that they would never get a job anywhere. He promised to blackmail them for life. The guy was very controlling and the women knew he meant it. Apparently they knew what he had done to some other woman in the area who reported him. At any rate, they stayed at Marsh Ridge and found comfort in each other. But, they each desired to have Dwight dead. They wanted their lives back.

"A couple of weeks ago Judy met one of the golfers at a gambling casino in St. Ignace, and she learned that Reggie Macleod was in that group and was playing golf in the Gaylord area. She also had heard from Billy Wingate that Dwight had a bad encounter with Bill Wallach the day before. The women and I, who just happened to be with them on this particular evening, began to plot a way to get rid of Macleod and Dwight. We discovered that the mystery weekend was at Marsh Ridge and we knew that that would help confuse things for the investigators, and for the guests.

"I learned from Janice that Judy had applied for a special education job in Alpena and it looked very promising, but the interviewer said they would have to talk to her previous employer. That would be this Macleod guy and Judy was sure he would ruin this opportunity for her. The chance to shut him up was too good to pass up.

"We needed a person to help fool the guests so that the murder would look like it had been staged as part of the mystery weekend.

Liz had an actor friend in Battle Creek who she thought could help. We pooled some money to pay him. I called and asked him if he wanted the work and after he agreed I gave him directions. Janice agreed to go to the 14th tee when she got a call from Stacy who could see the 13th hole from the window in Jac's. "

"Where did the placemat come in?" Harrison asked.

"We saw him writing on a placemat with his friend Mark Thompson. So we had Heather tell you that he wrote on the placement that Wallach would be killed. He wouldn't pass a lie detector test because he did write on the back of a placemat, but he didn't write what Heather told you he wrote."

"Talk about the set up."

"We were trying to set Dwight up and we did it by having the group with Bill Wallach right in front of him. This way, he could see where they were and anticipate the cooler on 14. We could kill Macleod to revenge what he did to Judy, and at the same time set up Dwight for doing the killing. Dwight would be convicted on circumstantial evidence and go to jail for life and then he'd no longer be a problem to the women."

"Lou or Maggie, any questions?"

Lou spoke first, "So you told the lady on the putting green Saturday morning that the murder would take place on the 14th tee to set up Dwight?"

"Yeah. I said that I heard it from Dwight. I wanted to implicate him for the murders. It was planned."

"When the plan backfired, was there any plan to kill Dwight?" Maggie asked.

"Yeah, they were going to kill him at a picnic at the county park Friday evening. They figured that Janice was going to get it for killing Reggie, and she might bring them into it. Dwight would still be free and they couldn't handle that, so they decided to hold him under water. They expected the authorities to rule it an accidental drowning. They planned to get him drunk first."

"Did Mr. Austin know that his life was in danger?" Lou asked.

"Since I'm spilling my gut, I guess you might as well hear the whole story. When I heard of the women's plan, I wrote Dwight and told him about the threat on his life and that in appreciation for this information I expected to receive five million dollars. I was going to use the money to help the women get on with their lives. You know, move from here and get set up in some other community. Instead of killing Dwight, I thought we could get his money and use it to start over. I guess he got suspicious and decided to kill them before he got killed himself. So, in a sense I'm responsible for the death of the pilot and the women. This is just one terrible nightmare."

"You say he decided to kill them?" Harrison asked. "You're saying that Dwight caused that plane to crash?"

"Seems pretty clear to me. He had the plane rented for the morning of the crash. At least that's the rumor I've heard. You're the investigators, you know more than I do. Anyway, I'm using common sense, and I figured that he did something to the plane between the mailrun flight and renting the plane yesterday morning. If he kills the women nothing comes out about his abuse and harassment at Janice's trial. The plane crash looks like an accident due to engine failure. Hey, you guys are the detectives, not me. But, it makes sense, don't it?"

"Yes, it's a logical scenario," Lou admitted. "My advice to you, Shorty, is to get a lawyer to guide you through the next month or so."

"Thanks. I'll consider it."

The three thanked Shorty for his information. They said that they would be in touch if more information or clarification was needed.

Back at the sheriff's office, they called Mark Thompson. Harrison suggested he get hold of his attorney, they would be in Vanderbilt in about twenty minutes.

The three arrived at Mark's home and were greeted graciously. Kara Ingram, Mark's lawyer was present. "Thank you for seeing us on such short notice," Harrison said.

"You're welcome. Still trying to get over the death of my coworkers at Marsh Ridge. Having six people you know die in one day is a bit unsettling."

"Yes, we imagine this is a difficult time for you," Harrison said sympathetically. "We won't bother you for long. We're very close to solving the murder. We think you can help us understand a few things."

"I'll try if I can. I want to get all of this behind me, too. Time to get on with some healing."

"Yes, it is."

"What questions do you have for me?"

"We still have concerns over why you wouldn't talk with us about the plan that Dwight was developing."

"Well, now I think I have to. My conscience is bothering me. With the approval of my lawyer, I'll explain." He looked at Kara who nodded affirmatively.

"I'll tell you what was happening and then I'll tell you why I had to keep it a secret. Dwight had a run in with Mr. Wallach a day or two prior to the murder. He was very upset with the man because he said guys in the Wallach group hit into him several times during the course of 18 holes. We met at Jac's on Friday night and he knew that this Mr. Wallach would be playing on the Marsh Ridge course the next day. He took a placemat and turned it over. He began to write a plot and talked with me about it. He was going to get some girlie magazines, cut out a bunch of pictures, put them in a large plastic envelope with a sticker on it saying 'Property of Bill Wallach.' He was going to put this in an envelope and mail it to Mr. Wallach's school board president. Dwight thought this would put him in real trouble back home and would undoubtedly lead to his public humiliation and the end of his job. Dwight was that upset with the man. I tried to reason with him, but he would hear nothing of it. He wanted revenge and this seemed to do the trick."

Mark continued, "Now, I didn't want to tell you this because number one, he asked me not to tell a soul and I promised I wouldn't, and secondly, if I did tell someone and it got out, Dwight would seek some type of revenge against me. I've just given you an idea of what he is capable of doing."

"I understand, thanks for explaining."

Maggie said, "Another witness said that you met briefly with Don Dailey and Judy Austin. The witness said that Judy gave you a small white container or package. The three of you talked for a short while and then you left in the direction of the 14th tee."

"I remember that. That was a part of the real mystery weekend. We were asked by the mystery writer, I think his name was Mr. Growe, to take that to the pool area and leave it on a table. I did that. I think it was a clue for the guests who were trying to solve the 'Mystery at the Marsh.' That's all that was."

Harrison asked, "What can you tell us about your friend Dwight in the last week?"

"He asked to see me a week or so ago. He said that he believed his life was threatened and he wanted me to be the executor of his estate if something were to happen to him."

"That's all you know?"

"Did he say who was threatening him?"

"No."

"Who do you think would threaten him?"

"I think it was the friends of the guy who died. I think they think Dwight did this and they're wanting to take the law into their own hands and kill him. They could have learned that he had rented that plane and were expecting him to be in it when it crashed."

"That makes sense," Maggie said.

"I trust that you have no need to speak further with my client," Kara said. "He had nothing to do with the murder at Marsh Ridge and nothing to do with the deaths of the women. I expect he will not be bothered with anymore questions."

"I think we have what we need, Miss Ingram," Harrison said. "Thank you for being available on such short notice." Kara smiled and nodded.

Maggie said, "I'm sorry, but I have one last question, if I may?" Mark smiled and nodded. "Was Judy Austin, Dwight Austin's daughter?"

"That has been a well kept secret. Dwight and his wife, Arlene never had any children even though they wanted desperately to have kids. Dwight always wanted a boy. He dreamed of having a boy and watching him grow up. In fact, I think the neighbor boy, Jimmy

Shekleford, served as a son substitute for all of his sixteen or seventeen years. Anyway, Arlene proposed that they adopt Judy who was about ten at the time. Dwight initially was not in favor of the idea, but Arlene was insistent that she wanted to adopt this young girl. From the day she arrived, Dwight was a problem for her. I don't know all of their problems, there are rumors of course. I think Dwight loved his adopted daughter, but it sure wasn't mutual, I'll say that. She seemed to hate him. I don't know why. I think Dwight told me once that she had been placed in a number of foster homes and I think she may have been abused by some of the foster parents. Don't quote me on that, but I think she had a very troubling past and was quite an angry girl. Frankly, I was amazed that she seemed to get hold of her life. She put herself through college and looked like she was into a promising career.

"In fact, I'm no psychologist, but it seems to me that her being fired by the guy who was poisoned was a terrible blow to Judy. Here she had survived all of this abuse growing up in foster homes. She gets her life together by putting herself through college and she earns a certificate to teach and then, just like being in a foster home, she gets leveled again, only this time in a profession. The firing must have been traumatic and I can see where it would lead her to plot the guy's death. I'm not condoning it, don't get me wrong, but I can understand it.

"I was always kind of amazed that the family could exist with such anger and hatred. He never publicly claimed her as a daughter. Arlene died about two years ago and Judy and Dwight have been bitter enemies ever since. Very sad. But, no, Judy was not his natural daughter."

"Thank you. No more questions," Maggie said, closing her notebook.

⌇

Harrison called Dwight and arranged to talk with him. Of course, Dwight wanted his attorney, Lawrence Norwood, to be present. A time was agreed upon and the meeting was planned to be held at the sheriff's department in Gaylord.

When all gathered and introductions were made, Harrison began, "Mr. Austin we have some questions for you." Dwight looked down but nodded in response to Harrison's comment.

"We've learned that you had some sexual relationships with the women of Marsh Ridge. Is that correct?"

"Lies, lies. You see, this is all a set-up for a fall guy. It's bad enough that I have to grieve the loss of my daughter and people I knew at Marsh Ridge, but now you have to suggest that I would have some inappropriate relationship with these women. First, you think I may have something to do with the death of that golfer in front of me and now you suggest some illicit relationship. Can't you see that I'm being framed?"

"I suppose it's possible, Mr. Austin. That's why we're talking with you," Harrison explained. "We're trying to learn all we can. What information do you have to suggest that you're being framed?"

"Blackmail for one."

"Blackmail?"

"Yeah. I got a letter from someone who demanded money from me claiming he was informing me that my life was in danger."

"Who is 'he'?"

"Well, I don't know if it's a guy or a woman, I guess. I just assumed it was a guy. I'm convinced it was one of the friends of the guy who died."

"Tell us more about this threat."

"I got a letter saying I was being set up to die and I would be killed at a party. The invitation was signed, 'The Marsh Ridge Recognition Committee.' I got the invitation to a party last friday. The person blackmailing me said that I would be contacted and if I didn't pay five million dollars, this person would not alert me to the next threat. He or she hasn't contacted me yet."

"Who do you think this could have come from?"

"As I said, from the golfers who were friends of that guy who died."

"Because?"

"Well, because they're convinced that I killed him."

"You know this for a fact?"

"No, but they would surely believe it. You see, we had a run in a day or two before the guy died. I was furious with them for hitting into us. We had a shouting match and I threatened them. Well, the big guy in the group did hit into us again which sets me up to follow through on my promise. So, then a guy dies in the group in front of me. You know, I have thought a lot about that afternoon, gone over and over it in my mind and I recall seeing a guy coming toward us on 13. He was in a cart and as he passed I could tell he was wearing the same Payne Stewart style of clothes that I was wearing. Not many guys wear knickers. I'm sure that information has gotten to you and others who are investigating this thing. They're probably convinced that I drove up to the 14th tee and poisoned their friend. So, they're plotting my death."

"So, you think Reggie's friends are plotting to kill you?"

"Yeah, this phony recognition party is to be held in some county park. They can't have it at Marsh Ridge because they aren't members. They can go to a public park, claiming they want to honor me, and when they get me to that setting, they'd kill me. Except one of them or all of them sees a chance to get my money and they are using this revenge to blackmail me. You guys are the investigators and here I am making it all clear for you."

"You have a logical scenario, Mr. Austin," Harrison offered. "We'll get right on it. Tell me again. When is the party supposed to take place?"

"I got a call saying it was off because of the plane crash, but that another opportunity to end my life would be coming up. I was instructed to wait for instructions to drop off the five million dollars."

"Was the voice from a male or female?"

"You know, this is going to sound strange to you, but I really don't know. It was hard to tell. I've got a hearing loss in the high frequencies and sometimes I can't hear too well. I think it was a man's voice, but I couldn't be certain."

"I've checked my calls and all coming into the department and you didn't report this threat to us?"

"No, I didn't call. I did tell Mr. Norwood, here. But nobody knows. I'm trying to think of how I could get the money. If I decided not to pay, I'd call and see what protection I could get."

Lou excused himself from the group; he knew that Maggie would brief him later. Lou called Doc at his office in Bay City. It was the middle of the day. He explained to the receptionist that the call was very important and asked to be put through to him.

"Hi, Lou. Calling to set up a tee time?" Doc asked, in a light manner.

"No, Doc. We're still working on the investigation up here in Gaylord."

"I thought it was solved. Word is that the nurse did it, isn't that what happened?"

"She's the suspect and has been arrested. But I don't know if you've heard that six women, including the nurse, and a pilot were killed in a plane crash yesterday morning."

"No, didn't hear that. Is this related to Reggie's death?"

"Could be. We're waiting for the FAA to finish an investigation to see if it was human error or mechanical failure or, well, we just don't know."

"What can I do for you, Lou? Got a patient with novocaine about to wear off."

"I need to know if the seven of you have taken any action against Dwight Austin?"

"The crazy guy who said we hit into 'em?"

"Yeah. Until you and Maggie figured it was the nurse, we were thinking of seeking revenge of some kind."

"Did you blackmail him, Doc?"

"What do you mean?"

"I mean, did you tell him you wanted money to save his life, anything like that?"

"We did think about getting him in some way and through the pocketbook was one way. We felt certain that he was the killer. He left the course that afternoon. He didn't even allow the cops to talk to him. He was right behind Reggie, and he had promised to do something drastic if we ever hit into him again. While we're law-abiding citizens, we did spend some time in our grief thinking about revenge."

"But did you send him a letter extorting money from him?"

"It was drafted, but I don't know if Art sent it. He might have called instead."

"Doc, I need you to trust me. I need you to contact the others and get me information about the exact action that you've taken. It's very important and please don't do anything more. We're close to solving not only the death of Reggie, but possibly the women of Marsh Ridge."

"Okay. I'll contact the guys and we'll do whatever you direct."

"Thanks, Doc, go back to that patient and better give him or her another dose of the novocaine."

"I think I will, Lou."

Later that afternoon, after all of Doc's patients had left the office, he picked up his phone and called Jeff Gooch.

"Jeff, this is Rich Lewis."

"Yeah, Doc. How're you doing?"

"I'd rather be playing golf, but I'm doing okay. Listen, I got a call from Lou Searing earlier today. He asked me if I knew about any plans we had for getting some revenge from the old man in knickers."

"Yeah, and you told him?"

"Well, I was less than honest. I did tell him we were angry at the guy, and thought about getting back at him. You know, I did tell him that."

"You didn't tell him about the plane, I hope."

"No, of course not. I may have a hearing loss, but I'm not stupid."

"Good. Did Art go to Gaylord?"

"I think so. He left home a day or two ago. He said he was going to settle up. He can't seem to accept the murder. The last time I talked to him, he was pretty disturbed about it. It wouldn't surprise me if he went up there to find that old man and confront him."

"Art would probably do that, Doc."

"Did you hear about the women from Marsh Ridge dying in a

plane crash near Gaylord?"

"No, didn't hear that."

"Yeah, six women who worked at the resort died along with the pilot. The FAA is investigating."

"Well, I sure hope Art's not involved. We can't contact him. He's been gone for awhile, like I said, and other than leaving a message on his answering machine, he can't be reached."

"What do you want me to tell Searing?"

"Oh, tell him you've got nothing to help him. That's a true statement."

✍

Doc called Lou in Gaylord. "I couldn't learn much, Lou. Listen I want to help you, but I don't want to be a traitor to my friends."

"How would you be a traitor, Doc?"

"Well, truth is, we knew the old man killed Reggie. It had to be him, he was the closest person and he vowed to act out his threat. We decided to let you and the sheriff handle it, figuring it would be a simple case to be solved within a day or two. But, when nothing got solved and we could see this old man literally getting away with murder, we got frustrated and angry."

"I understand your emotions, Doc, but..."

"We learned that Dwight had a plane in Gaylord. Art's a pilot, too. When you told me the women died in a plane crash I was afraid that Art may have been involved."

"Is Art up here in Gaylord?"

"I think so."

"Thanks, Doc. You've been helpful. I appreciate your sharing the information."

✍

Harrison told Lou and Maggie that the FAA and the National Transportation Safety Board had already done a preliminary review of the damage. He said, "While they have not mentioned anything to the media, they did tell me that they're quite certain that the crash was caused by engine failure and that the failure was caused by something in the fuel, possible sugar or water. This happened at the time of ascent where the plane is in almost a forty five degree angle to the ground. They basically told me this wasn't an accident or human error, at least not as far as the pilot is concerned. Somehow, foreign matter got into the fuel tank between the mail run at 4:00 a.m. and the take off at 9:56 a.m. yesterday morning."

"So what you're saying is that having just solved the murder of the golfer on the 14th tee, we now have the murders of the six women of Marsh Ridge and the pilot to solve," Lou said, shaking his head in disbelief.

"You got it."

"Well, let me tell you what I've learned and maybe Dwight's paranoia is not far from reality. I've learned that the guys who lost their golfing buddy were thinking of possibly taking the law into their own hands. They're convinced that Dwight murdered Reggie. They learned that the nurse killed Reggie, but one of them may not have heard the news before taking action into his own hands. In fact, he's been gone for a few days and folks can't reach him. He could be involved. His name is Art Williams."

Maggie interjected, "Did the records at the airport show that Dwight chartered a plane for yesterday morning?"

"Yes, that's right," Harrison said, "He paid to have the six women of Marsh Ridge taken to Mackinac Island. So, someone may have learned that he was taking the plane. If that someone expected him to be flying the plane or to be on board and they wanted to finish him off, he may be the one who put water or sugar in the fuel to assure Dwight's death."

"Exactly. Except Dwight wasn't in the plane as pilot or passenger."

"I know. But, it could also be, as Shorty said, that Dwight now sees that he's in big trouble with Janice in court and her perhaps exposing all of his harassment and abuse. He may not want any of that and so he arranges to kill them, you know, 'I'll have the last word strategy.'"

"I'm going to suggest that the perpetrator is not Shorty," Harrison said. "He sees Dwight's money, and my guess is that he wants that money to do what Dwight would want done, and that is to make this all go away, nothing said. There's not going to be any court case since Janice is now dead. So, there is no way for Dwight's abuses to be exposed, as you put it, Maggie. Shorty has his eye on the money and taking Dwight out of the picture wouldn't allow him to get the money. My guess is that Shorty did not sabotage that plane."

"Makes sense and I would agree," Maggie said.

"Does that leave Dwight himself or Art Williams?" Lou asked.

"Those are the logical ones that we know about. Anybody could have done it or it could be an accident by the lineman at the airport."

CHAPTER 21

Thursday, July 28
Gaylord, Michigan

It was about ten o'clock Thursday morning when the phone rang in Dwight's home.

"It's time for your money or your life. Pretty simple choice, Mr. Austin. Listen carefully. You are to give me five million dollars at four o'clock this afternoon at the 14th tee at Marsh Ridge. I will be there in a golf cart and I want the money in one thousand dollar bills. Now, understand this. If you do anything to interfere with this transfer, your life is set to be ruined. You see, I'm just as creative as you are in messing up people's lives. So, any involvement of the police will set in action a plan to ruin you, Mr. Austin. It's your choice. I get five million and you have golf in your future for the rest of your natural life. One slip by you, even a phone call to the police will be monitored, and your life will be shortened big time. It's the least I can do to avenge the death of Reggie and the seven beautiful people on that plane yesterday. Repeat. Five million dollars this afternoon at four o'clock at the 14th tee. You will recognize me when I say, "Nice day for golf, isn't it." If you understand what you are to do, say, "I understand."

Dwight took a deep breath and said, "I understand." The phone went dead.

Dwight got in his car and drove to Lawrence Norwood's office. Dwight explained in detail what the man had said on the phone. The two men discussed options.

"I think we immediately work with the authorities to apprehend this guy," Norwood advised.

"I can afford it, Larry. How about if I just give him the money and then I can get on with my life. Sure it's a loss, but I can afford it. If he's caught, then there will be a trial and out may come my behavior with the women at Marsh Ridge, and I can't bear to have the public embarrassment that this disclosure would create."

"Well, ultimately it's your choice, but remember that you are now subject to his control. If it works this time, there's always next time and you're always wondering with each call or confrontation what this guy is planning. You're now in his control. Plus he already admitted that he can ruin lives. Since he seeks revenge for the death of Reggie and the women, he can wake up any morning and decide to ruin your life. My advice is to confront the guy and get him in the hands of the police and the court."

"What would happen?"

"That's up to Harrison and the detectives he's working with, I guess. I imagine they'd record the transaction and then arrest the guy as he leaves. I'm not skilled in apprehending extortioners. I give advice and defend you and my advice is to confront this guy."

"I've trusted you all these years, Larry. I guess I should continue to do that. But, this guy could know I'm here now, he might be monitoring everything."

"We'll work around that. I know how to work with Harrison and he'll know how to work behind the scenes. This extortionist is an amateur. We'll pull it off. Don't worry. I suggest you go home and come back here about two this afternoon. If I need to see you earlier, I'll call and let it ring three times and then hang up. So, if you hear a three-ring phone call, come on over. Understand?"

"Yeah. I hope we're doing the right thing. I still think I'd rather pay the five million. My money has gotten me my way in the past. It can continue to do that."

"It's your call, Dwight. We've got time. Go home and think about it. I'll see you at two o'clock unless I ring three times."

꒰꒱

Harrison, Lou, and Maggie were sitting in the sheriff's office thinking of their next steps when a letter arrived by courier for Harrison. The letter was brought to him with "Immediate Attention Requested" typed on the envelope. Harrison opened it, read it, and then said, "Well, this letter from Norwood is a new development. Listen to this." He read the letter to Lou and Maggie.

"How do you advise we proceed?" Lou asked.

"My first thought is to put a mike on Dwight and to have him initiate some conversation during the transaction at the 14th tee. We'll be at a distance with binoculars and once the money is transferred we can move to arrest for extortion. The guy will have the money in his possession."

"Sounds too simple," Maggie said. The guy is crazy to make this transaction out in broad daylight with acres of land all about him. It's almost like he's trying to be caught."

"I agree," Lou said. "Aren't we risking Dwight's life with quick intervention?"

"No, just the opposite, a quick response and we've got him in our custody. We'll converge on him with golf carts just like we normally would with squad cars."

"He could have a weapon and put us all away, if we're not careful."

"True, but our approach will be a surprise. He won't have an opportunity to draw on us. I'm very comfortable with the apprehension and arrest. If Dwight doesn't change his mind, it will be clean. By suppertime, we'll have this all wrapped up."

"I don't feel good about this," Maggie said, looking quite concerned. I think this guy, whoever he is, is sharp. He sees a chance for millions. He has to be aware that Dwight could risk public embarrassment and decide not to let him get away with the blackmail. Maybe we record it and hold off a bit on the arrest."

"Not my style, Maggie. If I see the crime committed, I'll act. Once the guy has the money from Dwight, then I want the arrest. Letting him go weakens our case."

The remainder of the morning was spent planning every step of the arrest. Harrison communicated with Lawrence Norwood that all was in place for the apprehension of the extortionist. He gave Lawrence very precise instructions for Dwight. He was to wear a hidden microphone supplied by the department. Dwight was to try to get the guy to dialogue a little. He was not to be confrontational. Dwight's instructions were to arrive at the 14th tee at four o'clock, listen for the code sentence, try to exchange some dialogue, hand over the money, and stay put. That was all he was to do.

Dwight arrived at two o'clock. He sat down with Lawrence Norwood and discussed the plan. He left for the bank around three o'clock, picked up five hundred thousand dollars and drove to Marsh Ridge. He got into his personal cart, and eventually, around 4 p.m. waited at the 14th tee for the man who seemed to hold his life in his hands.

In the meantime, Harrison, Lou and Maggie made arrangements for the use of a number of golf carts and video equipment to record the hand over so it could be used as evidence at the trial. The officers involved were in golf clothes. They were to report to the pro shop as if playing golf at three-thirty. Officers arrived in ten minute intervals. They were assigned to carts, clubs put on the back, and assigned spots on the Marsh Ridge course to await the action. Everyone communicated using hand-held radio devices.

Maggie and Lou stayed in Maggie's van. They agreed that their presence could be a clue to the person extorting the money that there was interference. Lou and Maggie could monitor the activity with two-way radios.

It was about ten minutes to four when Lou looked to his left out of the van and said, "Oh, my God, look who's here."

"Who, Lou?"

"That guy over there in the knickers and red hat is Art Williams. He's one of Reggie's friends. Doc told me they couldn't find Art. He thought he might be planning to take some action to revenge Reggie's death."

"Looks like he's the mystery man."

"Do I intervene, Maggie? Should I go out and stop him. I mean, I know him and he's about to commit a crime that will be devastating to him and his family for no reason at all."

"Boy, that's a tough one, Lou. I guess it would be better to intervene and stop a crime than to clean up after it."

"Yeah, I guess I'll try to stop him." Art got in his cart quickly and was heading away from the parking lot. By the time Lou got out and shouted, Art was too far away, and quite frankly, Lou didn't know where Art had gone. Lou looked at his watch. It was three minutes to four. Lou couldn't get to the 14th tee by four o'clock.

Lou followed Maggie's advice and got on the radio to let Harrison know that he had seen Art Williams in the parking lot and that he could be the guy meeting Dwight Austin at four o'clock.

At five minutes to four Dwight was alone at the 14th tee. Golfers were approaching the tee. He allowed them to hit and when they left, a man drove up and parked his cart next to Dwight. "Nice day for golf, isn't it?" he said.

"Here's the money you demanded," Dwight said as he handed over the money. The man opened the container and looked in to be sure the money was there.

"It all had better be here, and not a word, old man. Your life is over the minute I'm confronted. Is that clear?" Dwight nodded. "Oh, one more thing, I hope you can live with yourself for all the pain you brought to my friends, my very innocent and God loving friends. You're one sick and evil man, Dwight Austin."

"You've got my money, but you've not seen the end of me. You'll never see the end of me. Understand?" Dwight replied, full of anger.

The man chuckled, shook his head and pulled away leaving Dwight sitting in his cart to the left of the 14th tee.

Within seconds, six golf carts converged around the man.

Harrison was the first to reach the cart. "You're under arrest for extortion. Get out of the cart. Down on the ground, now!" As the extortionist began to get out of the cart, he took a garage door opening device from beside him and pushed the button. The cart holding Dwight Austin exploded, killing him instantly.

"Thought I gave him plenty of warning. I told him if I was confronted, his life was over. Some people just don't understand cause and effect, stimulus and response. My friends can now rest in peace. It's over."

Shorty Gross was arrested and taken to the sheriff's department for booking. The ambulance was called once again to the 14th tee. The bloodied and mutilated body of Dwight Austin was put into the ambulance and taken to the hospital and morgue. Shorty went into silence after making his statement at Marsh Ridge. He would not talk to anyone, not even a court appointed lawyer.

⌇

An elderly man came into the sheriff's office. He was unshaven and his clothes were tattered. "Can I help you?" asked the receptionist.

"I'd like to talk to somebody about that plane crash a couple of days ago."

"Have a seat, please. I'll get someone."

The receptionist called Harrison on his radio and asked him to come in as someone was there to see him. Harrison said he'd be right there and to ask the person to wait.

A few minutes later Harrison arrived, walked up to the man and said, "Understand you'd like to talk to somebody about that plane crash. My name is Harrison Kennedy. Come on back."

The disheveled man rose and followed Harrison back to a conference room. He sat down and began, "My name is Jerome Brown and my conscience has been bothering me."

"How's that, Mr. Brown?"

"Well, I seen something that's been on my mind a lot."

"Tell me what you saw, Jerome."

"Well, I get up pretty early and I live out by the airport. Sometimes when I get up early I can't get back to sleep. A couple of mornings ago I looked out to see that mail plane coming in. It usually comes in around four o'clock. I know the pilot, Tom. Well, he taxied up as he always does. I kinda watched him through my binoculars and I seen him leave like he always does and then I seen this small light, you know like a flashlight. I was curious so I kept looking at it. Then I seen this fuel truck come up to the plane and it didn't have its lights on. I thought that strange. It wasn't normal. I usually head into town when I can't sleep to get some coffee at the Marathon station. So, I done that and as I went down the road that passes the airport entrance I seen this car parked by the road. Again, that's strange. I never seen no car out there on my way into town. I seen the license in my headlights so I took it down. Then around noon the next day I heard about that plane crash and those women dying and that famous pilot, Frank, getting killed and I wondered if that strange car and the fuel truck with no headlights had somethin' to do with it. Anyway, here's the license number that I seen."

"Thank you, Mr. Brown. We really appreciate your giving us this information."

"Well, I didn't want to get involved. But, I got some daughters and granddaughters and having them women die like that, I couldn't live with myself if I didn't say what I seen."

"We appreciate it, Mr. Brown."

Harrison took Jerome's phone number and asked the man to call him if he knew anything else. When Jerome left, Harrison went to the computer to see to whom the car with the license JJM-67F was registered. The computer screen instantly pulled up the name Samuel H. (Shorty) Gross with an address in Gaylord, Michigan.

Lou and Maggie followed Harrison to the sheriff's department but waited in Harrison's office while he talked with the visitor. After the old man had left, Art Williams appeared and asked if Lou Searing was there. The receptionist said he was and that she would get him and to have a seat.

Lou and Maggie came out and greeted Art. "You doing okay, Art?" Lou asked.

"Yeah. I hoped I'd get to see you two before I left for home. I'm glad I did."

"Tough adjusting to the loss of your friend, isn't it? I lost a good friend a few years ago and I'm still not over it, Art."

"I knew Dwight killed Reggie and would have killed others if they had been in the wrong place at the wrong time. I knew he did it. You guys weren't fast enough for a crime that was so obvious, so I talked to the guys about doing it ourselves. They didn't think it was a good idea, but I didn't listen to them. I thought about doing something to his plane out there at the airport. I thought about trying to get some of his money. I thought about killing him for killing Reggie and bringing such grief to his family and to all of us."

"That's normal I guess, Art. Grief causes people to think and act out of character sometimes," Maggie said, realizing she had those feelings after she was attacked by the customer of her old insurance company.

"I came up here to do something and then this morning I kind of came to my senses. I realized it wasn't going to help me any to pay lawyers and court costs and then to spend time in prison. Late this morning I decided to go back to Marsh Ridge. I thought that maybe if I faced the place again some healing could begin. So, I went out there and played a round of golf. I finished about 3:45, but before going back to Greenville, I thought I'd try to find you to thank you and Mrs. McMillan for helping us out."

"No thanks needed, Art. We're just doing what we need to do. It's all over now. We've got the man and we'll let the judicial system take it from here. Harrison Kennedy is a real pro. Maggie and I have much respect for him. Time will heal, Art. It takes a lot of time, but time will heal. Trust me," Lou said.

"Please thank Carol for me too, will ya?" Art said shaking Lou's hand.

He then leaned down and giving Maggie a hug said, "You're one phenomenal investigator Maggie, thanks! The guys really appreciate your being there for us."

"You're welcome. Have a safe trip home."

CHAPTER 22

Saturday, July 30
Gaylord, Michigan

T he Nelson Funeral Home in Gaylord was the site for the visitation for Dwight Austin. Surprisingly enough, for all the people who knew Dwight Austin, the funeral home was almost empty. His golfing friend Billy Wingate was there with his wife Willetta. Mark Thompson from Vanderbilt was also present talking to Billy. Lawrence Norwood stopped by earlier to pay his respects.

The two men were talking about the craziness of the last two weeks. The door to the funeral home opened and in walked Jimmy Shekleford. He was dressed in a suit, tie and his shoes were shined. He nodded to the two men and walked over to the closed coffin. The explosion, in addition to Dwight's already deformed face, caused the funeral director to think it best to leave the casket closed. Jimmy stood there for a few seconds and tears formed in his eyes. He remembered how Mr. Austin believed in him, gave him a job cutting his grass, talked about the Detroit Tigers, gave him a car and provided him a college education. Other than his dad, there wasn't a finer man on this earth than Mr. Austin. Jimmy Shekleford felt empty inside.

A part of him had died, too.

He glanced at the few flower arrangements around the casket. He read the notes and didn't recognize the people, but then his eyes fell on the nice display of roses and the note that read, "*It was our joy to share our son with you. Jimmy was as much your son as he is ours. Thank you for your kindness, The Sheklefords.*"

Jimmy took out his handkerchief and wiped his eyes. He lightly touched the casket as a farewell to the man who was his friend.

The End

Epilogue

Shorty Gross was convicted of the murder of eight persons: Wendy Blackman, Janice Ketcham, Judy Austin, Heather Abraham, Liz Lake, Stacy Hammonds, Frank Jackson, and Dwight Austin. During the trial it was revealed that Shorty had learned that Dwight had reserved the plane for the morning of July 26. He fully believed that Dwight was taking the Cessna on his own. He had often called and reserved the plane for private flights. Shorty put sugar into the gas tank believing that Dwight would be flying and be killed shortly after takeoff. He drove the fuel truck up to the plane in case someone got suspicious. A fuel truck going up to a plane would be normal. Shorty decided to kill Dwight in the plane crash to save the women the task of killing him on Friday, July 29. Shorty knew his plan was fail-safe, but he feared that the plan of the women to drown Dwight would backfire. He would either get Dwight's life and free the women or Dwight would save himself and pay Shorty five million dollars. Either way, the women would be free.

The explosion of Dwight's golf cart was set off by a bomb that Shorty had planted under the seat early in the afternoon of July 28. The golf cart was stored in the electric cart barn on the course. Everyone knew Dwight's cart. The inscription on the driver's side read, "The Knickers Carrier." When Shorty pressed the garage door opener like device, the bomb detonated instantly. Shorty was sentenced to life in prison without parole.

Ben Hall defended Shorty in court. While his client was convicted and sentenced to life in prison, Ben gained tremendous respect as an attorney willing to defend a citizen accused of a major crime. From that point on, Ben Hall was destined to become a great public defender and his aspirations for high political office would no doubt come to pass.

ADMINISTRATION CAN BE MURDER

A monument was erected at the Otsego County Airport in honor of **Frank Jackson**. He was a man who served his country in war and his community in peace. The names of the six women who died in the crash were engraved on the monument as well. The city council was considering changing the name of the airport to Frank Jackson Memorial Field.

Janice's mother died about a week after the plane crash. Her heart couldn't take the accusations that her daughter was a murderer. When Janice died, it was just too much for her to bear. Life didn't seem to carry any meaning anymore. The meals on wheels driver became concerned when she didn't answer the door. He called the food distribution office who in turn called the police. The police found her at her kitchen table in a coma. She died later that evening at the hospital.

The Marsh Ridge Golf Resort quickly reestablished its reputation. Mr. Workman personally saw to it that Janice's daughter received sufficient scholarships to allow her to successfully complete her schooling to become a nurse. Waiting lists continued to grow as people from all over the country wanted to experience the ambiance of Marsh Ridge and to participate in one of Mr. Growe's famous productions of "Mystery at the Marsh."

Matt Maloney, Doc Lewis, Jeff Gouch, Art Williams, Dan Dillon, Walt Wilcox, and **Bill Wallach** decided to work toward establishing an annual golf tournament in memory of Reggie. The proceeds would go to the Council Against Domestic Assault. The golf outing is held on the second Saturday in July.

Lou and **Maggie** felt satisfaction in solving the murders. Maggie continued to wonder when the phone would ring to once again invite her to solve another murder. She enjoyed working with Lou.

Lou settled into his writing studio in his Grand Haven home overlooking Lake Michigan. He looked at Carol, comfortably seated in a rocking chair by the bay windows, reading her novel. He reached down and patted Samm on the head, then ran his hand over the furry backs of Luba and Millie, the mother and daughter cats sleeping near his writing area. As predictable as the sun rising in the morning, he reached for a few M&Ms, his creativity pills, turned on the computer and began to type.

All that he had experienced in the last month would become his third book. Sitting in his writing studio, with Carol and their pets close by, views of the expansive and beautiful Lake Michigan holding up yachts and craft of every description, and the opportunity to tell a story was pure bliss. He hoped that the family to come after him would know the joy that writing gave him, and how much he appreciated his family, who believed in him and supported him in his pursuit of creativity. Life was good. It was time to tell a story about Lou and Maggie and a complicated mess in Gaylord, Michigan.

Coming Soon

You won't want to miss the next murder mystery with investigators, Lou Searing and Maggie McMillan. An advocate, Jessica Williams is attending a gala ball on Mackinac Island when she takes a cruise in the Straits of Mackinac. She doesn't return.

Even though Lou and Maggie are threatened if they choose to get involved, they settle onto Bois Blanc Island in the Straits of Mackinac and solve the case.

If you've enjoyed Lou and Maggie's investigations to date, you're sure to enjoy their fourth adventure in the beauty of northern Michigan.

Buttonwood Press Order Form

To order additional copies of *Administration Can Be Murder* or earlier mysteries, *The Principal Cause of Death* and *A Lesson Plan for Murder*, visit the website of Buttonwood Press at www.buttonwoodpress.com for information or fill out the order form here. Thank you.

Name_____

Address_____

City/State/Zip_____

Book Title	Quantity	Price
A Lesson Plan for Murder ($12.95 – Softcover)		
The Principal Cause of Death ($12.95 – Softcover)		
Administration Can Be Murder ($12.95 – Softcover)		
TOTAL		

Rich Baldwin will personally autograph a copy of any of his books for you. It's also a great gift for that mystery lover you know!

Autograph Request To:

_____

_____

_____

Mail Order Form with a Check payable to:

Buttonwood Press
PO Box 716
Haslett, MI 48840

Fax: 517-339-5908
Email: RLBald@aol.com
Website: www.buttonwoodpress.com

Questions? Call the Buttonwood Press office at (517) 339-9871

Thank you!